Artistic Licence

Dread clasped at Carla's heart as Piero approached her. 'You gave good head, boy. Now let's see if you can give good arse!'

She trembled as the covers were torn from her. Now her gender would be discovered and she would have to take the consequences! She was terrified, and yet the hot excitement was building up once more.

'I won't hurt you, lad,' said Piero. 'A fellow can take another's prick without shame when the need is great. It doesn't make you less of a man.'

If only he knew, thought Carla. If only he knew.

D0813944

TRADE
Books & CD's

BOOK NOOK

Artistic Licence

VIVIENNE LAFAY

Black Lace novels are sexual fantasies.
In real life, make sure you practise safe sex.

First published in 1997 by
Black Lace
332 Ladbroke Grove
London W10 5AH

Copyright © Vivienne LaFay 1997

The right of Vivienne LaFay to be identified as the
Author of this Work has been asserted by her in
accordance with the Copyright, Designs and Patents Act
1988.

Typeset by SetSystems Ltd, Saffron Walden, Essex
Printed and bound by Mackays of Chatham PLC

ISBN 0 352 33210 7

*All characters in this publication are fictitious and any
resemblance to real persons, living or dead, is purely
coincidental.*

This book is sold subject to the condition that it shall
not, by way of trade or otherwise, be lent, resold, hired
out or otherwise circulated without the publisher's prior
written consent in any form of binding or cover other
than that in which it is published and without a similar
condition including this condition being imposed on the
subsequent purchaser.

Chapter One

Carla Buonomi had been walking all night. Hungry, thirsty and tired, she sank on to a rock jutting from the hillside and rested her aching feet. The boots she wore were her own, but the rest of her clothes were unfamiliar, men's clothes, stolen from her cousin Stefano while he slept. She regarded them as her due, hoping they would protect her now she had left home and set out to survive as best she could in the great city of Florence.

The sun had come up over the horizon, although it was still dark where she was. Carla could see the city swimming in a bath of gold, seemingly just a stone's throw away. She took out the chalk and charcoal that she kept in the purse at her belt and began to sketch on the rock where she sat. Two of the buildings stood out from the rest. On the left she could see the russet dome of the cathedral, its seductive curve topped with a jutting lantern. To its right, the thrusting tower of the *Signoria* proclaimed the power of the city-state. Carla felt a shiver of excitement travel down her spine. There was something almost sexual in that juxtaposition of feminine roundness and phallic potency.

Aware that such an idea would not have occurred to her if she were still a virgin, Carla blushed to recall what

1

Father Andrea had said to her at confession, that not just her reputation but her soul had been sullied. It was true, she saw the world differently now. Never again could she view life with innocent eyes, which was why she had decided to conceal her woman's body beneath Stefano's dark tunic and itchy hose. She scratched at her groin and felt the soft folds of her sex beneath her knuckles, which made her pause for thought. She would have to do something about that.

Despite her eagerness to arrive at the City of the Lily, Carla felt utterly exhausted. After scrubbing out her brief sketch she made a pillow of the small sack of possessions she carried then lay down on the rock for a nap. It was hidden from the track by a clump of umbrella pines so she felt quite safe, and soon the sun would reach that spot with its welcome warmth. She intended only to doze for five minutes, but soon she drifted into a state of sleep where dreams and memories intermingled freely . . .

As long as Carla could remember, Stefano, the handsome son of her father's brother, had egged her on to perform daring deeds and naughty pranks. As children they had climbed trees together, raided birds' nests, put fir cones in people's beds and generally run wild. He had made her life exciting, but when Carla reached adolescence her mother had warned her against spending time alone with him.

'It is not seemly for a young girl to behave like that,' had been her only explanation.

When her father warned that Stefano would 'get her into trouble', Carla had shrugged. What was so new about that? They had been making mischief together for years. So, although she was careful not to be seen with him, it was relatively easy to find ways to meet in secret. She would watch and wait until she saw him go up into the hills then casually remark that she was going to look for wild herbs or berries. The pair would then meet far from prying adult eyes and spend a couple of hours chasing rabbits, paddling in streams or climbing trees, just as they had always done.

But one summer afternoon, when Carla was sixteen and Stefano seventeen, their high jinks took a new turn. Carla found a trinket on the road, a golden tassel that must have fallen from the bridle of some nobleman's horse, and said she would make a pendant of it.

'No you won't!' Stefano teased her, trying to snatch it. 'I saw it first!'

'But I picked it up. Finders keepers!'

She ran with it up the gentle slope of the hill towards an olive grove. Stefano followed, his strong thighs making light work of the gradient, and by the time they were amongst the gnarled trees he had her pinned to the ground.

'Now, yield!' he demanded, his black eyes glittering with amusement as he prised her fingers open and snatched the tassel.

Annoyed at being deprived of her treasure, Carla bit his hand. He slapped her cheek and she kicked out at him, just missing his codpiece.

'Vixen!' he snarled, pulling her roughly into his arms. 'Don't you know never to kick a man in the crotch?'

'Why not?' she asked, cheekily.

'Because you could ruin his family jewels, that's why!'

'Well you stole my treasure, why shouldn't I spoil yours?'

She struggled free, giggling and breathing heavily, but he caught hold of her again and this time his hand brushed the taut swell of her breast. Carla felt a tingling between her legs and a swooping sensation in her stomach. It had happened several times recently when she was in Stefano's company but she had thought little of it until now. Faced with her cousin's sensual smile and knowing eyes she suddenly understood, at some intuitive level, why her parents had warned her against him.

Stefano's gaze was smouldering at her wickedly and his hand returned to her left breast, where the nipple

3

was clearly outlined beneath her linen shift. He gave it a gentle squeeze, intensifying the dizzy heat that was suffusing through her veins. Suddenly everything seemed to be in slow motion. Like a rabbit mesmerised by a fox Carla could only stand there in a daze, wondering why she felt such a strong yearning for him. His lazy thumb moved back and forth across the hard bead of her nipple, while her legs seemed to melt beneath her.

'Well, well, Carla. You are a big girl now, aren't you?' he said in a low, insinuating tone that was a bit like his old wicked coaxing, only more wicked. 'And a naughty one, too. I think I'm going to have to spank you. Oh yes, indeed!'

She was suddenly afraid, not of him but of the sense of being at the edge of an abyss. 'No Stefano, please!' she murmured, but not very convincingly.

He ignored her, pulling her down on to the ground beside him then over his lap. Carla struggled as he lifted up her skirt, but the more she wriggled the more she could feel his cock harden beneath her, pressing into the soft flesh of her stomach. She had seen men's things before, when they peed or washed, but she had never been in such close contact with the alien organ and the effect on her was arousing. Somewhere in the mat of hair between her thighs a secret pulse was throbbing wildly.

Stefano pulled up her skirt until her bare buttocks were exposed to the warm sunshine, and a deep thrill passed through her. Although she could no longer see her cousin's face, Carla knew he was enjoying this turn of events as much as she was. His scent was in her nostrils, crude and yet beguiling, a male smell composed of sweat and earth and something indefinable.

'Naughty, naughty girl!' he whispered as his palm caressed her behind. 'You've given me a monstrous hard-on, you little hussy. I intend to punish you severely for this!'

He began to tap her lightly on alternate buttocks with the flat of his hand. Carla lay prostrate, enjoying the feeling of helplessness and the sensual warmth that came not only from the sun on her bare bottom and the light pummelling, but also from somewhere inside her. Again she felt that tormentingly delicious melting, and knew that she wanted him to do more to her. Her body was crying out for something, but what? In her ignorance she could hardly imagine.

The slapping grew more forceful and soon her bottom was smarting, but Carla remained in her drowsy state, lulled by the rhythmic beating accompanied by the humming of the bees. She was enjoying this feeling of surrender, of letting Stefano do what he liked to her. And all the time she was aware of what she was doing to him, keeping his prick hard and strong so that it formed a great ridge beneath her belly.

The token punishment ended but Stefano was in no hurry to release his cousin from his lap. His hands stroked her tender bottom with gentle rhythm, making her sigh, and soon she felt his lips on the nape of her neck, tickling her as he whispered, 'Did you enjoy that spanking, wicked girl? Or do you prefer what I'm doing now?'

She turned and grinned at him. 'I like both.'

He pretended to be shocked. 'Shameless creature! How can you be taught right from wrong if you like both pleasure and pain equally?'

Carla giggled. 'You didn't hurt me. Not much.'

His eyes glistened at her. 'You want me to hurt you? They say a woman always bleeds the first time. Is that what you want, cousin?'

'I – I don't know.'

Carla felt confused. She sensed that the way he was treating her, talking to her, would have earned her parents' disapproval, yet she didn't know how to stop him. The old Stefano had undergone a transformation into this sly, seductive creature who had a strange hold over her that she could not explain.

He pulled her off his lap and put his arm around her shoulders as they sat, side by side, beneath the ancient olive trees, then he kissed her cheek. 'Don't worry, Carla. I won't go any further than you want me to.'

His words confused her even more. Go? Go where? But now he was kissing her mouth and his warm, moist lips tasted of honeyed wine. Carla let him slip his probing tongue into her mouth and slide around inside, making her feel light-headed. At first she surrendered passively to the invasion but after a while she was giving as good as she got, her tongue duelling with his while their lips moved against each other urgently. The kiss went on and on, becoming more passionate as she responded.

At last he pulled away, allowing her to gulp down some much-needed air.

'Good!' he grinned, his eyes filled with grudging admiration. 'That was pretty good, for a first effort.' His expression grew first doubting, then teasing. 'It *was* a first effort, wasn't it? Don't tell me you've kissed another boy before me or I shall throw you across my knee again.'

'No,' she giggled. 'I've never kissed anyone like that before.'

'Nor shown anyone your nice new titties?' She shook her head shyly and her hands instinctively went to cover her chest. He pulled them away. 'No, don't hide yourself. They look really nice. At least, as far as I can tell beneath your clothes. Will you let me have a proper look at them?'

Chary of him, Carla shook her head. He laughed. 'All right – an improper look, then!'

Echoes of her parents' warnings prompted her to say, 'Stefano, I don't think I should. It's not right.'

'Just a feel, then. There's no harm in that, surely.'

He had them in his hands before she knew it, kneading them softly, making the nipples stand out like hard, unripe olives. Carla was unprepared for the tingling sensations that spread from her breasts down to the secret niche between her thighs, the fluttering in her stomach that was a bit like hunger pangs only far more

6

exciting. She gave a soft moan, and soon his lips were enclosing hers with crushing insistence once more while his fingers continued to work eagerly on her nipples, fanning the flames of her desire for him.

Stefano plucked her breasts out from her chemise like fruit from a tree and began to lick them. Carla lay back on the grass in sensual abandon. The sensations were sweeter than she could ever have imagined. Her whole body was yearning for more of the wonderful lightness and warmth that made her flesh feel as if it were made of something rare, ethereal.

'Carlotta!'

Stefano murmured her baby-name in a voice thick with desire. His legs were pressing hard against hers, his crotch moving restlessly so that the bulging rod rubbed against her and his appetite for her increased. Carla felt a stab of fear. Her cousin was like a runaway stallion who could scarcely be stopped in his headlong course. She was afraid he might turn on her if she tried to stop him, to snarl and spit at her like a wild beast. She had once seen him like that in a fight with another boy and the horror of it had impressed itself upon her memory.

'Stef . . .' she began timidly. His lips instantly pressed against hers, stifling all protest.

His hands were lifting her skirt now, eagerly smoothing a path up her clenched thighs which he proceeded to prise apart. Carla could feel the open folds of her sex moistening and swelling with excitement, and when he touched her there a shudder of blatant lust went through her. It was an intensification of the peculiar feeling she'd been having for the past few years, a feeling that was half pleasure and half torment, an urge that awakened a craving for something immensely powerful and mysterious.

'Oh God!' she heard Stefano mutter, his breath hot on her lips as his finger probed the last defence between him and his goal. There was a stab of pain and then a feeling of wetness.

'Are you bleeding?' he asked, looking down at her.

She gasped in horror: what had he done? But a smile spread over his handsome face as he pulled out his glistening finger. 'No, not blood. Just your runny love-juices, you little hussy! You can't wait for it, can you?'

She felt him fumbling with his belt, and then he pulled down his hose and exposed his long, thick member. Wonderingly she took its silky strength between her fingers, gazing down in fascination at the way its red valve reared up at her. In the tiny slit she could see a smear of liquid. The loose skin moved beneath her fingers and, as she experimentally pushed it up the column of his cock, he gave a loud groan.

'Don't! You'll trigger me off!'

'What do you mean?' She stared at him, wild with curiosity, and the ache inside her mingled with the itch outside.

He grinned, his eyes dark and knowing. 'I mean it would be a waste if I came before we'd both had some fun. Come on, Carla, don't be shy. It's too late for that now. Lie back and open your legs to me, there's a good girl.'

'W – what are you going to do?'

Her voice was faint, and the hum of the bees was disturbing now. Carla had a feeling that she was about to cross some irrevocable threshold. Was this what her parents had meant by getting into trouble?

Stefano seemed to read her thoughts. 'Don't worry, I won't get you into trouble. I'll pull out in time.'

'Out? Out from where?'

But his face grew hard and determined as he knelt between her limp thighs and pointed his erection at her private parts. Passive now, Carla let him place the red tip of his penis right between her folds. It felt very soft and melting down there, but at the same time she could feel an insistent pulse that was urging her on. Clasping his shoulders she pulled him down into her.

'Oh!' he groaned, as the head of his prick slipped past the vestige of her virginity and into the wet warmth beyond. Carla clutched at him fiercely, steeling herself against the slight twinge of pain, then relishing the extraordinary sweetness that was slowly overtaking her senses. Being touched inside, right inside, felt wonderful.

Stefano's hand was on her breast, caressing its rounded fullness and making her nipple tingle, but the contact between their outer flesh was nothing compared to what was happening internally. Carla gasped in wonder as he began to thrust into her, over and over again. The way he was sliding in and out of her was pure bliss, and soon her hips instinctively moved to maximise her pleasure. After some initial awkwardness she found that she could match her thrusting pelvis to his, and soon they were following a pattern of four shallow, restrained thrusts followed by one long reckless one, as if they were engaged in a horizontal galliard.

Carla felt herself becoming wetter, and there was soon an odd squelching sound that made her giggle. Stefano frowned at her, and pulled out abruptly. 'Look, you made my cock go limp with your silly giggling!' he complained, pouting.

She stared down at the flaccid organ. It was strange to think how stiff it had been, seconds before. What a curious phenomenon a man's thing was, with a wayward life of its own. But when Carla reached out and touched it she felt it stir.

'That's better!' he smiled at her. 'Give it a good pulling and maybe things will improve.'

But as she stroked the penis back into full erection it twitched in her hand and then shot a stream of sticky liquid over her hand. She squealed and pulled her arm away.

Stefano laughed. 'That'll teach you! At least you didn't get any of that inside you.'

Carla wiped her hand on the grass, but she felt sorely disappointed. Something that should have happened, hadn't, and she had no idea what it was. All she knew was that when Stefano had been inside her body it had produced the most exquisite feelings in her, feelings that she longed to explore more fully.

He drew her close and she lay there in the crook of his arm, gazing up into a clear blue sky. Playfully Stefano dangled the golden tassel over her open crotch. It tickled her still-sensitive labia, making her restless and desirous once more.

'Here, take this in exchange for your cherry,' Stefano whispered. 'Just remember you're mine now, mine alone. I can have you whenever I want.'

She looked up at him with scared eyes. 'What do you mean?'

'A girl always belongs to the first man who takes her, didn't you know?'

'Belongs?'

'Yes, body and soul.'

'You mean, like man and wife?'

He gave a sardonic laugh. 'Oh, I doubt they'll let us wed! My folks have another girl in mind for me, and I heard your Papa say he had his eye on the youngest Bardoni boy for you. What's his name – Federico, that's it. But you mustn't tell anyone I broached your barrel. No man wants to be palmed off with soiled goods. That's our little secret, eh cousin?'

Carla wriggled uncomfortably, hating the sticky feeling between her thighs now that her excitement was waning. His words troubled her. She was on uncharted seas without a compass, and the only man who knew the course seemed bent on wrecking her life.

'What's the matter, Carlotta?' His grin no longer seemed beguiling, more menacing. 'Don't worry, you won't fall for a child. If you're worried I'll use my fingers on you, then you can use yours on me. We'll have plenty of enjoyment without any of the risk.'

The fear that she had been harbouring came out in a timid question. 'Stefano, have we done wrong? What would Father Andrea say?'

Her cousin laughed, with a cruel edge. 'He'd say you were in mortal sin, my girl, and had better say ten Hail Marys in double quick time or be prepared to languish in hell!'

She could not tell if he was teasing her. The old Stefano that she had been able to read like a book had almost vanished, to be replaced by this enigmatic, dangerous young man. Confused and vaguely miserable, Carla wanted to go home. She got up, smoothing down her skirt, and mumbled some excuse.

'Best go on your own then,' he said, casually. 'We daren't risk being seen together. But any time I want you I'll let you know.'

Want you ... want you ... His voice echoed in her ears as she slowly followed the dirt track down the hillside towards the village. There had been such arrogant presumption in his words, as if she were a mare that could be saddled for him to ride whenever he desired a gallop in the hills. Carla felt her heart rebel. The pleasure he had given her had a price attached to it, and she was unsure what that was. Yet she feared him now, feared that their 'secret' gave him a power over her which might be abused.

Stefano had talked of getting her with child – was that the risk they had taken? Yet he had also made it clear he had no intention of marrying her. A cold fear gripped Carla's heart as she recalled a girl who had been ostracised by her neighbours for bearing an unwanted child. The babe had been given to nuns but the taint had remained, making the girl a permanent outcast.

'I will tell Father Andrea,' Carla decided. 'He will know what to do.'

The following Saturday she went to confession, but instead of the usual catalogue of peccadilloes, Carla Buonomi surprised Father Andrea with her open admission of sexual depravity. In her naivety, she described the act she had performed with her cousin Stefano in frank detail.

'I let him put his thing inside my private place,' she murmured. 'I had a feeling it was wrong, Father, although he told me no harm would come of it. And he wasn't inside me for long.'

'You have transgressed in ignorance,' came the priest's

solemn voice from behind the fretted screen. 'But that is no excuse. Like Eve, you are guilty of original sin and must be purged. Tell me, child, how did you feel when your cousin performed this shameful deed upon you?'

'I did not know I should be ashamed,' Carla said. 'So I enjoyed it.'

'You *enjoyed* it?' Father Andrea sounded outraged.

Carla continued, defiantly, disliking his tone, 'Yes. It felt nice.'

'Holy mother of God, your plight is graver than I had supposed. You are in mortal jeopardy, my child, and must take care not to sin again. If you see your seducer about the village make sure you turn away so you are in no danger of repeating the evil deed.'

'Oh, then he'll follow me. He said I am now his, to take whenever he pleases.'

'Wicked youth! Do not be misled, dear child. Stop your ears if he should speak. Say three Hail Marys and two Our Fathers every night and morning, to give you strength. And if your flesh should be in danger you must make the sign of the cross to remind you of the mortification of the flesh suffered by Our Lord. Think on his agony, not of your own pleasure, and your soul will be saved.'

Carla listened in silence to his admonition. It seemed that what she and Stefano had done was more serious than she had at first thought. Yet she could not blot from her mind the memory of those blissful feelings. And how could she possibly avoid her cousin when he lived next door, and was forever popping in and out of her home? The very sight of him would remind her of what they had shared, and if he winked or smiled at her she knew she would follow him, be damned with him. Carla knew she was powerless to resist the sensual spell he had cast over her. Her body craved him, and her soul must pay the price.

But when she left the church that night Carla was less concerned about the priest's warning than about her own fear of the future. Stefano had said he would not wed her, that her parents planned to marry her to Federico Bardoni. But that lad was stupid, and ugly. After Stefano he would seem a dull partner, but she could see no way out. There was no one else in the village whom she could propose as a better candidate, not so long as Stefano seemed determined to keep her only for his clandestine pleasure.

Realising that she had got herself into an impossible situation, Carla's thoughts turned to the wide world beyond. The thought of leaving home was daunting, yet she was aware that she had become an economic burden to her parents who had four younger mouths to feed than hers. Marriage to Federico would certainly occur within the year if she stayed at home, and that made even the unknown dangers of the city a welcome prospect.

If, through no fault of her own, she had fallen into sin then she would remove herself from the source of temptation. Not only by leaving the village, but by pretending to be of the opposite sex. Dressed in a boy's clothes she would pass as a man, her small breasts safely concealed beneath a baggy tunic and her hair cropped so that it curled about her earlobes. Her parents would think she had run off with a pedlar or a musician, since she was always hanging around such types. They would miss her for a while, but not for long. They were always far too busy to give her more than a passing glance or brief word.

Once the idea had come into her head, Carla could not ignore it. She longed for a life of freedom, rather than the restricted round of child-bearing and toil that marriage to Federico would bring. And Florence was a magical city. Although she had never visited it Carla had heard tales of the beautiful people who lived there, of their fine clothes and magnificent houses filled with statues and paintings. Perhaps there would be room for a street artist there, one who could make lightning sketches of passers-by to amuse their friends . . .

* * *

The sun was streaming down on Carla in full force, bringing her back from her reverie. She stretched her aching limbs and sat up. It had been hard to leave home, to turn her back on everything, and everyone, she had ever known. Yet she felt she had already outgrown a household which revolved around the younger children, making her no more than an unpaid nursemaid. Besides, there was a yearning in her soul that would not be denied.

When she had crept into her uncle's house before dawn and stolen the garments that lay in a heap beside her sleeping cousin, she had feared he would awaken and confront her, but he had continued snoring soundly. She had trembled when she ventured out into the alien night, as much from fear as from cold but now, having survived the danger of the dark, she was eager to begin her new life.

In Stefano's old clothes she felt safe, close to him and home, yet safe from other men. Although she had not yet put her disguise to the test, she felt sure that in Florence, where strangers arrived every day to seek their fortune, she would pass for just another young lad on the make. Jumping up, she took her last swig of wine from the leather bottle on her back and walked down the fragrant hillside with bold strides, imagining how it must feel to be Stefano. Some of his cocky self-assurance seemed to have transferred to her from his clothes, for as she hit the road she assumed a swagger that made her feel strong and exhilarated. The rhythm of her walking soon translated itself into a phrase that repeated itself insistently, first in her head and then on her lips: '*Mi chiamo Carlo! Mi chiamo Carlo! Mi chiamo Carlo!*'

But beneath her male attire the golden tassel, symbol of her lost virginity, swung teasingly between her breasts from its leather thong.

14

Chapter Two

*I*t was strange being in such a great city and knowing no one. At first Carla joined the other beggars on the streets of Florence, but they were an unpleasant crew and she endeavoured to keep her distance. Although everyone took her for a boy, she sometimes had her bottom pinched or ribald remarks were made, making her uneasy. The sights, sounds and smells she experienced were varied and unusual, filling her with bewilderment, but she did not dare to ask too many questions. She had slipped into Florence through one of the toll gates by hiding behind a laden pack horse, and she didn't want anyone challenging her right to be there.

She soon found the market place, where there were rich pickings to be had. The statue of Abundance which stood on a pillar nearby was not a sham, for the wealth of produce that came into the old market from the countryside was enormous. It was easy to cadge an over-ripe fig or spotted peach from a fruit stall, or to scrounge leavings of broth from a soup kitchen or a hunk of yesterday's bread from a baker, but Carla was not content to settle for a life of beggary. She had set her sights higher than mere survival.

For several days, Carla remained in a state of constant wonder as she watched the coming and going around her. Everyone looked busy and prosperous. Even the beggars seemed fat and contented. Merchants hurried between the warehouses, inspecting stock, while a whole army of fullers, carders, dyers and weavers transformed the wool from its raw state into fine and luxurious cloth.

On Sunday, when she hung around the cathedral, Carla saw the sumptuous wools and silks made up into the most beautiful clothes, worn by the rich nobles. She gazed in envy at the carefully protected virgins of good family, who were shepherded into the dark interior of the *duomo* wearing veils, and wondered what it must be like to lead such a sheltered life. The matrons and city fathers walked with their heads held high, their sons were swaggering youths who wore their hair to their shoulders and were clean shaven. In their tight, jewel-bright jackets and contrasting hose they seemed to enjoy flaunting their well-toned buttocks and shapely legs.

Seeing them, Carla felt strange yearnings, the kind she had felt for her cousin, only now she regarded such feelings with suspicion. It would not do to give in to those urges and make herself even more vulnerable than she already felt. Sometimes, curled up in a doorway at night, the ache inside made her moan and shift her thighs restlessly. She was plagued by tormenting dreams of Stefano. She still feared the powerful force that had driven her out of the familiar comfort of her village and into this strange and alien city.

After she had been there almost a week, Carla decided it was time to prepare for her chosen trade. She disliked being idle in the midst of so much industry. Reasoning that the best friend she could have right now was an apothecary, since that was where the artists bought their pigments, she made her way to the *Via dei Speziali*, where they had their shops. It was in the very heart of Florence, midway between the great dome of the cathedral and the tall tower of the town hall, in the territory of the powerful wool merchants.

Carla entered the first shop she saw and was amazed by the variety of merchandise. The apothecaries sold spices, stationery, cosmetics and other trinkets as well as medicinal potions. While she browsed amongst the pomanders and amulets, skin creams and perfumes, she made an interesting discovery. Packets of pink centaury were labelled *Biondella*. Now she knew why so many of the fashionable ladies appeared to have golden hair!

As she was inspecting the pretty notepapers she overheard an artist's apprentice ordering pigments for his master: 'He wants equal quantities of your Venetian and Tuscan red, more of your raw umber than last time and the same amount of ochre. Oh, and some verdigris. Not as much as last time.'

'What about my ultramarine?' the old apothecary asked.

'He said you palmed him off before, with azurite mixed in.'

'I did not! It was best lapis lazuli, I swear! If he can find better elsewhere, let him try. I guarantee he'll send you running back to my door.'

The banter continued for a while and Carla made mental notes as a plan formed in her mind. She had been successful in posing as a youth, why should she not pretend to be an apprentice too? It was surely worth the risk to get her hands on some of those wonderful-sounding colours.

As soon as the shop was empty she went up to the counter, where the apothecary was weighing out some herbs. 'Excuse me,' she began.

The old man peered at her over the scales. 'You're new, aren't you?' he said, gruffly. 'Don't recall seeing you in here before.'

Her nerve failed her at once. How could she weave an elaborate story to explain her presence in town? This man undoubtedly knew all the artists in Florence and would soon call her bluff. Instead, she decided to throw herself on his mercy.

'Yes, I only arrived here last Friday,' she admitted. 'And I have to make my living somehow. I can draw, so I thought I would make some portraits, but I need colours. Some chalk and some ochre, and maybe charcoal if you have it.'

'Do you have money, then?'

'A little.'

She took the paltry coins she had made begging out of her belt-pouch. The apothecary gave a derisive laugh, dashing her hopes. 'I don't know what you expect to buy with that!'

'Isn't it enough?'

'Not nearly enough. But look, I'll tell you what I'll do. There are always some bits left in the empty tubs. If you want, you can scrape them out and mix them with gum. I'll let you go out to the back and find them if you'll agree to mind the shop for a while. Can I trust you?'

'Oh yes!'

'Right. Don't attempt to sell anyone anything. Just tell them old Bondino will be back soon. Stand behind here and don't you budge until I return. All right?'

She watched the man leave. Almost as soon as he had gone, two fashionable ladies entered. Carla could see their manservant hovering just outside the shop. They paused at the door, staring in amazement at Carla. Both women had dyed blonde hair coiled up in elaborate plaits with little bells incorporated that jangled as they walked. Their dresses were of dark blue and green brocade, embroidered with flowers like a spring meadow. Their sleeves were slashed and trimmed with bows, showing a contrasting lining beneath, and they wore gloves and pretty, high-heeled slippers. Carla was daunted by their sophisticated air.

The taller of the two ladies spoke to her companion. 'I thought I saw Bondino sloping off down the street. It seems he's left this pretty boy in charge. Well, isn't this our lucky day!'

'Mm!' the other said, her dark eyes bright with mischief. 'How far do you think we could get with him before his master returns?'

'He looks a bit green about the gills, don't you think?'

'It's not his gills I'm interested in, Francesca!'

Carla could scarcely follow their conversation, but she knew she had to address them and she was terribly afraid that her secret would be found out. Clearing her throat she said, in as low as voice as she could manage, 'Can I help you, ladies?'

The pair approached the counter, their faces full of guile, and Carla's heart sank. The one called Francesca leant right over the wooden barrier, exposing her cleavage. She clearly read Carla's embarrassment as sexual, and gave a knowing smile.

'Well, my dear,' she said, beckoning her forward in a conspiratorial manner. 'What we want is some of old Bondino's very special perfume. Isn't that right, Livia?'

The one called Livia tossed the feathery ornament she'd been playing with back into its tray. 'Oh yes. Yes indeed!'

'Th – the perfumes are over there, ladies.'

The women exchanged a look of amused complicity. 'No, you don't understand. Those are for other women, ordinary women. We want the special stuff. You know. He keeps it under the counter.'

Carla pretended to look but there were so many drawers, all with Latin labels, that she was confused. 'Maybe we'd better help him find it,' Livia said.

Before Carla could protest, both women were behind the counter and far too close for comfort. Francesca put her hand casually on Carla's behind as she scrutinised the drawers, and gave her buttock squeeze. 'Mm, not bad!' she told her companion with a wink.

'I can't see any useful goods round the back,' Livia said. 'Maybe we should look in the front. Do you think he's well stocked?'

Francesca gave a dirty laugh. 'I should say so, by the looks of him. Shall we find out?'

There was no doubt about their innuendo now and it was making Carla extremely nervous. Her coarse brown tunic came only halfway down her thighs and she had taken the precaution of fashioning a codpiece out of wool scraps that she had secured inside her hose. Visually, the

19

prosthetic helped her pass as male, but she knew that if anyone as bold as Stefano tried to grope her, she would be lost.

'Won't you give us a peep at your booty?' Livia asked, giggling. 'I'll bet you've got the best medicine any woman could have.'

'Better watch out he doesn't give you a dose then!' Francesca cackled.

Carla had never met women like this before, never even dreamt they existed, and she knew she was out of her depth. They spoke a language she could scarcely understand, full of double meanings, and they looked at her with such frankly shameless expressions that she was as embarrassed for them as she was for herself.

'This – er – perfume you require,' she began, in desperation. 'What is it called?'

Francesca gave a knowing smile. 'It's not what it's called that matters. It's what it does that counts. The stuff is guaranteed to have any man swooning at our feet in seconds, isn't it Livia?'

'Oh yes, it's powerful stuff all right. Shall we try it out on this young fellow? Always assuming we can find it.'

'If you'd care to wait until the apothecary returns, I'm sure he'll find it for you,' Carla said. 'He said he wouldn't be long.'

To her great relief she saw the old man framed in the doorway, a huge smile further wrinkling his already lined face. 'Ladies, ladies! I pop out for a moment and miss the sun coming out from behind a cloud. How you brighten my day, Monna Livia, Monna Francesca.'

Carla was sickened by his obsequiousness but knew she must hide her feelings if she were to get her reward. She stood aside while he found the perfume, and soon a heavy cloying scent filled the shop. The ladies seemed delighted, but Carla didn't care for it at all.

When the women had gone, well pleased with their purchases, Bondino said, 'Did they tease you, lad? Never mind them. They're just candle courtesans.' In response to Carla's mystified look he explained, 'Prostitutes, you know. They sell their bodies to men. You must have seen them hanging out in the candle makers' shops round the market.'

Carla was amazed. She had taken them for noble-women, but now she realised that their fine clothes had been acquired sinfully she was not so much in awe of them. The idea of letting a man do what Stefano had done to her for the sake of a few *lire* appalled her. Did they enjoy it, or just endure it? Her curiosity was roused, but she would never contemplate doing such a thing herself. She had set her heart on making money from her talent.

Bondino went into the back of the shop and brought out some small wooden boxes which he dumped on the bench. 'Here you are, scrape around in there and see what you can find.'

Carla was pleased to salvage the pigments. She care-fully mixed them with gum and Bondino helped her put them into small screws of paper. He gave her a quantity of chalk, too, and some charcoal. Finally he let her have some tattered sheets of paper that he said he couldn't sell. 'Mind you make good use of them,' he told her. 'They are best quality, only that fool of a delivery boy managed to ruin them in transit.'

Delighted with her good fortune, Carla left the shop and set out for the great square of the *Signoria*. She planned to set up shop there, where she could easily be seen by the crowd. Under the high-vaulted *loggia* at the side of the paved square she would be protected from the weather too. She felt sure she would make her reputation as a portrait artist in no time.

It was noon and the streets were almost deserted as everyone fled the scorching sun. The *loggia* was reserved for the city fathers during public ceremonies and dis-plays, but artists and beggars occupied it at other times. Carla was glad of the shelter as she gazed out across the huge expanse of paving in front of the town hall. There were a couple of artists sketching, so she moved towards them hesitantly, wondering if they would accept her as one of them.

'What do you want?' one of them asked, rudely, as she approached.

'I want to be an artist.'

The man laughed, displaying his gappy teeth. 'Do you belong to the Guild?'

'Guild?'

'That's right.' The man continued with his drawing of the sun between two lions, depicted on the plaque over the door of the *Signoria*. 'They'll never let you practise as a proper artist if you don't belong to the Guild, and that costs money. If they catch you practising illegally you'll be fined for idleness and if you can't pay you'll go to jail.'

'Are you a Guild member?'

'Used to be. Got thrown out.'

'Why?'

'Don't ask so many questions, young 'un.'

'I want to know how to become an artist, that's all.'

'The most you can get to be outside the Guild is a two-bit dauber and scribbler like me, Claudio the piss-artist. If you're lucky, you'll make a few florins a year. But don't get your hopes up. You'd probably earn more by straight begging.'

Carla refused to be discouraged. She sat herself down near the man called Claudio, who seemed friendly enough in a lugubrious sort of way, and took out her paper and pigments, deciding to use him as her first model.

The man regarded her askance for some minutes and finally said, 'Where did you get your materials – did you steal 'em?'

'No!' she said indignantly. 'I helped an apothecary and he let me have them.'

'Which one?'

'Bondino.'

'You picked a good one there, anyway. He supplies

some of the best artists in town. Get on the right side of him and you might just get somewhere.'

'Really?'

Claudio leaned over to look at what she had done. Although there was little more than an outline in red ochre on the buff-coloured page he nodded his head in approval. 'You have the talent, I'll give you that. How did you learn?'

'I just used chalk and charcoal and began to draw my brothers and sisters, on anything I could find. My first efforts weren't very good, but I improved over the years.'

He nodded, calling to his friend. 'Hey, Lucca. Come and look at this!'

Carla felt self-conscious as the two artists discussed her work over her head. She was not sure whether their praise was genuine, or whether they were mocking her, but she went on steadfastly completing her sketch and when she had finished, Claudio asked if he could keep it.

'I'll let you have some more colours in exchange,' he grinned.

'Thank you!' she beamed.

'A gift like yours should be encouraged. Just one thing, though. Promise you'll stay away from the *loggia*. Go and ply your trade somewhere else.'

'Why?'

The two artists grinned at each other and Lucca said, 'You're too good, that's why. We don't want the competition. Bugger off and find another pitch, there's a good chap.'

Carla knew it was no use arguing. They might turn nasty if she objected. So she put the scraps of pigment into her bag with the rest and sauntered out into the sunshine again. Although she was disappointed at losing her spot in the shade, at least they had not tried to beat her up or rob her of what little she had.

She was encouraged, too, by their approval of her work. If real artists saw merit in it, surely others would be prepared to pay good money for their portraits. She wandered through the half-deserted streets until she found herself amongst the leather workers' shops. There all kinds of luxurious leather goods were sold, from beautiful supple boots to tooled belts and purses of softest suède. Nearby was the street of the spice merchants, where the apothecaries were. It seemed an ideal place to attract the attention of the rich and fashionable.

She found a quiet corner with a flight of steps and sat down where she could watch people passing by. At first she felt very conspicuous, but after a while she realised that most people were far too busy with their own affairs to bother about her. Carla took out her chalks and began to draw on the flat paving stones in front of her, making the outline of a madonna and child. Soon she was absorbed in her work, so much so that she failed to see the small crowd that was gathering around her.

'He's good!' someone said, making her look up. 'Look how delicately he's drawn the features. But what's he doing on the streets?'

Carla gave a shy grin. The man seemed prosperous, judging by his elegantly quilted green jacket embroidered with gold at the collar and cuffs. She seized her chance. 'Would you like your portrait painted, sir? I have paper, and colours. It will only take me about a quarter of an hour, if you have the time.'

The man laughed, and she was afraid he would turn her down. But a young man next to him said, 'Go on, Agnolo, why not? Your wife will love it.'

'Not as much as my mistress!' Agnolo laughed. 'All right, I don't mind helping a budding artist. Where do you want me to sit?'

Embarrassed, she realised she could hardly expect him to squat in the dirt like herself. But then a man who had been listening from a doorway brought out a folding stool and the nobleman sat on that. The crowd thickened, some of them recognising Messer Agnolo, and all of them curious about the street artist they had never seen before.

Carla knew she must do her very best work as her

future reputation, and therefore her livelihood, was at stake. Carefully she observed her subject's features: slightly bulbous forehead receding into dark, straight hair; small brown eyes beneath beetling brows; straight nose. She began to sketch it out and soon the fine detail was appearing, every little furrow and shade faithfully represented as far as her materials permitted. Lost in her art, she saw nothing but the face taking shape beneath her fingers, heard nothing but the beating of her heart in calm concentration.

At last, satisfied with the likeness, she held it up for all to see. There were gasps of admiration. 'More lifelike than the man himself!' someone said. 'A flattering study,' said another. 'He's hoping to get a good fee!'

As the crowd started to move on, Agnolo took the portrait and studied it carefully. 'You have talent, young man. How much do you charge for your fifteen minutes' work, eh?'

'Whatever you care to give me, sir. What is it worth to you?'

He turned to his friend. 'What do you reckon?'

'His materials are cheap, but I'd give him 25 *lire* for his brush.'

'For my brush?' Carla was nonplussed. 'But I only used crayons.'

Both men laughed. 'It's a figure of speech,' Agnolo explained. 'He means for your skill and labour. 25 *lire* it is, then.'

It seemed a small fortune. Carla took the money gratefully and once the men had passed on down the street she squeezed the coins to her chest in glee. The man who had lent the chair came back to collect it and noticed her joyful expression.

'Your first commission?' She nodded. 'Well it's a more honest living than some, I suppose. But if you want to get on in this city you need to get off the streets. They're no place for a good-looking lad like you. Sooner or later someone will want you to do more for them than just paint their picture.'

Carla knew he meant well, but she did not want anyone to spoil the joy of her first real wages. What should she spend it on: a good meal, some new clothes, a bed for the night? It was hard to make her choice but eventually she decided on some new hose with a treat at a pie-shop if she could afford it.

Over the next few days Carla found herself a small, but steady, stream of customers. Most gave her very little money but one or two were more generous, and she was beginning to save her earnings in the cloth pouch she wore at her belt. Soon her chief fear was that, without a secure hiding-place, someone would steal her hard-earned wages. If only she could earn enough to get off the streets, to rent a room where she might stash her money beneath the floorboards or up the chimney, she would be quite content with her way of life.

Then, one fine June morning, a young man walking by with a jaunty stride paused to watch her sketching a pretty young whore at the request of one of her customers. Carla was making a good job of it, conveying the subtle contours and proportions accurately and suggesting the fresh radiance of the girl's skin with chalk highlights. When the job was finished, and the people had dispersed, he came up to her.

'Good morning, it's nice to watch a fellow-artist at work,' he began, pleasantly enough.

Carla blushed, still not used to being thought of as an artist. 'It's kind of you to say so, sir.'

She looked up into the young man's open, handsome face and felt a faint stirring within as their eyes met. He had very expressive eyes, dark and velvety, that were regarding her with an admiration she found flattering. But his next words threw her into confusion. 'Are you apprenticed? I haven't seen you in the Guild. Who do you work for?'

Suddenly she was afraid that he had been sent to spy on her from the Guild, that she would be accused of working illegally. She gathered up her things quickly, ready to make a dash for it if things turned awkward.

'Wait!' His hand was on her arm, making her heart beat all the faster. 'Please don't go. I wanted to talk to you.'

Something made her trust this stranger. He didn't seem unkind. 'I belong to no Guild, sir,' she confessed. 'If I am breaking some law it is through ignorance. I'm just trying to get by as best I can. I have no family to look after me.'

'You are an orphan?' She nodded, ashamed of the lie yet not knowing what else to say. 'What is your name?'

'Carl – o!' She caught herself just in time.

'Well, Carlo, my name is Marco and my master is Piero Cortoni. I have a feeling he would be very glad to meet you.'

'To meet *me*?'

'Yes. He's looking for a lad to help out. You wouldn't be apprenticed, not yet anyway. More of a labourer than an artist. But it has to be better than being on the streets. You'd get bed and board and, who knows, once he discovers your talent he might take you on officially.'

It did not take Carla long to make up her mind. She knew she might wait a long time before she got a better offer. Marco seemed the sort she could trust, and she could do with a friend. She thought wistfully of Stefano. He had been her great companion when she was young. Oh, why did he have to spoil things? He had changed her life forever but at least he hadn't ruined it, as he would have done if he had got her with child.

Then she remembered the cheerful bustle of her home, and sighed. Were her family missing her? Perhaps one day she would return to visit them, but for the moment she must remain in exile, with loneliness her greatest enemy. How she longed to be part of some kind of household again!

'Cheer up!' Marco grinned. 'Is it yes, or no?'

'Oh yes – please!'

Marco was on his way to Bondino's and invited her to join him. He was surprised when the apothecary recognised his companion. 'So, you are a bona fide artist after all!' the old man said, seeing her enter with the apprentice.

'Not yet!' She made a face. 'But I hope to be some day.'

She listened attentively while Marco reeled off the list of his master's requirements and, when the time came to leave, she didn't mind being given a couple of packages to carry. They walked back down the street of the shoemakers and began to cross the town hall square. There, in the *loggia*, Carla saw Claudio sketching a woman with a basket of produce. Beside him, to her astonishment, was the study she had made of him displayed on an easel. There were some words scrawled on a tile underneath it, but Carla couldn't read.

She tugged at Marco's sleeve. 'See that painting next to the man in the *loggia*,' she said. 'What does it say on the tile?'

He squinted at it then read aloud, 'Self portrait.'

'What!'

'Why, don't you think it's a good likeness? It seems very like the man to me.'

Carla smiled to herself but decided to say nothing. Let Claudio pass her work off as his own if it brought him more custom. She could afford to be generous now that she had far better prospects than those poor souls in the *loggia*.

They continued through a dark warren of narrow streets with Carla fending off her new friend's questions as best she could. She did not want to lie to him, but her answers about where she had lived before were evasive. At last they ended up near Santa Croce outside a tall, narrow building that bore an escutcheon over the doorway.

'This is both home and workplace to me,' Marco said. 'All four floors of it. Piero rents it from the Pazzis. Come in and meet the gang!'

There were five apprentices in the Cortoni workshop and Carla was introduced to them all. The baby was Antonio who, at twelve years old, had only been apprenticed three months. He had an open, moon-round face and a mass of light brown curls. Carla thought he looked like a little cherub. The two juniors, Matteo and Luigi, were strapping lads who looked as if they enjoyed a good joke and a bellyful of wine.

More sober was Giovanni, the eldest of them all. At eighteen, Marco explained, he was old enough to matriculate, but the fee of 25 *florins* could not yet be met so Piero paid him wages. Carla had the impression that this prolonged indenture rankled with him, that he would rather be a journeyman, working for himself. He was the only one of the apprentices that she felt wary of, distrusting his brooding expression and the haunted look in his eye.

At last it was time for her to meet the master. After climbing past rooms full of materials, tools and evidence of work in progress in which Carla longed to linger and inspect, they reached the upper floor which was entirely occupied by Piero.

'Let me go in first,' Marco whispered, outside his workshop.

Carla strained to hear the conversation through the half-open door. She suffered an apprehensive few minutes before she was invited to join them. When she went in she saw a room filled with all kinds of brushes, canvases, boards, pestles and pigments in terrible disarray, but, in the midst of it all, two wonderful works of art were in progress. In one corner was a marble statue, the rugged face and figure half chiselled out, and in another was a triptych obviously intended as an altarpiece. It gleamed with warm tones of red and gold.

Piero Cortoni was a strikingly handsome man, well built and with a burning energy that seemed to fill the room. Carla looked into his gold-flecked eyes and saw lurking there a huge appetite for life, in all its forms. For some reason, it scared her a little. She reminded herself that this man could be her passport into the Guild and a proper training as an artist, so she would do her level best to make a good impression.

'So, you're this Carlo who is so talented an artist that my man here wants to rescue you from the gutter!' he began. 'Well you look like a guttersnipe, that's for sure. Has he explained I don't want any more damned apprentices right now? Got my hands full with this lot. But when one of them goes there will be a vacancy. Until then, you'd have to be general dogsbody. Are you prepared for that?'

'Oh yes! I'm sure I'll learn a great deal just by watching.'

'I'm not keeping you just to watch, you cheeky young fellow!'

'Oh no! I didn't mean . . . It's just that if I can't do any real painting yet at least I can see how it's done.'

Piero grunted, reaching for his carafe. He poured himself a generous measure of white wine but did not offer them any. Carla looked out of the window and saw the giant tower of the *Signoria* in the distance. What would Claudio and Lucca say if they knew how soon she'd fallen on her feet? They would be green with envy!

'He'll have to sleep up here, there's no room with the rest of you lot,' Piero continued, thoughtfully. 'I'll have a trestle bed made up.'

Marco winked at her. 'Lucky you!' he muttered under his breath, with a grin.

'Now take him downstairs and make him earn his supper,' Piero said, with an impatient wave of his hand.

It was surprising how quickly Carla felt at home amongst the apprentices. They all seemed keen to show her how things were done, and by supper time she knew how to grind and mix some of the pigments. She had also made a couple of hogshair brushes, not as well as the others, but of a passable standard.

'Tomorrow you'll get to prepare some of the boxwood panels with ashes of chicken bones,' Marco told her. She made a face. 'Don't worry, you'll get used to it. It's vital work. Wood isn't fit to paint on until its been treated in various ways. You'll soon learn all there is to know.'

He smiled at her and, once again, she felt the old tug

of desire in her belly. Of all the apprentices he was the one who attracted her most, but Carla knew she must keep her feelings well under control. With everyone living in each others' pockets she must be extra careful to get along with everyone, and most of all with Piero. Already she was in awe of the master, who ruled all the lads with quiet authority. He had only to frown and the least of them hastened to apologise, or rushed to do his bidding.

The thought that Carla must sleep upstairs in his quarters was daunting. As dusk fell and the meal ended, she grew more and more nervous. She helped clear the table and swill the dishes in the big stone sink, then Piero beckoned to her. 'Come along now, Carlo. I'll show you to your bed. Bring that taper.'

She picked up the lighted candle from the table and followed him out of the door. As she went she thought she could hear whispers and sniggers behind her, and her heart fell. Were the others jealous of her because she seemed to be getting special treatment? She had vowed not to do anything to upset anyone, but it was hard when she was unaccustomed to their ways.

To her dismay, Carla found that Piero had made up a bed for her near to his own. She had presumed she would be sleeping next door, but now she would have no privacy. What would happen when her courses came and she was obliged to dispose of her blood-soaked rags? The problem had been worrying her ever since she arrived and now it seemed even more formidable. Well she would have to find a way round it somehow.

Piero sat down on his bed with his legs apart. 'Help me off with my boots, there's a good chap.'

Carla struggled to pull off the leather boots and when she had succeeded she was horrified to see him take off his hose right in front of her, exposing his private parts.

'What's the matter – never seen such a fine set before?' he grinned. 'Well, you shall strike up an intimate acquaintance with my cock and balls. Fetch that bowl of water over here and give them a good washing.'

She stared at him, disbelieving, but the frown that shadowed his brow when she hesitated sent her scurrying across the room to the washbowl. Carla knew she could not afford to get on the wrong side of her new master, but her heart was protesting loudly in her ears. As she knelt before him to perform the task his prick reared up and began to swell, attaining mighty proportions. She stared at it fascinated. It was even larger than Stefano's had been. But it stank of stale sweat and semen, making her wrinkle her nose.

'What are you waiting for? Get on with it!' Piero snapped.

Carla took the sodden sponge from the bowl and began to wash the glans while she held the shaft with her other hand. The penis throbbed and jerked with a will of its own, and Piero gave a grunt of satisfaction. She grew bolder and sponged the whole of his shaft then started on his balls.

'Go easy!' he warned her, as her hands fumbled with the soft scrotum. 'You should know how to handle a man's tackle by now. I dare say you never stop handling your own!'

His words only increased her trepidation. How could she hope to keep her gender a secret when they were living at such close quarters? And when her secret was out she would no doubt be given a beating and turned out onto the street again, or worse. Her fingers trembled as she clasped the sponge and water trickled down Piero's thigh.

'Watch what you're doing!' he grumbled. 'Here, use the corner of this sheet to dry me.'

His phallus felt cool beneath her fingers and, now that it was washed and there was no unpleasant smell, Carla felt those strange excited feelings return. The reddish-purple eye looked up at her from his lap, seeming to offer a challenge. She started to get to her feet, thinking the job was done, but then Piero put his hands on her shoulders and pushed her down again. There was a weird smile on his face and his eyes looked blank and distant.

'You've not finished yet,' he said. 'Act like a cat and give it a good licking for me. A sucking too, if you've a mind. Just make me feel as good as you can and I'll let you stay.'

The excitement within her intensified at his words. All the time she had been handling his prick Carla had been filled with a vague longing, and now Piero had put it into words. Yes, she secretly desired to kiss this wonderful organ, to lick and suck at it until she knew every contour, every crevice. The urge had been there with Stefano, but then she had been too timid, too afraid of upsetting her parents. Well, now she was on her own and she knew a bit more about such things now.

A vision of the two women in the apothecary's shop came into her mind and she bent her head over the erect penis and gave it an experimental lick with the tip of her tongue. Was this what men would pay for? The long moan of delight that issued from Piero as she began to lick more boldly convinced her that this was, indeed, what men liked women to do for them. At first it seemed alien to be tasting living flesh, almost an act of cannibalism, but she soon got used to it and then began to enjoy it.

The musky flavour filled her mouth and, when Carla tasted the first bitter fluid that issued from the slit in his glans, she almost liked that too. He began to thrust hard into her mouth and at first she was afraid he would choke her, but she soon learnt to accommodate the bulbous tip which stroked the roof of her mouth like a caress. While she sucked at his glans she ran her tongue up and down his shaft, eliciting more exclamations of pleasure. It was very gratifying to please a man so.

Before long, Carla was fellating him with abandon, becoming quite expert at manipulating her tongue around the smooth column of flesh while she learnt to tolerate the glans pushing at the back of her throat without gagging. She was unprepared for his climax, even so. When the hot liquid spurted down her throat she squealed and drew back in alarm.

Once Piero had recovered from his ejaculation he regarded her with mocking amusement.

'What's the matter, didn't you think I'd come? You can't give head like that, idiot, and not expect there to be consequences. Here, wipe your mouth. You did a good job, I can tell you that. If you work with as much enthusiasm in other ways you'll fit in here very well. Now get to bed. We rise at dawn, and then you'll soon discover the meaning of hard work. Blow out that candle.'

Carla lay down in the dark on the horsehair mattress and covered herself with a single sheet of hempen cloth. She could not sleep for thinking of what she had just done and how it reminded her of Stefano. Soon she was imagining how it might have been between them, on that sunny hillside, if she had known what to do. Perhaps she could have made him love her, take her as his wife. She began to understand, for the first time, what power a woman could have over a man.

The empty feelings inside her were unbearable, and she thrust her hand between her thighs and squeezed hard. It seemed to relieve the ache a little. Somehow she knew that down there, between her legs, lay the source of both her strength and her weakness, a force that both frightened and delighted her.

In the morning the apprentices were up at first light. Carla heard the bustle on the floor below and sleepily opened her eyes, only to be rudely awakened by Piero. He pulled the sheet off her saying, 'Hands off, lay-a-bed. There's work to do. Get yourself up and splash some water on your face, that'll wake you. Then go down and help get breakfast.'

But when she joined the others they looked at her with sly, grinning faces and whispered to each other behind their hands. Carla was mystified until Giovanni said, 'Did you have a good night then, with the master?'

'I slept well, thank you,' she answered.

'It's what happened *before* you went to sleep, that's what we want to know about! Did he make you suck him off?'

Carla blushed. Had they been spying on her? She looked round at their leering, impudent faces with horror, then Marco came up and put a reassuring hand on her shoulder.

'Don't worry,' he said, with a wink. 'We've all been through it. Think of it as a kind of initiation rite, if you like. At any rate, you're one of us now.'

She gave him a weak smile. He, at least, seemed to be her friend. If this was what being an artist entailed, Carla wasn't sure she liked what she had got herself into. This was a very strange household. It seemed the kind of place where anything could happen, and the fact that she was there under false pretences could get her into a lot of trouble some day.

Chapter Three

*B*y the end of the first week at Piero's, Carla felt accepted as one of the lads. She soon showed herself to be competent at all the small tasks they gave her, from preparing the painting surfaces to making brushes and mixing pigments, and she never grumbled if she was asked to do something menial like sweeping the floor or washing out rags. Although she was the butt of their jokes at first she bore it all good-naturedly and laughed with them. She was very contented with her new way of life.

Although she was kept busy from dawn to dusk, Carla was still able to observe a great deal of what went on around her. There were always half a dozen examples of work in progress in the big, airy workshop on the second floor, and a couple more in the master's room upstairs. The two senior apprentices were working on a picture of Tobias and the Angel. Whilst Marco painted the figure of Tobias, Giovanni was applying jewel-bright colours to the robe and wings of Gabriel, or putting golden high-lights into his curls. Marco told her the work had been commissioned by a silk merchant to mark his eldest son's first business trip abroad and it would be a kind of talisman, to ensure his safety and success.

Carla paid even more attention to what the juniors

were doing, since she hoped to join them before long. They were not allowed to touch the main features of the paintings but worked on backgrounds and minor figures. She noticed how they positioned themselves around a large painting so they could keep out of each others' way. She watched how they held their brushes, sometimes supporting their painting hand with the other on their elbow when the detail needed to be finely executed. She saw how they worked with small quantities of paint on their palettes so it would not dry out, and how careful they were to match the shades to the samples Piero had given them. When Piero finally allowed her to wield a brush Carla was sure she would know what to do.

Meanwhile, there were more pressing concerns, such as how to ensure she kept her female identity a secret. Her period came six days after she arrived, but the flow was never heavy and there was always a good supply of paint rags around the studio. She spirited some away when she went to the privy and then put the soiled ones in with the others when she washed them in the bucket at the end of the day. If the water ran more red than any other colour nobody noticed.

It was at night that she was most afraid of being discovered as a woman, but after her 'initiation' Piero kept his distance. Carla often heard him labouring in the dark to give himself satisfaction, but after a couple of nights it ceased to bother her. Her own desires were another matter. She was having disturbing dreams about the other apprentices, and when she woke she felt ashamed at having enjoyed them.

A favourite fantasy had her posing as a nude model while all the others sat round her in a ring. As they drew her figure they commented on it.

'Small, firm breasts,' one would say. 'Just the way I like them. And such pretty nipples.'

'I go for her bottom,' said another. 'I'd like to take her from behind with those pert buttocks pushing against me.'

'I'd want to see her face. I'd like to watch her pleasure, it would increase my own.'

'I want her to satisfy me, the way she satisfied Piero.'

As the talk continued, Carla would find herself becoming more and more aroused in her dream. Sometimes she would wake in the night and her body would be in a feverish condition, the nipples hard upon her breasts and an itch in the secret channel between her thighs. It was then she would stroke and rub herself, trying to ease the intolerable irritation, but it only seemed to make it worse. Exhausted, she would drop asleep again but in the morning she would feel tired and fractious.

It was in such a mood that she had her first confrontation at work. Giovanni asked her to pick up some delicate gold leaf on a brush and hand it to him, but she breathed too heavily as she was transferring it and the wafer-thin gold floated on to the floor where it disappeared.

'Clumsy oaf!' Giovanni snarled. 'Have you any idea how much that stuff costs? Piero makes me account for every atom of it. Now he'll dock it from my wages.'

'He couldn't help it,' Marco said. 'He's never handled gold leaf before. You should have told him exactly what to do.'

'Any fool can see the stuff is extremely fragile.'

'I'm not a fool!' Carla said, near to tears. 'And I'm not clumsy either. How was I to know how thin the gold was? Where I come from we never saw gold, nor silver neither.'

'Where did you come from – the gutter?' Giovanni sneered. 'I've noticed you never talk about your family. Kick you out, did they?'

'That's enough, Giovanni!' Marco said, his voice surprisingly firm. 'You may be the senior one amongst us, but that doesn't give you the right to bully the new boy.'

'Wait till Piero hears what he's done.'

'You mustn't tell him. It wouldn't be fair on Carlo. Anyway, the master probably won't even notice, but if he asks, say you put an extra layer on the halo. He won't quibble.'

'Why are you taking his side like this?' Giovanni asked, his sallow face dark with suspicion. 'Fancy him, do you?'

'Oh, don't be so ridiculous!'

Marco turned away in disgust, and Carla felt her heart go out to him. She wanted to tell him how grateful she was that he had defended her, but it was impossible with Giovanni looking on. He was scowling at her with the mean-eyed look of a wolf deprived of its prey.

The quarrel blew over, but from then on Carla was wary in her dealings with Giovanni. She tried to keep out of his way as much as she could. He was the only one of the apprentices about whom she had any misgivings. Even Piero seemed less intimidating now she had performed that very personal service for him, seen him naked and heard him belch, fart and snore all night. Most of the time he left her pretty much alone, as if she had become part of the furniture.

Carla did not spend all her time cooped up indoors, however. On Sundays the apprentices accompanied their master to church at Santa Croce and afterwards there were often exciting events in the square such as flag-tossing contests, bear-baiting or jousting. She loved being in the company of the young men, with their infectious energy which expressed itself in jokes and tussles and songs. Before long she knew the words to several of the bawdy songs they loved to sing as they roamed in a gang through the streets, such as the 'Song of the bakers':

> *'Into your oven goes my shovel,*
> *While I knead your pretty pies,*
> *Soon your bread will start to double,*
> *No need to show such surprise!'*

One afternoon there was a *Giuoco del Calcio*. The *Piazza Santa Croce* had been made into an arena with benches all round, and from the windows of all the houses facing on to the square hung banners of fine embroidered linen in bright colours, making the scene look very festive. Carla stood with the others at one of the corners, and soon the two teams came running into the ring dressed in their coloured uniforms of red and blue, and green and yellow, preceded by their team flags.

The crowd roared, getting to their feet with much cheering and jeering. 'Which team are we supporting?' Carla asked Marco.

'The reds, of course!' he grinned. 'Down with the greens!'

There were 27 players on each side and play began at a furious pace which was kept up throughout. As they chased the ball from end to end of the arena Carla tried to work out the rules, but the only thing she was sure of was when one side or the other scored a goal. The game was exhilarating to watch even so, and everyone was in an excited mood by the time it came to an end. Marco was particularly pleased because the reds had won hands down. He put his arms around Carla and hugged her tightly, which made her happy, but the physical contact with him aroused feelings in her that she did not want to explore right then.

After the match they all hung around to watch the entertainment and the other boys flirted with any girls they could find, some of them making secret assignations.

'How can he possibly get to see her again?' Carla asked Marco, when she overheard Luigi arranging to meet a pretty young girl.

'Wouldn't you like to know! I'll warrant that next time he goes off to market he'll be a long time gone. Or maybe he'll steal out under cover of darkness. You know what they say, "Love will find a way!"'

'Does this often happen?' she asked, surprised.

He gave her a wink. 'More often than Piero dreams of. That's the beauty of having him tucked up in bed upstairs. Sometimes we have two or three girls smuggled in!'

'I can hardly believe it.'

'What's the matter, are you jealous? Maybe we'll sort one out for you sometime. You could easily creep downstairs once old Piero is snoring away.'

'Oh no!'

Too late, Carla realised that the dismay in her voice was too strong. Marco grinned. 'You're still a virgin, is that it? Perhaps you should visit a whore. I know a good woman. She's used to helping young boys through their first time.'

Carla said nothing, afraid of giving the game away. But Marco did not forget their conversation. One afternoon he said casually, in front of the others, 'Why don't you come down tonight, after Piero's asleep? We've got two girls coming and we'll arrange some good sport for you.'

Carla didn't know what to say. If she refused they would think her a prude or a weakling, but if she accepted she might get herself into deep water. She said she would, but then reasoned that she could pretend she had fallen asleep and forgotten all about it.

She wasn't to be let off that lightly, however. When she didn't appear, Matteo crept up to the master's bedroom and shook her awake. Piero was still snoring away, so Carla had no excuse not to follow him downstairs where the older apprentices were whispering and flirting with two young girls. She felt weird, seeing them sitting in the laps of Luigi and Marco. A sudden feeling of jealousy took her by surprise when she saw Marco kiss the pale neck of his girl and stroke her blonde, curly hair.

'I've brought Carlo down for kissing lessons,' Matteo announced, making her blush horribly.

'Only kissing?' Luigi said. He glanced at his girl and she giggled. 'Nina's a good kisser, aren't you sweetheart? Are you prepared to show a novice how to do it?'

'Mm, maybe. It depends what I get in return.'

'Saucy minx!' Luigi pushed her off his lap. 'Go over there and give him a proper tonguing. Make his toes curl

41

and his cock stand up, then you might get a good time later. Off you go.'

There was no way Carla could get out of it without looking a bigger fool than she already felt. She stood there, stiff as a board, while Nina sidled up to her with an amused grin. 'Have you really never kissed a girl before?'

Carla nodded, wanting to sink through the floor. Yet the girl intrigued her, with her knowing brown eyes and mature, voluptuous body. Here was someone of around her own age who already knew far more about love and life than Carla had dreamt of. She felt as much in awe of her as she had of the two whores in the apothecary's. But beneath it all she was still terrified of discovery.

'Come on,' Nina said, taking her by the hand. 'Over here where we can be comfortable.' She made Carla lie down on one of the boys' beds then lay alongside her. 'Take me in your arms, then! Now slowly bring your lips towards mine until they meet in a kiss – that's right.'

Carla was amazed to find that kissing another woman was not so different from kissing Stefano. When she thought about it, there was no reason why it should be, but somehow she had imagined that men and women's bodies were totally different all over. It was a revelation to her to be able to kiss quite passionately without worrying about the fact that Nina was of the same sex as herself.

The other girl's mouth was fresh and sweet, her little tongue active and probing. Soon Carla was enjoying the kiss immensely, letting her lips move against the softness of Nina's while their tongues duelled playfully. Then, when the other girl drew away, she felt a definite twinge of disappointment.

Carla looked up to see the faces of the apprentices ranged all round the bed, regarding her with amusement. She looked away, abashed, and they all laughed at her.

'If that was really your first time you put up a jolly

good show!' Luigi said. 'How was it for you, Nina? Did you prefer this young virgin's kisses to mine?'

In response, the girl hurled a pillow at him. This gave him the excuse for a pillow fight and soon the couple were attacking each other with abandon while the other apprentices warned them to keep the noise down.

Their warning came too late. The heavy tread of Piero was heard on the stair, accompanied by his grunts and mutterings. The two girls were unceremoniously bundled out through the back door to make their escape into the night. By the time the master appeared all candles had been extinguished and the lads were apparently asleep in their beds.

Piero sniffed the air. 'What can I smell? Candle wax, sweat and a woman's perfume. Have you been up to your tricks again?'

Only a stifled giggle answered him. He re-lit one of the candles and held it aloft. Carla held her breath as she huddled beneath a blanket in the corner. 'Carlo, what are you doing down here? Back upstairs, this minute!'

She did as she was told and soon the house was quiet again. Before Piero got back into bed he forbade her to leave the room at night again. 'Those boys are a bad influence on you. Before I know it you'll be carousing and whoring with them, and not concentrating on your work. I've seen it happen to Luigi and Antonio, but I'm damned if I'll let it happen to you. You've got real promise!'

Carla was secretly pleased that he valued her so highly, but she had no intention of giving up the company of the other apprentices. She might stay in her bed at night, but during the day she would relish the easy camaraderie that she had with them, especially with Marco. They were developing a real friendship, and if he had to go out of the workshop for an hour or two she could hardly wait for him to come back. She took every opportunity she could to talk to him or help him with his work, and when he acknowledged her with a smile or word of thanks it made her day.

Around the middle of June the workshop suddenly became a hive of frantic activity. Marco explained that Carnival was approaching and there was a huge demand for all kinds of painted scenery, traditional-style towers of paper and wax, elaborate masks and head-dresses – all of which Florentine artists were well able to provide. Piero's workshops became stuffed from floor to ceiling with columns, arches and backdrops made out of wood or plaster and painted to look like the real thing.

Carla enjoyed helping out. She was given free rein with some of the items and was particularly pleased with a beautiful female mask she made. The skin was like porcelain delicately tinged with pink, and the eye-holes had real lashes fixed around them which she had made from horse-hair. Even Piero admired it, and his next words astonished her.

'It's too good to waste on any customer, you shall wear it yourself!'

'*Me*?' Carla exclaimed. 'But where? How?'

'You shall ride on the float with the other lads. They need a woman for the masque they're going to perform. You'll do perfectly. Your figure is quite womanly, since you've not got your manly muscles yet.'

She did not know what to say at first. The others began to agree with Piero, saying she would be perfect for the part of the pretty young girl married to the rich old man. When Carla discovered she was supposed to cuckold her husband, played by Giovanni, with a younger lover, played by Marco, she began to find the prospect more attractive.

'You'll be riding on the float in the procession,' Piero explained. 'It will stop every so often and the masque will be performed, with the others providing the music.'

'The crowd throw coins and gifts,' Matteo added with a grin. 'I ate so many sweetmeats last year that I was sick as a dog afterwards.'

'Trust you!' Marco said, cuffing the boy affectionately.

'So, will you do it?' Piero asked her. He was smiling at her quite benignly, for a change. She nodded. 'Good fellow! Or should I say, "Good girl!"?' To Carla's surprise he planted a juicy kiss on her mouth. 'Mm, your lips could make me believe you were a woman – in the dark!'

'You watch him, Carlo!' Luigi grinned. 'He might come on to you after lights out!'

While they all worked hard at the preparations the lads began talking about what happened at last year's carnival. It sounded as if the Feast of Saint John the Baptist was a celebration marked by licence and excess. Carla listened, goggle-eyed, whilst the older apprentices went into detail.

'Remember that girl with the enormous breasts, Marco?' Luigi said.

'How could I forget?'

'While you tupped her from behind she let me rub my cock between her tits.'

'Yes, and what an arse she had! Great fleshy buttocks you could really get a handle on. And she squeezed me with her cunt as if she were milking a cow. Gave me the most fantastic climax, I can tell you!'

'What was her name? I've forgotten.'

'Er . . . was it Emilia?'

'Yes, that's it! I hope we'll see her again this year.'

'Me too. This time you can fuck her while I get to come between her fat breasts. I can hardly wait!'

Hearing their frank talk Carla was assailed by mixed emotions. She was curious to know what went on between a man and a woman, but at the same time she felt absurd pangs of jealousy at the thought of Marco making love to another woman. She knew it was ridiculous, but she couldn't help herself.

Marco caught her eye and must have sensed something of what was going on inside her. He gave her a wink, saying, 'Don't mind us, Carlo. We work hard and we play hard, that's just the way we are. Some day I intend to settle down with a good woman, but until then I shall have as much fun as I can find.'

'You'll find plenty on the 24th!' Luigi grinned. 'It's a

shame you're going to be dressed as a woman, Carlo, or you might get your share too. But I doubt any girl is going to be attracted to a man in a gown.'

'Oh, I don't know,' Giovanni put in, with a wry smile. 'Some of the priests don't do so badly!'

That night Carla was in a turmoil. It was bad enough having to pose as a boy, but to be dressed as a girl would be quite an ordeal. She guessed that she was going to have to take some ribbing from the other apprentices. If they only knew! Most of all she was upset at the thought of Marco making fun of her. She had begun to desire him passionately. She was quite sure of that now, although the knowledge had come as a shock to her. But hearing him talk about being with other girls had awakened such fiery longings within, that it was all she could do to avoid flinging off her tunic and hose and revealing her woman's body to him there and then.

She moaned softly in her distress, safe in the knowledge that Piero was out on the town. He had gone off to the tavern – on one of his binges, as Luigi had described it. Apparently they happened once a month or so. It was the first time Carla had been alone at night and she lay sombrely examining her feelings while she hugged herself beneath the thin coverlet. Her body was warm and soft to the touch. Would it please a man like Marco?

Slowly her hands crept to her aching bosom, where the nipples were sticking out like bronze finials on the alabaster domes of her breasts. Carla brushed them experimentally with her fingertips and felt a hot spasm of energy flood down towards the tingling niche between her thighs. She tried to remember what it had felt like to have Stefano inside her, but the memory was already becoming blurred. Her old life seemed a lifetime away, the village where she had been born and bred more like a foreign country.

Sighing and moaning, Carla played with her nipples with one hand while the other one parted the overheated labia and felt the soft, damp warmth within. Something was throbbing steadily down there, a small nub of flesh

46

at the top of her private place that seemed to have a hot appetite of its own. Tentatively she began to rub the spot, and the tingling sensations intensified. How strange it felt to be giving herself pleasure in that way! But she reasoned that if a man's fingers could caress and stroke her the way that Stefano's had, then her own could do it just as well. And there seemed no other way to quench the fire that had been kindled in her body.

Suddenly she heard noisy footsteps treading heavily upon the stairs and she knew that Piero had returned from his drinking bout. He came swearing and grunting upstairs and Carla knew that her chance of finding relief must be postponed if she were not to attract his unwanted attention. So she turned over onto her stomach, pretending to be asleep.

Piero flung the door open and then cursed a few times. Making no attempt to light a candle he sat on his bed and struggled with his boots, cursing again until he had managed to remove them and fling them across the floor. Carla listened to the succession of noises in resignation, hoping he would just tumble into bed and settle down. He was bound to snore, but she had more or less got used to that.

'Wench!' she heard him mutter. 'That's what I could do with, a nice fat wench!'

Carla heard him stagger to the piss-pot and fill it, then he flopped down heavily on his mattress, making the floor shake. Relieved, she flexed her legs and rustled the sheets, preparing to sleep, but that was her undoing. As if he had suddenly realised that he was not alone, Piero rose from his bed and came over to hers with an evil-sounding chuckle. Dread clasped at her heart with a tight grip.

'I might not have a wench, but I've got a boy!' she heard him mutter. 'And he's mine, to serve me any way I want. You gave good head, boy. Let's see if you can give good arse, too!'

Carla trembled as the covers were torn off her, exposing her prone body in its thin shift. Now her sex would

47

be discovered and she would have to take the consequences! She felt the weight of Piero's knees on either
side of her own, but still she dared not speak or move.
His hands pulled up her shift but she kept her thighs
close together and her buttocks clenched. She was terrified, and yet the hot excitement she had been feeling just
minutes before was still with her, ready to be ignited
once again. Torn between fear and desire she wondered
what would happen next.

'If I use some oil it won't hurt you,' she heard Piero
say. 'Open your legs, there's a good lad. I've got a stiffy
fit to paint with.'

Strong hands pushed her thighs apart and then a
warm, oily finger was placed in the crack between her
buttocks and began to burrow its way in. At first she
resisted, but soon the feeling changed from being painful
to being pleasurable. Piero began to wind his finger
round and round in her, loosening her up, and she began
to move her mound against the mattress, finding the
friction most gratifying.

'That's right!' Piero cooed. 'You get used to it, lad. A
fellow can take another's prick without shame when the
need is great. It doesn't make you any less of a man.'

He was pressing a second finger into her, opening her
anus and making the wild throbbing in the front of her
body accelerate to fever pitch. Carla stopped worrying
about whether he would discover the truth about her.
She stopped caring what he was about to do to her. All
she wanted was to wrest every bit of satisfaction from
the experience that she could.

So when Piero's thick tool began to worm its way into
her backside, Carla relaxed and let him enter her without
obstruction. His thrusting soon produced exquisite feelings in her, both back and front, so that the twinges of
pain that accompanied them hardly mattered. She raised
her pelvis and thrust back against him, glorying in the
heightened sensation that this activity produced.

It didn't take long for her master to achieve his climax.
With a volley of curses interspersed by gasps and groans,

Piero clutched so hard at her thin shoulders as he came that she squealed aloud. He mistook her anguish for protest and pulled out of her rapidly, mumbling apologies.

'Didn't mean to hurt you – gone too far – sorry . . .'

He rolled off her bed and on to the floor with a thud. Carla lay in stunned silence, feeling the darkened room whirling about her ears as she tried to recover from her frenzy of sensuality. Her body was still hot and needy, but she was also exhausted and continued to lie, face down, until the feelings subsided and drowsiness took their place.

She was vaguely aware of Piero clambering back into his own bed and of everything going quiet again. With a deep sigh, Carla turned on her side and prepared for sleep. Her bottom was sore, and would no doubt feel worse in the morning, but at least Piero had not explored further than her arse and was still under the impression that she was a boy. For that, at least, she was grateful.

Next day Piero was contrite. Although he was obviously in a bad state himself, he gave her some apothecary salve for her inflamed anus and brought her a posset of healing herbs. 'Sorry I was a bit rough with you last night,' he said, gruffly. 'You can stay in bed for a bit if you like.'

But Carla didn't want to lie in bed like a mardy child. She had dreamt of Marco all night and was eager to see him again. In her dreams he had been taking her from behind, not like Piero, but the way he had with the big-bosomed girl. His hands had played with her breasts while he thrust into her, making the hot throbbing grow more and more urgent until something burst within her like the sun filling the horizon, flushing her through and through with flurries of voluptuous warmth. She had never had a dream like it before, and the memory of it was still with her like a glorious flower, blooming secretly in her head.

When she went down into the workshop Marco was there with young Antonio. Both Luigi and Giovanni were out on business. He looked at her strangely when she appeared, and her heart seemed to revolve like a tumbler. His quizzical face searched hers for clues until he said, 'There's something different about you this morning, Carlo. You didn't lose your virginity last night by any chance, did you?'

Carla stifled a giggle, since this was ironically near the truth. But she shook her head. 'No, of course not.' She didn't want to tell him what Piero had done to her.

Marco grinned, tousling her hair affectionately. 'You know, you're going to make an awfully pretty girl at the carnival. I wouldn't be surprised if I don't end up quite fancying you. Better mind I don't get too drunk, or I might make a pass at you!'

The smile that Carla gave him back was knowing, secretive. It was proving a sweet pain to conceal her sex from this man. She longed for the day when she could be open with him, when they might stand a chance of being lovers. But, for the time being, she could only dream. And dreams, however sweet, could never quite satisfy.

Chapter Four

They were short-handed in the workshop, with so many commissions for the carnival on top of their other work. The place was littered with curls of paper, blobs of wax, wood shavings and string. One morning Piero took Carla aside and said the words she was longing to hear.

'I'm prepared to let you paint in some background to one of my jobs. The other lads are too busy, with this cursed carnival practically upon us. Come on upstairs, and I'll show you what needs to be done.'

She followed him gladly, aware that she was about to be given her first real painting job. In the upstairs studio stood Piero's personal commissions. The statue had disappeared but the triptych was still there, almost complete, and there was a half-finished portrait of a man in hunting costume. Behind him the Tuscan hills were sketched in, and figures of dogs and horses. Piero gestured towards the work.

'This is the one. I want the hillsides filled in. You'll need several shades of green, and then I want flowers scattered, mostly white, yellow and purple. Do you think you're up to it?'

'Oh yes!'

'Better not tell the others, eh? This will be our little

secret.' His dark eyes gleamed at her in friendly conspiracy. 'We don't want them complaining to the Guild, now do we? If you manage it well I might think about taking you on officially. I'm making no promises, mind!'

Carla just nodded, but her heart was singing loudly. An apprenticeship! She quashed the thought that she would be in big trouble with the Guild if her gender were ever discovered, vowing to cross that bridge if and when she came to it. For now it was enough that Piero trusted her to work on his precious portrait, if only on the background.

She worked happily all morning, her palette filled with pigments mixed from malachite and copper. Piero showed her how to make another shade, green lake, by boiling verdigris in larch resin. Soon the grass and foliage were glowing like the first flush of spring.

'That's good, very good!' Piero smiled. 'I knew you'd repay my faith in you. Now mix up some Naples yellow and white lead for the flowers.'

When she had gone as far as she could with the portrait, and Piero declared himself well satisfied, he decided to trust her with an even more important task.

'I need some blue, not azurite but ultramarine. Will you mix some for me?'

Carla knew how expensive the deep blue pigment was, and how much he trusted her to let her mix it. It was made from ground lapis lazuli and only used for very important subjects, such as the blue of a Madonna's gown. While Piero worked on his triptych she went to fetch the carved wooden box in which the costly powder was kept. She brought it down from the shelf and took it over to the workbench where the pestle and mortar were.

After grinding it to a fine powder Carla mixed the pigment with egg yolk and a little water, the way she had been shown, until it was smooth and thick. She took the little bowl in her hand and walked towards Piero who was concentrating on his painting, the tip of his tongue protruding slightly as was his habit. Suddenly she tripped over a loose floorboard and the bowl went flying. The precious paint went mostly over the floor and some of it splashed on the triptych, just where it was not wanted.

Shock turned Carla into a frozen statue. She couldn't believe what had just happened, but there was the accusing stain to prove it and the little bowl smashed into fragments. After what seemed like an endless hiatus, a furious cry broke from the master.

'You stupid bastard – look what you've done! How could you be so careless with the most expensive pigment of all? Dolt!'

He cuffed her round the ear and Carla burst into tears but this only inflamed Piero more. 'Stop blubbing, you fool! There's no use crying over spilt milk. Get a cloth and clear it up at once.' Then he saw where it had splashed onto the corner of his painting and he gave another roar. 'Mother of Christ, you've ruined my painting, too!'

Carla stammered her apologies, but her words sounded futile even to her ears. She could hear her pulses hammering in her ears and the sight of Piero's dark face, screwed up in fury, only made her heart beat all the more. Trembling she fetched a rag and began to mop up the deep blue paint.

'You deserve a thrashing!' she heard Piero say, as he examined the damage to his painting with an incredulous expression. 'You're supposed to be helping, not hindering. What a fool I was to trust you. Perhaps a good beating will knock some sense into you.'

He picked up a fretted fly swatter and a deep dread filled her. Her father had never beaten her, and Stefano's chastisement of her had been more playful than painful. But Piero was very angry. When she cowered away from him, backing slowly towards the door, his eyes glittered cruelly at her. 'Come here!' he snapped. 'And take your punishment like a man!'

He seized her wrist and dragged her over to the bench where he made her bend over. His rough hands pulled at her clothes until her hose was around her ankles and her buttocks were bare. Carla remembered what he had done to her before and hot shame ran through her, but when the first slap of the reed implement came she found it did not hurt as much as she had feared and the now-familiar feelings of arousal happened again.

'I'll teach you!' Piero snapped, swatting at her bottom once again. 'You deserve my belt, not this flimsy thing.'

There was a pause and, for one dreadful moment, Carla thought he was unbuckling his belt to use that on her. But something had caught his attention. He suddenly pulled her round, lifting her tunic, and she knew with a horrible sinking certainty, that her game was all over.

'God's body, I don't believe it!' he was saying, his expression totally incredulous as he stared at the bushy hair hiding her private parts. 'A woman! You're a bloody woman!'

Carla could not meet his eyes. She stood there trembling like a leaf, unable to say a word. All kinds of terrible punishments filled her imagination, every one far worse than a mere thrashing. Although she had only been in Florence a few weeks she had seen the dreadful penalties that certain miscreants had to pay under the Law. There had been public mutilations, pillories and hangings. She had no idea what punishment might be meted out to impostors like herself and she was quite certain that Piero would hand her over to the authorities forthwith.

So she was utterly astonished when he burst out laughing. 'The cheek of it!' he kept saying. 'The brazen cheek of it!'

'I'm sorry,' she said, hanging her head with tears flooding her eyes. 'It was very wrong of me. But I did so want to become an artist.'

'You fooled me good and proper. You fooled all of us! To think I had you in the arse, when I could have taken you like a woman! You had the last laugh on me, wench, didn't you?'

'I – I meant no harm . . .'

'Sure you didn't. But harm will come to you if this gets out. The Guild would make an example of you, and it wouldn't be a pretty sight, I can tell you!'

Instinctively Carla dropped to her knees. 'Please don't report me, master. I'll do anything for you. I'll work for you for nothing.'

'What? Do you imagine you can go on keeping your sex a secret indefinitely?' Piero looked thoughtful for a moment, then continued, 'Well, and why not? If I hadn't stripped your lower half just now I'd never have guessed. I was looking for your cock and balls dangling down, you know, and suddenly I realised they weren't there.' He laughed again. 'Damn me! You really took me for a ride, young woman.'

'The others wouldn't have to know,' Carla assured him. 'We could go back to how it was before. I'd go on working as if I were your apprentice.'

'You can never be that,' Piero said, solemnly. 'But I suppose you're right about the others. If they haven't sussed you by now there's no reason to suppose they ever will. Still, I don't like it. I don't like it at all. A woman's place is in the home, not in the workplace. Whatever possessed you, Carlo – hell's bells, I don't even know your real name!'

'It's Carla. I came to Florence in men's clothes for my own protection. I wanted to make my own way in life, and I had my own reasons for wanting to leave my village.'

'I'm sure you did,' Piero said, not unkindly. 'Well, Carla, if we are to continue with this charade – oh my goodness! To think I wanted you to dress as a girl for the carnival!'

He went into hoots of laughter again. Carla was disconcerted, still not knowing what the outcome of all this would be. She watched his face keenly for clues and once he stopped laughing his expression took on a thoughtful cast. The dark eyes looked her up and down, as if seeing her for the first time, and then his mouth curved into a wicked grin.

'All right, here are my conditions,' he began at last. 'I shall say nothing about your – small deficiency, but you must let me come to your bed whenever I fancy. You shall be my woman, to fuck whenever I please. But that will be our secret. I swear no one will ever know.'

Carla sighed, remembering what Stefano had said to her. Now she seemed to be in just the same position, a man's plaything to be used or discarded as the mood took him. The spirit of rebellion that had led her to abandon her home and family and escape to Florence flared again briefly, but then she had second thoughts. In many ways she was happy in Piero's household. She was learning her craft, although mostly by proxy, and she enjoyed the company of the other apprentices, especially Marco, while the thought of facing life on the streets again was utterly depressing.

But to submit to Piero's will, to let him ravage her whenever he liked – could she bear that? Carla felt a little shiver run through her, but it contained more excitement than fear. Secretly she longed for those wonderful feelings she had experienced with Stefano and perhaps Piero would be a good lover. He was older than her cousin had been, and she knew he frequented whores from time to time. He was quite good looking too, and there was a raw, virile energy about him that fascinated her.

He misunderstood the reasons for her hesitation and broke in with a smile, 'You needn't worry about getting with child. I can control myself.'

'Then – I will accept your offer,' she said. 'So long as I can go on helping out in the workshop. I wouldn't want any more than bed and board.'

'Fine, so long as you realise you can never be apprenticed. I don't know how I'll explain it to the others as time goes by, but I'll think of something. So it's agreed. Let's shake on it like gentlemen, even though you're a cursed female!'

His wry grin and the dancing light in his eye led Carla to think that becoming this man's mistress might be less of an ordeal than she had at first thought. As she went about her tasks that day she even found herself looking forward to the night, hoping that Piero would come to her bed as a lover for the first time. When she joined the other apprentices, however, she felt even more of an impostor than she had before.

'What was all that shouting about earlier?' Marco asked her quietly, while they were preparing the table together.

'I spilt some ultramarine.'

Marco whistled through his pursed lips. 'Shit! Did you get a beating?' She nodded. 'That's what I was afraid of before, when you spoilt that gold leaf. I got you out of a thrashing then but this time I couldn't help you, I'm sorry. Piero does everything on a shoestring because he tries to undercut the other artists to get more work. So if you waste any materials he goes wild. We usually cover up for each other if we spill anything.'

'I'll be more careful in future.'

'I bet you will!'

Marco's smile was warm and comforting. Carla longed to throw her arms around him and declare her feelings along with her secret, but she dared not. It would be even harder pretending to be a boy now that Piero knew the truth, but Marco, who held the key to her heart, was still ignorant of her true nature. If only he'd been the one to find out instead! She would have had no hesitation in accepting *him* as her lover, in exchange for his silence.

For the rest of the day Carla tried to behave normally but her mind and heart were in turmoil. When the time came for them all to retire, she made her way up to the top floor as usual and performed her toilet at the wash-stand. Then she lay down in her shift and waited, in some trepidation, for Piero to finish drinking his wine downstairs.

At last she could hear his tread upon the stair. She lay quietly in the candlelight and soon he appeared, a formidable figure in the doorway. His crudely handsome face was grinning at her, and she felt her heart sink as she realised that she was completely at his mercy. He stripped off his clothes until he was stark naked and she saw his sturdy cock rise to attention as he approached her bed.

'Get that thing off!' he said, pulling at her shift. 'Now I know you're a woman I want a good look at your body. You can't be much of one, I suppose, if you've kept us all in the dark this long.'

He brought the candle near and, blushing, she pulled the thin shift over her head until her body was completely exposed. He proceeded to comment, as if he were buying an animal at market, but the situation was so like that of her dream of posing nude for the apprentices that Carla began to feel aroused and her nipples stood stiffly on her small breasts.

'You've not much in the way of a bosom,' Piero observed. 'But what you have got is shapely enough and the rest of your figure is pleasing. I wouldn't mind making a study of you sometime.' He grinned. 'Turn you into a madonna, maybe. How would you like that?'

She smiled but said nothing. Already she felt like his possession, as if she had no rights of her own. He put out his hand and caressed her breast with his palm, sending shivers of anticipation down her spine. 'Don't worry,' he said. 'I won't hurt you. You're still a virgin, aren't you?'

Carla wasn't altogether sure. Although she believed Stefano had taken her virginity, somehow it did not seem to count. Afraid that Piero would not want her if he thought she had been with another man, she nodded.

'Thought as much. I wouldn't have been so rough with you the other night if I'd known what you really were. This time I'll be more gentle.'

He made her spread her legs then felt between them. Carla was aware of the folds of flesh opening up to him, revealing the secret of her sex, proving to him that she was what she claimed to be. Piero laughed again, softly, the kind of laugh a man gives when the joke is on him, and his finger pressed harder into her. She could feel how soft and wet she was down there, the way she had been with Stefano, and deep inside her the slow building-up of tension began as her body prepared itself for pleasure.

Piero's lips fastened on one of her erect nipples, intensifying her desire for him. She could smell the male odours on him, sweat and musk, and her heart rejoiced at the primitive meeting of male and female. His eagerness for her was very gratifying, and as his tongue laved her breast and his fingers worked at the moist lips of her pussy, Carla marvelled at her own increasing lust for him. So this is what being a woman means, she told herself.

Up to now she had believed that the attraction was all one-way, that men craved and women endured, but now she was discovering new urges within herself. The flame that Stefano had ignited was burning brightly and she could hardly wait for Piero to come inside her. She began to moan and push her mound against his groping fingers, longing for her need to be assuaged.

'Are you sure you're a virgin?' he asked, grinning. 'You seem suspiciously hot for it.'

'Mm, it feels so good!' she murmured.

'It'll feel even better soon.'

He knelt between her outspread thighs and placed his glans at her entrance. Carla felt her womb twitch at the thought of that hard flesh plunging into her, filling up her emptiness. He eased his way in, inching slowly into the welcoming interior with a groan of satisfaction, and she pushed her breasts against his chest, feeling the rough hairs tickle her nipples. At first there was some soreness, and she moved awkwardly trying to synchronise her hips with his. But once he was snug inside her she began to work her mound against him more smoothly, instinctively moving to increase her own excitement.

Soon Piero was grunting and sweating his way

towards a climax, his heavy balls slapping against her thighs as he rode her like a mare. Carla exulted in his energy, his whole-hearted concentration on the task in hand. She had seen him look like that when he was painting, as if nothing else in the world mattered but what he was doing right then. She had felt the same, absorbed in her own artistic tasks. But now he was obsessed with her and she with him, and it felt wonderful to have their two minds and bodies working in harmony.

But then, just as he was puffing and panting the loudest, Piero suddenly pulled out of her and shot his seed over the sheets. Carla was shocked. She felt as if someone had thrown cold water over her, all her senses reeling at the sudden withdrawal of stimulation. She lay there listening to her deafening heartbeat, feeling the perspiration trickle down her breasts and a great sadness overwhelmed her. What had begun as a glorious consummation suddenly seemed just an animal act, a crude encounter that was over in a few minutes.

'There, I said you'd be safe!' Piero told her with some satisfaction. He evidently expected her to be pleased that he'd managed to get out in time. Carla nodded, but what she was feeling inside was too overwhelming to speak of. There was a great sense of loss, of frustration and a sudden realisation of just what she'd let herself in for.

She wanted him to stay in her bed and cuddle her for a bit, but as soon as his breath was back Piero rose and shuffled over to the piss pot. After he'd relieved himself he sank back on to his own bed. In the darkness Carla felt a tear trickle down her cheek and she was only slightly comforted when he said, 'You'll be all right here, you know. Goodnight.'

The next day was hard. Mixing with the other apprentices Carla already felt different. Up to now she had hidden her secret well, but now that Piero not only knew she was a woman but was treating her like one, her secret had become a conspiracy, and that made her uneasy. She was constantly looking out for searching glances, or listening for pointed remarks. At every moment she expected someone to notice the swell of her breasts under her tunic or to smell the odour of her sex, although she had scrubbed herself almost raw to remove all trace of it.

It was worse when they talked of the show they would put on for the carnival. They ribbed her mercilessly for being cast in the rôle of a woman, their comments being rather too near the mark at times.

'You'd better watch out for Piero on Carnival night,' Giovanni said. 'He might just forget you're a boy dressed up as a girl and take you for the real thing.'

'Yes – he'll "take you" all right,' Matteo grinned. 'If he's drunk enough he won't know the difference between a cunt and an arse.'

'Shut up, don't frighten the lad!' Marco intervened. 'I think we should start thinking about his costume, not putting the frighteners on him. He'll need a wig to go with his mask, and some sort of padding to go under his gown. And we should be rehearsing, as if we were on the float. There's only a few days to go.'

'He can make his own wig, can't he?' Giovanni grunted. 'We're all far too busy.'

So Carla was set to make a 'womanly' wig for herself. Marco helped her design it. They fashioned it out of flax dyed bright yellow, and she twisted bunches of the fake hair into the semblance of an elaborate coiffure, studded with 'pearls' and 'diamonds.'

'I'm going to look a fright in this,' she told him at last.

'That's the whole idea. We're all going to look like exaggerated versions of real people. It helps the crowd to understand at once what sort of characters we're playing. When you've only a couple of minutes to tell a story you need bold effects and big gestures. It will be very effective, you'll see.'

As night-time approached Carla found herself growing impatient for the newly-discovered joys of the bedroom. Despite the fact that her last night with Piero had

61

left her more frustrated than satisfied she couldn't wait for more of the same.

He seemed eager to get her alone too, making an excuse to take her upstairs as soon as the evening meal was ended. Once they were alone he fell upon her, his lips ravishing her neck with kisses and his hands tearing off her clothes.

'You've awakened such an appetite in me,' he confessed. 'Seeing you dressed up as a boy all day, and knowing what you really look like under your clothes, only makes me want you more.'

He took her to his bed this time. It was larger and more substantial, and she sank on to it with a sigh. Soon he had her spread-eagled on the mattress while he took her from behind, not in the arse but passing between her thighs to the smooth, warm channel of her sex where he plunged in with gusto. Carla moaned, writhing against the bunched bedcovers and feeling the rough cloth abrade her swollen nipples. Then his hands passed beneath her and he squeezed her breasts, sending new tremors of delight throughout her willing body.

'Oh, I could get used to this!' he grunted, as she moved her buttocks in rhythm with his thrusts. 'You may have been a virgin, maybe not. Either way, you're learning fast how to please me. I love a woman that moves her hindquarters the way you do.'

His words inflamed her lust so that the throbbing sensations grew stronger, inflaming her to fever pitch. She was dangling on the edge of satisfaction, sure that a few more of Piero's lusty thrusts would bring her whatever consummation her body craved, but then came his sudden backward slide and the soft curses as he spurted all over her naked buttocks.

'God, I nearly didn't make it that time!' he exclaimed, as he rolled over onto his back beside her.

She lay quietly while he wiped himself with the sheet then made his way over to the piss pot once again. The light of a full moon was flooding the attic room, and Carla felt its coolness on her overheated flesh, but it wasn't enough to soothe the disappointed ache deep within. What was it that she wanted? She had no idea, yet the sense of being left high and dry was overwhelming.

Sleep came slowly that night. Carla spent hours lying in the eerie moonlight, wondering where her life was going. A part of her felt trapped, obliged to serve her master in bed while being unable to serve him properly as his apprentice. Yet she knew it had always been a wild dream of hers to become a *bona fide* artist. Women were banned from such work, and she had been a fool to think she could get away with her disguise for long. Perhaps she should count her blessings and settle for a life under Piero's protection, doing such work as he gave her and being his mistress in private.

Carla might have accepted such a fate willingly if it wasn't for the presence of Marco in the household. Her feelings for him were growing daily, strange longings that she had only been able to identify properly since Piero came to her bed. If only it were Marco making love to her she would be perfectly happy. His kindness and friendship had kindled a deeper desire in her than the merely physical and she was sure that, if only she were given the chance, she could give herself to him body and soul.

It was far too dangerous to think that way in reality, but nothing could stop her fantasising. When she finally fell asleep her imaginings pervaded her dreams, and she replayed her love-making with Marco taking Piero's place. This time the sweet sensations haunted her all night long and were still with her when she awoke next morning, feeling stiff and sore. She washed and went downstairs to prepare Piero's breakfast, as she always did, and the sight of Marco in his shift made her blush.

He looked at her closely, then took her aside. 'What is it, Carlo? You look so strange this morning. Is it something Piero has done to you?' Carla shook her head but she could tell he was not convinced. His expression grew more concerned. 'He's abusing you, isn't he? Buggering you. Is that it?'

'I – I'd rather not say.'

'Don't worry, I won't get you into trouble. But tonight I'll get him off down the whorehouse then he won't come to your bed. Perhaps he can be persuaded to let you sleep downstairs with us in future. I'll see what I can do.'

Carla was grateful for his offer but she knew it would be futile. Piero had no need of a whore while he had her, and he certainly wasn't going to let her sleep elsewhere. As she looked into Marco's dark, kindly eyes she longed to tell him the whole truth but she dared not.

The apprentices made a sortie into the streets of Florence to see how the carnival route was being prepared. Carla was amazed to see blue canopies hung between the houses bearing patterns of suns, moons and stars like a false sky. The carnival was only days away and there was a general air of excitement throughout the city. Stands were being erected in the main squares where the spectacles were taking place, and there were floats being constructed in yards and back alleys everywhere. Jugglers and fire-eaters were practising their skills, singers, musicians and actors were rehearsing and all the bakers were busy making extra pies and sweetmeats for the hungry masses.

Carla was thrilled at the thought that she would be a part of it all. Yet she felt apprehensive too. What if people found her a bit too convincing as a girl? Would they suspect the truth, or would they think she was one of those effeminate males who preferred lying with other men? Worst of all was the fear that she might not be able to trust Piero to keep her secret. He had already been making suggestive remarks to her. He had told her not to worry about her costume, that he would borrow clothes from a whore to dress her up in. What if he dropped hints to the others that she not only looked the part of a whore but she acted it too?

That night Marco did succeed in dragging Piero out

for a night on the town, and when he finally returned to his bed he was too drunk to do anything more than lie there snoring the night away. Although he kept her awake, Carla was relieved that her body was to be given a rest. The exciting feelings that he aroused in her were like a drug: she couldn't get enough of them, but they left her only craving more.

Sometimes she felt disgusted with herself and wished she had fled instead of remaining to become Piero's sex-slave. He was not unkind, but his treatment of her was purely selfish. After a few preliminary gropes to make sure she was wet enough for him to slip in easily, he was inside her and pushing away. She longed for him to kiss her breasts more thoroughly, to give her gentle caresses instead of rough ones, to whisper endearments instead of grunts and curses. She knew she was being unrealistic, but she feared that their animalistic couplings were damaging her soul.

Always the hot craving for him was there, forming a torrid undercurrent to her day and coming to a head at night. Even as she lay there, relieved that he was too incapacitated to make love, her body wanted him, blindly and hungrily like a beast that must be satisfied. She began to fear that she would never be free of the bonds of lust that bound her to him.

Chapter Five

Carla woke one morning to the sound of music, singing and laughter. At first she was mystified but she soon remembered: it was the Feast of St John the Baptist, Carnival Day! Last night they had joined the candlelit procession through the town to the cathedral, walking behind the priests who bore holy relics, including the thumb of Saint John. It had been a magical evening, full of mellow light and music, but now the day itself had dawned and promised to be even more exciting.

Carla leapt from her bed only to find that Piero had already left his. While she was splashing water over her face and hands he entered, with a bundle of clothes over his arm. 'Here are your carnival togs – fit for a lady!' he grinned at her, first dumping them on the floor then picking up a dusky pink *cioppa* which he held out to show her.

'I'm to wear *that*?' she exclaimed in wonder.

The overgown was of rose sarsenet trimmed with green brocade. Under it she would wear a white chemise with full, embroidered sleeves and a pale green underskirt. There were green velvet slippers to match. The whole outfit was far more luxurious than she had ever worn before and, despite her misgivings, Carla was excited at the prospect of dressing up like a lady. There was padding for her hips and a corset, which Piero said he would have filled out with wadding if she were a boy.

'But since you're not, you can fill it with your own titties,' he laughed. 'Fortunately they're not so large as to give the game away. Put this lot on then, and be quick about it.'

He helped her get dressed. It was even stranger being in ladies' garments than in men's because the fashionable clothes were quite different from the loose-fitting shifts and woollen gowns that she used to wear at home. The long, heavy skirt meant she could not move quickly and the tight corset restricted her breathing. But what alarmed her most was her womanly shape. Although the neckline of her chemise was not particularly low it showed the swell of her small breasts quite plainly.

'I can't wear this!' she protested. 'No one will believe I'm only a boy dressed up!'

Piero was leering at her. 'Oh yes they will, if I tell them so! They'll marvel at how much like a fine lady you look in that get-up.'

'But I shall be discovered!' she moaned. 'Let me wear something else, please! Or at least take off this corset.'

'You wouldn't say that if you knew the trouble I went to to get hold of all that finery.'

'But I *can't* wear it!'

She was near to tears, terrified that if she were on public display with the other apprentices she would be arrested as an impostor and clapped in jail.

But Piero was growing angry. 'You'll wear those clothes and like it!' he snapped. 'No more of your mealy-mouthed excuses. Put on your wig and bring yourself and your mask downstairs. They'll be loading the float soon and you must practice on it with the rest of them.'

By the time she descended to street level the float was parked outside the house and the other apprentices were hanging up the last of the decorations. Garlands of fresh flowers were suspended from the four posts at each corner, and the platform was decorated with shields alternating between the apothecary's emblem of a jar with two spoons and the artist's emblem of palette and brushes. The horse that was to draw them along was caparisoned with a surcoat showing the Madonna and Child – the arms of the Apothecaries' Guild.

The others greeted her with cries of surprise but the only one she paid any heed to was Marco. He came up and examined her closely, his eyes widening as they drifted to the shadow of a cleavage above her neckline and the curve of her bosom below. 'I'd never believe you were a boy,' he murmured. 'You appear so feminine!' His smile grew cheeky. 'I'll have no difficult pretending to be your lover now!'

Although she knew it was futile to feel cheered by his words, nevertheless Carla drew comfort from them. She realised with pride that had he known she were a woman, he would find her attractive, and what had seemed like an ordeal to come now seemed more alluring. She thought about the part she was to play, that of a young wife shackled to an impotent old husband and responding to the advances of a handsome young lover – an artist, who had been hired to paint her portrait. Piero had put the finishing touches to the 'portrait' that morning, once he had seen Carla dressed up in her costume.

Carla was confident that she could play it convincingly, since all she had to do was respond with exaggerated cries and gestures to what the other characters did or said. Her face would be hidden by the grotesque mask.

'Here,' Marco said, 'let me colour in your lips to blend with the red lips of the mask.'

Carla stood still while he gently applied some rouge to her mouth. The touch of his fingertips was soft and sensuous, making her whole body tingle with light arousal. She saw the warm light in his brown eyes and her soul trembled when she remembered that, at some point in the masque, he would kiss her.

They practised standing on the float in their positions, making sure that they could go through their moves without hindrance, then the cart was drawn away to some secret destination until later, when they would be joining in the procession. Carla took off her mask but she kept her dress on. She was going to be a woman all day!

Meanwhile there were many other sights to see. The streets resounded with music from strolling players or the thunder of hooves from the hectic horse races that ran from end to end of the town. There were wedding parties too, since many chose to marry on that day, and in the Square of the Signoria the elaborate gilded castles and huge wax candles were displayed, each representing a town that was subject to Florence.

Carla walked with Marco through the crowds and felt so happy she wanted to laugh and cry at the same time. At last she could show herself in her true colours and, although he believed her to be a boy and was constantly marvelling at her womanly appearance, it was easy for her to imagine that they were a couple of lovers, just like the others she saw around her. He even put his hand on her elbow to guide her through the crowds, and warned her of puddles or mud in the road to protect her gown.

'He's treating me just like a real lady,' she thought, and her heart glowed with pride.

The time came for the apprentices to join in the grand procession through the streets, and as Carla climbed up on to the stage she felt a wave of apprehension. Was she courting disaster by putting herself publicly on show? They arranged themselves in their positions for the tableau, which showed Giovanni as the old husband in a long beard hunched over his walking stick while Marco, dressed in a wine-red doublet and grey hose that showed off his shapely calves and thighs, kissed the young wife's hand. In the background was a chorus of gossipy neighbours, played by the other apprentices who also doubled as rough-and-ready musicians.

Piero was driving the horse, an old nag he had borrowed from a friend. When they were ready to go he led them through to the main procession where they found their place amongst the other floats. Although she was supposed to stand stock still, not moving a muscle until the time for their little play began, Carla squinted at the floats in front and behind, marvelling at what she could make out.

Immediately in front of them was the decorated car of the barbers' guild, with the appropriate theme of 'Samson and Delilah'. Behind were the furriers, showing off their wares even though it was the height of summer, their theme 'Orpheus taming the wild beasts', with one of them playing his lyre while the rest of them crouched submissively beneath animal pelts.

The cart went rocking on its way through streets lined with cheering onlookers. Some tossed coins and sweetmeats onto the floats but sometimes the occupants of the floats themselves distributed gifts. The bakers threw little fancy pies decorated with crescent moons into the crowd. At certain set points the procession halted and some of the tableaux came to life, performing brief scenes, while others burst into song. Priests threw holy water over the crowds or sang special hymns before the small statues of the Virgin that were found high up in niches on some street corner buildings.

When the time came for their play to be performed Carla was very nervous. Shaking like a leaf she moved over to Giovanni and pretended to fuss over him while the 'neighbours' sang a bawdy song about her ancient husband not being able to get it up any more. Then her 'husband' beckoned to Marco and the easel was set up. While Giovanni retreated behind a curtain held by two of the neighbours, Marco pretended to paint her portrait but kept coming over to steal a kiss.

At first he kissed her lightly on the lips, but as the play progressed he grew more bold. Carla was delighted to see how eagerly he threw himself into the performance. Soon he was kissing her with a feigned passion that nevertheless roused her thoroughly, and he even began to caress her upholstered breasts, much to the

70

delight of the crowd. His lips fastened on the bare flesh of her cleavage and the crowd roared obscene encouragement.

'Go for it, lover boy! Give her what her husband can't provide! Make the young woman happy and the old man a cuckold! Show her what a real man can do!'

They were entering into the spirit of it with gusto, and Carla began to relax and enjoy herself. This might be the only chance she had to get real kisses out of Marco, and she was determined to make the most of it. Her lips parted through the mask and she savoured the taste of his tongue as it probed into her mouth, making her knees weak. His hand squeezed her right breast and she could feel her nipple harden with desire. Oh, how she wanted him!

To be simulating passion in front of the crowd was one thing: to be really experiencing it was another. There was a sweet torment in her predicament that only made her want him more and more. She was surprised at the strength of his performance and began to wonder if he could possibly have guessed her secret. His lips moved near to her ear and he whispered, 'Your padding's very realistic, Carlo. I could well believe your tits were real!'

Their dalliance was suddenly broken off when the cuckolded husband appeared and became the laughing-stock of the audience as he ranted and raved in his despair. Carla felt disappointed as their little show drew to its close but she knew it would not be long before the whole thing was re-enacted again. She took up her statuesque pose and the cart rattled on its way to its next destination, but beneath her cool exterior Carla was feeling very hot and bothered. She could scarcely wait for their next stop!

There were to be four playlets in all, at various points in the city, and each time Carla fancied that Marco was becoming increasingly amorous. Had he forgotten that she was supposed to be a boy dressed up? The way he kissed and caressed her could not be more convincing. Each time he seemed to hold her more firmly, to kiss her more passionately and to caress her more intimately. Was he becoming as aroused as she? Carla certainly liked to think so. While they performed she began to imagine what it might be like if he knew her real identity and was truly in love with her. She knew she would go on imagining such a situation for weeks to come, after Piero left her alone at night. Marco was giving her plenty of fodder to feed her dreams!

Piero followed along behind the other floats, acting as cheerleader for the crowd although they hardly needed it. Carla noticed him watching her with increasing mirth as the afternoon progressed towards evening. He drank frequently from a wineskin and his face was flushed in the heat, his hair tousled. Even as she dreamed of what she and Marco might do together if they were lovers in real life, not just in fantasy, the spectre of her nights with Piero continued to haunt her. He had awakened a hunger in her that he could not assuage, and she increasingly believed that only her make-believe lover could really satisfy her.

The carnival procession came to its final resting place near the cathedral and the apprentices were free to leave the float and enter the Baptistery, where the votive candles and other offerings were displayed. Carla was disappointed that her love scenes with Marco were at an end. She stuck close by him as they entered the candlelit building and he winked at her, whispering, 'I can't get over how like a girl you look, Carlo!'

'What if I *were* a girl,' she responded, daringly. 'Would you fancy me then?'

He gave her a bashful look, which pleased her immensely.

The celebrations continued late into the night, with side-shows, ceremonies and concerts. At midnight the apprentices practically had to carry Piero home. He kept insisting he was fit to find his way to the whorehouse, but he was obviously incapable of doing any such thing. In the end they bundled him on to an abandoned cart and wheeled him through the streets.

Carla was secretly relieved that she would have no trouble from him that night. She had spent the day dreaming of making love with Marco, savouring every one of his kisses and caresses, and she had no wish to have it all spoilt by the carnal demands of their master. She watched with amusement as Luigi and Matteo lugged him up the narrow stairs to his bed.

Down in the apprentices' quarters Marco and Giovanni were warming up the little cakes they had bought and putting on a hot posset. The youngest boy, Antonio, was already sleeping in his little alcove, overcome by drinking too much wine. Carla sat before the fire in her long dress, looking forward to her supper, but soon she became aware of Giovanni's eyes upon her. They were hard and lascivious, and sent a cold draught of fear through her.

'What do you think to our young impostor here,' he said to Marco out of the blue, making her quail. 'If you didn't know he was a boy, wouldn't you swear he was what he appears to be, a rather beddable young girl?'

Marco laughed. 'I've already told him that. It's been weighing on my mind all day. I had to keep reminding myself that he has a cock and balls under those petticoats.'

Giovanni's next words chilled her even more. 'Maybe we'd better check, just to make sure! I didn't like the way Piero kept looking at her, as if he knew something we didn't. You don't suppose he'd be keeping something from us, do you?'

Carla was terrified. She stared into the red heart of the fire, trying to pretend she could not hear what they were saying, but then Matteo and Luigi appeared and Giovanni enlarged on his suspicions to them. 'What do you fellows think of our sister, here? Seems she's become our master's favourite ever since she gave him good head. Piero keeps her all to himself up there, doing heaven knows what to her and giving her all the best jobs. Doesn't it make you sick, lads? I know it does me.'

The others thought it a great game and joined in with

enthusiasm. 'Maybe she'd give us good head too,' Luigi grinned. He pulled down his hose and waved his flaccid cock. 'Can you breathe life into this thing then, little sister? I'd like to see you try!'

'Leave him alone,' Marco said, but it was only a token protest.

Carla sensed the mood of the company and it filled her with dread. They had all drunk a good deal of wine and were over-excited by the events of the day. In their eyes, the presence of a female impersonator in their midst was a poor substitute for the real prostitutes that they had been unable to engage since they were all occupied with more wealthy clients. They were full of the immoderate and indiscriminate lust of drunken men, and she could not predict what they might do next.

'How about a game of "blind girl's bluff"?' Luigi suggested with a grin. 'I don't see why Marco should be the one to get all the kisses.'

The idea was taken up with enthusiasm and before Carla knew it she was being blindfolded with a rag. Trembling with fear she stood before the warmth of the fire, wondering what they might do to her now she could no longer see.

'Turn her round three times!' Luigi commanded.

Dizzy and disoriented, Carla stretched out her arms in front of her and heard the giggles and scuffles of the men pushing each other out of the way. The game was repugnant to her. She was afraid of falling into the fire, afraid of being brutally seized and subjected to all sorts of indignities. Worst of all, she was afraid of discovery. Her heart raced like a downhill stream as she bobbed her way unsteadily around the room.

Someone touched her and she screamed aloud. 'Hush you fool!' she heard Giovanni say. 'You'll waken the master then we'll all be in trouble.'

'We can do something about that!' Luigi said.

Someone held her fast while another rag was pulled across her open mouth, effectively gagging her. She hated the oily taste and stink of the cloth but there was nothing she could do while they were pinioning her arms at her side, and she knew it would be futile to try and remove it. They were four strong men, and they had her at their mercy.

'Let her go!' she heard Marco say.

'All right, let's see who she catches this time,' Giovanni said.

She was spun round again and the room fell silent as she groped her way through thin air, feeling the masculine presence of the four sturdy apprentices even though she could see nothing. Every so often she would trap a tantalising scrap of cloth between her fingers, touch a lock of hair or skim a cheek, but every time they would be jerked from her grasp. She sensed that they were pushing each other away, but were they trying to escape her or vying to be the first to claim the sweet forfeit of a kiss? The game had a peculiar edge to it since they believed her to be a boy. There was a tension in the air, the atmosphere one of ambiguity, of simultaneous desire and repulsion, of pursuit and flight.

Despite her apprehension, Carla felt herself growing sexually aroused. What if Marco should be the one to catch her? She would give anything for another of his kisses, yet she sensed the others would not let him embrace her since he'd had more than his fair share already in their eyes. She fancied that she could sense his nimble form, pick him out from the others even though her eyes were bound.

The game was growing more hectic, with giggles and curses whenever Carla's outstretched hands lighted on a body. Once she touched someone's codpiece, felt the unmistakable profile of a hard cock within the pouch and withdrew her hand as rapidly as if she had plunged it into the fire, giving rise to a chorus of mocking laughter. Someone took her by the wrist and made her feel it again, made her cup the taut balls and stroke the length of the shaft, while he asked her, 'Can you tell whose packet this is?'

The others laughed raucously when she shook her

head. A familiar voice said, 'I think she has me by the balls. I claim my kiss!'

Carla knew it was Giovanni, and all the pent-up desire within her curdled then evaporated as she knew she must obey him. He took her in his strong arms and pulled her close, stifling her mouth with his own and thrusting his big tongue between her lips. She quailed, feeling the raw physicality of the man envelop her, body and soul. He was too strong for her, she couldn't fight him. While he rammed his tongue halfway down her throat, as if she were a whore to be used as he liked, his hands swept over her body in such an exploratory manner that she was terrified he would discover the truth about her.

At last he tore his mouth away. 'The boy kisses like a woman!' he declared, with an undertone of disgust. 'Feels like one too. What say we strip the little faggot and see what kind of creature it really is underneath all this frippery?'

Three pairs of hands were suddenly groping at her, pulling off her wig and fumbling with her skirt and bodice. A scream came from Carla's throat but it was instantly stifled by the filthy gag and became a strangled moan. She tried to pull away from the marauding fingers and her blindfold came awry revealing the hot, grinning faces of Luigi, Matteo and Giovanni, while Marco stood aside, scandalised.

'Let him go!' he barked. 'Leave the boy alone!'

'Keep out of it,' Giovanni snapped back. 'We're entitled to some sport on Carnival night.'

'Then find it on the streets. If you torment this poor lad any more I'll report you to Piero.'

There was hesitation then, just enough of a pause for Carla to spring free and stand by Marco's side, seeking his protection. He pushed her towards the door that led upstairs.

'Go on, up you go while you have the chance.'

She made an undignified exit, tripping over her skirt as she went, scrabbling up the narrow stairs on her

hands and knees like a hare fleeing from hounds. Downstairs she could hear the men arguing, turning on Marco
because he had deprived them of their prey, but Carla
did not stop until she was in the attic room with the
door closed behind her. Only then did she pause to catch
her breath.

Piero was snoring soundly on top of his bed in a
drunken stupor, still wearing his boots. Carla knew she
had nothing to fear from him. Wearily she stripped off
her fine clothes, letting them stay on the floor where they
fell, then sank beneath her coverlet. She felt sore all over
from the pinchings and pokings she had received, and
her pulses took a while to settle down after the shock of
being set upon.

Why had Marco come to her rescue? He was risking
being ostracised by the others, she knew that. Carla
wanted to believe that he had just been sorry for her as
the new boy in the household, but she couldn't help
wondering if he had guessed her secret. He, of all the
apprentices, had been most intimate with her, in friendship as well as physically. If anyone other than Piero had
divined the truth about her it would be him.

The door suddenly opened and Carla cowered beneath
her bedclothes, but then she saw Marco himself coming
towards her bearing a beaker in one hand and a cake in
the other. It was as if her thinking about him had
summoned him to her side. He knelt down beside her
bed and she propped herself up on her elbow with a
grin.

'I brought you some refreshment,' he whispered. 'I
reckoned you could do with it after all you've been
through.'

'You're so kind, Marco!'

Her eyes gleamed lovingly at him in the darkness and
he regarded her solemnly. 'I can't bear to see an animal
being tormented, much less a woman or a child.' There
was a pregnant pause. Surely he must know, she
thought. But then he went on, 'I know you're not a child,
Carlo, but there's an innocence about you sometimes

that makes you seem even younger than Antonio. I suppose it's because you've lived in the country all your life.'

She nodded and grinned, thankful to be let off the hook. 'You never talk about your family,' he went on. 'Don't you miss them?'

'Sometimes,' she admitted.

'So why did you leave?'

She shrugged. 'I didn't like the life they had mapped out for me. I've always wanted to be an artist, ever since I discovered I could draw. There was no chance back in my village, so I thought I'd chance my arm here. I was very lucky that you found me, Marco.'

He smiled, handing her the steaming mug of wine. 'Your talent deserved to be recognised. Maybe when I or Giovanni leaves you can take our place and be a proper apprentice.'

Carla gave a wan smile. She knew that was impossible, and her heart grew heavy, but she hid her feelings by taking a sip from the beaker. The mulled wine soothed her spirits and when she took a bite out of the little cake she realised how hungry she was and wolfed the rest down. Marco grinned, producing another from his pouch.

'I don't know how to thank you, Marco,' she murmured.

'I'll do whatever I can, while I'm still here. Giovanni has a down on you for some reason, and that's not good. But he'll leave and set up on his own before long. Even so, you mustn't get too dependent on me. I'll have to go myself some day. I'm just waiting for the right opportunity.'

He ruffled her hair then rose to his feet, looming over her in the dark. Carla murmured her thanks and watched him move like a shadow towards the door, cradling the hot mug to her breast. She didn't know whether to be glad or sorry that he was still ignorant of her true nature. It would have been a great comfort to share her secret with him as well as with Piero. But perhaps it was better this way. They could be friends without constraint and she would not be putting him in any danger.

Although her body was extremely weary after all the events of the day, Carla's mind was still awake and she lay there after Marco had gone thinking wistfully of how he had looked beside her bed. What if he had knelt down beside her and drawn back the covers, seen her breasts peaking beneath the thin chemise and had his suspicions aroused again? She knew that he regarded her as something of an effeminate child, but the way he'd kissed her on the float that day had half convinced her that he'd guessed at the truth.

A smile floated about the corners of her mouth as she imagined with what rapture he might greet the discovery that she really was a woman. How sweet his confessions of love would be then! How relieved he would be that the strange yearnings for her that he'd been experiencing were not prompted by some perverse and latent desire towards his own sex, but by those elemental promptings through which nature propagates the race.

Voluptuously Carla wriggled in her bed, letting the shift ride up until her thighs were exposed. She pictured Marco stroking her breasts in wonder, repeating over and over, 'So you *are* a woman after all!' Perhaps she would reach out and feel the springing cock within his hose, much as she had felt Giovanni's, only far more willingly. He would joke with her, let her take his member out and use it as her plaything, laughing to see it respond by growing even thicker and more full of rampant life.

What a pleasure it would be to suck at *his* cock instead of Piero's! The practice she had had would be put to good use, and soon Marco's desire for her would be unstoppable. He would clamber up on to her bed and take her in his arms, kiss her passionately and fondle her breasts until she gasped and moaned for him. Then, quite slowly and carefully, he would make his way into her willing cunny.

What unimaginable bliss that would be! If only he had

been her first lover, she would never want any other man. Her feelings for him would turn the event into the most ecstatic consummation she could imagine. As Carla thought of it her body seemed to become incandescent, glowing and throbbing with untrammelled lust. She threw off the coverlet and felt the cool night air caress her skin, but the empty ache inside her was a torment that nothing could ease. If only she had been bold enough to reveal her secret to Marco as he knelt at her side, to let him kiss and comfort her as he swore he would never betray her.

Carla hugged her breasts, put her hand between her thighs and squeezed it so that the wild pulsations hammered through her fingers. Desperate for some relief she thrust those fingers right inside herself and felt the moistly padded walls of the little cell within, where a man might be a prisoner and yet the happiest man alive. Over and over she whispered the name of the man who had won her heart, but the spell did not make him appear again. With a sob she turned on to her side and prepared for sleep, knowing that only he could satisfy her.

Before sleep came, however, she was brought back to the sordid reality of her fate. Not only was she enslaved by her secret to Piero but now she had made an enemy of Giovanni too. She had no doubt that he would find some way to get back at her, now that she had escaped his clutches and made him lose face in front of the other apprentices. To make matters worse, Marco would be leaving before long. He had told her not to rely on him, but what would her life be like in that place when she was alone and defenceless? As the church bells chimed in the night, reminding her that she had only a few hours left before she must be up and at work again, Carla felt as if her death knoll were being tolled.

Chapter Six

Carla went downstairs in trepidation next morning. She was sure that Giovanni would say something cruel to her but he scarcely paid her any attention, being busy with a new commission. Marco gave her a cheerful smile and Carla responded in kind, but now her heart felt torn in two when she was in his presence. It was bitter-sweet to see his handsome face, to watch him covertly as he worked and imagine how it would feel to be in his arms, yet not to be able to show her feelings.

Carnival seemed to mark a kind of watershed in Carla's artistic career. While she still prepared the boards with gesso, made brushes and mixed paint when required, Piero started to entrust more and more fine work to her. Perhaps he was testing her capabilities to their limit just to see if a woman could work as well as a man. Whatever his motive, she relished every new task that he set before her.

'How about making a portrait of me,' he suggested one day. At first she thought he was joking, but she soon discovered that he meant it. 'All my lads have used me as a model at some time,' he went on. 'And I remembered that you used to do sketches of people in the street before Marco brought you here. I'd like to see what you can do in that way.'

So she settled down with her chalks and charcoal, just as she used to do. Piero was a restless model, refusing to sit still but carrying on with his own work while she drew him, so she had to make quick impressions. An atmosphere of peaceful contemplation reigned as she became absorbed in the task in hand, constantly observing her model and correcting her handiwork until the finished product was the best that she could achieve.

At last he demanded to see her effort. 'Not bad at all!' he said, first holding the paper at arm's length and then peering closely at it. 'You've caught my likeness, no doubt about that. How would you like to do a full-scale portrait, in tempera?'

'Oh, do you really mean it?' She gazed at him in longing.

He nodded, brusquely. 'Not of me, though. I have a commission for a Saint Sebastian and I've no time to do it myself. I'd ask Giovanni, but he's busy with other work too. Of course, I'd have to pass your work off as my own. Only if it's any good though!'

'When can I start?'

'Today, if you like. I thought Marco could model for you.'

It was the best news she could have had. Piero suggested that she make the bedroom her temporary workshop, setting up her easel there and surrounding herself with everything she needed. The light was good during most of the day and she could work there undisturbed. Best of all, she would have Marco all to herself. She couldn't have wished for a better arrangement!

Marco seemed pleased too. 'If you do this well, Piero might apprentice you,' he told her. 'I should like that. It would mean I've brought you luck.'

Piero insisted that Marco should model in the nude. Carla was filled with secret apprehension, and she suspected that her master was enjoying her discomfort. Even so, she had to admit it made sense. She would have to portray the saint in his martyrdom, pierced with a dozen or so arrows, so it was important that she got the anatomy right. Even so she had to hide her blushes when Marco stripped unself-consciously in front of her. She'd had glimpses of the other lads' naked bodies before, but she had never been obliged to study them at close quarters as she would have to do now.

'How do you want me?' Marco asked, standing there in full nudity with his thick penis dangling before him and Carla almost fainting with suppressed desire.

'I – don't know. What do you suggest?'

'Well, I could put my weight on one foot, like this, with my hands behind me as if bound. I could raise my eyes to heaven, like so. Will you be portraying me tied to a stake?'

'Yes, I think so.'

'In that case I think hands behind is best, don't you?'

He was matter-of-fact about it but Carla could scarcely focus her mind on the job in hand. She was simultaneously embarrassed and fascinated by seeing him in the altogether for the first time. Once he had taken up his pose she did some preliminary sketches to get the angles right, but she regarded him from beneath lowered lids with fleeting glances, hardly daring to take a long, hard look at him as she used to with the faces she drew.

It had never occurred to Carla that a man's body could be beautiful but as she became lost in her work she grew bolder, staring intently at Marco's nude form, and she began to see the exquisite shape and texture, finding it most satisfying. He was not a big man but his chest was well-proportioned, with just a smattering of dark hair, his waist was slim and so were his hips. The muscles of his arms were well-developed, from carrying heavy loads when he was young, and his thighs and calves were both sturdy and shapely.

But what drew Carla's attention most was his beautiful prick. Even in its flaccid state it was pleasing to her eye, with its long, thick shaft of a tawny hue and the pink bud of the glans peeping out delicately. Beneath it swung the long sac that contained his balls, forming such an inviting trio that Carla longed to kiss and fondle it, to make that noble cock stand proud and free, to feel the soft heaviness of the testes in her palm. She knew Piero's intimately, of course, but whereas there was a kind of brute strength in his equipment that was not without its charm, Marco's genitalia seemed, by comparison, a work of art not nature.

'Do you mind if I take a rest?' Marco's voice had broken her reverie.

'Of course not!'

He came to sit companionably by her side while he viewed her efforts. 'It's coming on. I don't think you have the curve of my arm quite right yet, but that will come. A painting develops in its own good time, I find. There's no rushing the process. And you've made a good start. I'm glad Piero has so much faith in you, Carlo.'

'Me too.'

Carla could barely speak, she was so overcome by having a naked Marco beside her. He seemed so at ease with his body, casually arranging his cock and balls as he sat down so that they were not crushed under him. Her desire for him was making her miserable again, filling her with hopeless longings so that she could barely endure his proximity. So she was pleased when he began to distract her by talking about other works of art that he had seen in Florence.

'Lorenzo de' Medici has a fine collection. I saw some of his treasures when I visited with Piero. I wish you could see his ancient medals, his precious gemstones and artefacts. And his wonderful statue of David. It was made by the sculptor Donatello, and it shows him as a graceful young boy, not unlike yourself. I modelled my stance on him just now.'

'I wish I could go to his palace and see them too.'

Marco smiled. 'Maybe you will, one day. He is a good friend to artists. It's my fervent wish to produce something for him, to paint a family portrait or an altarpiece for one of his private chapels. But he only uses the finest artists and craftsmen.'

'I've not seen much of your work, Marco, but I'm sure it is very good.'

He shrugged. 'Much of what I have to do is hack work. I'd love to have the freedom to express what is in my soul. Maybe one day I shall paint something of which I am proud.'

They were close, very close, in the heat of the day and Carla could hardly contain herself. She stared at his red lips, longing to kiss them as she had before, but now she had no excuse and he would think her queer if she made advances to him.

Suddenly the door opened and Piero entered, wanting to know how they were getting on. He was pleased with what he saw. However, he needed Marco to do some more work downstairs. 'Can you manage without your model for a few hours?' he asked Carla.

She nodded. Marco did not have to be there in the flesh for her to paint him. His image had been imprinted on her retina through close observation mingled with extreme desire, and she knew she could manage perfectly well from memory. As the afternoon wore on the drawing began to take shape until she had it all sketched out and transferred to the prepared wooden surface. Tomorrow she would begin to apply the paint.

After three days' work the portrait was glowing with colour and form. Marco's image had been transformed into that of the martyred saint, his flesh showing the muscled frame beneath. Where the cruel arrows had pierced his skin there were ruby drops, and his face bore an expression halfway between agony and ecstasy. Carla looked at her own work and marvelled. This was the first time she had used pigment on a full-scale work of her own making and she was delighted with the results.

So was Piero. 'You have not failed me, Carlo!' he breathed softly, examining the work closely. Marco was standing by and gave Carla a brief hug, that cheered her immensely. He had already told her how much he admired her effort and his was the only praise that really mattered, although Piero's was of more consequence.

Just how much more consequence it was she soon discovered, when her master admitted that this portrait had been a kind of trial run. 'I've been offered a commission by a gentlewoman,' he told her. 'She wants her portrait painted. We are all so busy here that I was on the verge of turning it down when I thought of you, Carlo.'

'*Me?*'

'Yes. I thought I'd try you out first, to see if you were up to it. Now I believe you are. The job's yours, if you want it. I shall only take half the fee, and when the materials are paid for you may keep the rest. Interested?'

'What a wonderful opportunity!' Marco enthused.

Carla was dumb struck. A real commission, earning real money! But how could Piero dare to let her loose in the world as an artist when he knew she was really a woman? Was he gaining some kind of perverse satisfaction from the deception, regardless of the risk?

The minute Marco had left the room she voiced her fears. 'What if I'm discovered, Piero, and it's reported to the Guild? Won't you get into trouble as well as me?'

He grinned. 'Don't worry, no one will be any the wiser. If you've managed to carry it off under my roof you can surely fool some high-born lady. Just make sure her portrait is flattering enough, and you can't go wrong.'

'But what if . . .'

'Oh, don't be such a scaredy-cat! What do you suppose can go wrong? You'll be sitting at your easel and she'll be posing. Tell her you prefer to concentrate on your work, so you don't have to chat. There will be only two sittings, then you'll finish off here in the workshop. It's no big deal. Trust me.'

So Carla accepted the commission, despite her feelings of foreboding. She knew she could do with the money. There was no telling what might happen to her, and if she had a lump sum it would give her some security if she had to flee in the middle of the night to escape arrest. For, despite Piero's casual attitude, she didn't altogether trust him. If her sex were discovered there was nothing to stop him pleading ignorance and putting all the blame on her. She was pretty sure no one else in the house would gainsay him, not even Marco.

Besides, the thrilling prospect of working with colour again had completely seduced her. She knew that, despite Piero's praise, her first effort had been hit and miss. She had learned a lot but there was far more to discover about light and shade, tints and hues, brush-strokes and textures. There was a limit to what she could do in the workshop, with minor tasks always needing to be done and the all the interesting work still carried out by the senior apprentices. Carla had been given a second wonderful chance to improve her skill and she was duly grateful. She vowed to put every bit of talent she possessed into this portrait.

Monna Livia was the wife of Messer Bardarelli, a rich wool merchant, who had a sumptuous palace off the *Via Calimala*. Piero took Carla there himself, introduced her to the snooty steward as his 'boy' then left with a wink and a grin. Beyond the doorway was an open courtyard with a well in the centre and the living quarters rising up around it. There was much bustle on the ground floor, where business was carried out in the various offices, but upstairs the place had a more tranquil air. As she carried her easel and materials up the wooden staircase Carla caught glimpses of rooms with painted walls, of huge stone fireplaces bearing the arms of the family, of carved and painted chests and cupboards.

At last she was shown into a bedchamber on the third floor where Monna Livia was awaiting her. The room took Carla's breath away when she first entered. The walls were painted to look like an exotic garden, with birds and fruit trees. Even the rafters were painted in blue and gold. The huge carved bed that dominated the room was surrounded by chests of the same design, and there were exquisite rugs on the terracotta tiled floor. A vase of deep pink *rosa gallica* and myrtle stood on a chest at the side emitting their powerful perfume, and there were sweet herbs strewn around the privy corner, while in the opposite corner two turtle doves billed and cooed in a gilt cage.

In the midst of all this sensuous splendour stood Livia Bardarelli, dressed only in a white shift. Her dark blonde hair hung loose about her shoulders and her feet were bare as if she had only just risen from her bed. When she smiled her rather stern features softened into something approaching beauty.

'Welcome, young man!' she said, coming towards Carla with outstretched hands which she placed on her shoulders.

Beneath the fine shift the brown tips of her nipples were very obvious, crowning generously-proportioned breasts. The woman looked deep into her eyes for a few seconds then drew her over to the bed. While Livia lounged on the mattress, Carla sat on the chest looking up at her and wondering why she felt so uneasy in this imposing woman's presence. Was it just because she was wealthy and high-born? No, there was something else, but she couldn't tell what.

Monna Livia spoke in a low, enticing voice, first asking her name. She continued, 'Well, Carlo, this is to be a very special portrait. I shall talk frankly, but what I tell you must go no further than the walls of this room. Do you understand?'

Carla nodded, both overawed and mystified. The woman tucked her long legs under her and leaned back on the pillow, giving an impression of relaxed ease. 'Let me tell you a little about myself. I have been married to Messer Bardarelli for eight years and borne him two sons and a daughter. You might think that would make me happy, but there is something lacking in my life. Ever since our daughter was born he no longer comes to my bed, preferring the company of other women.' She sniffed, disdainfully. 'He thinks I have done my duty by him and cannot understand that I wish to receive him for pleasure, not just for breeding purposes. Can you understand that?'

'Oh, yes madonna!'

Monna Livia sighed. 'You are young, and probably still a virgin. What do you know of the desires of women?' Carla wanted to giggle, but she dared not. She gave a shrug and said nothing, wondering where this confession was leading. 'Well, suffice to say that I am not content to become a dried up old matron yet awhile. This is my plan. Do you know which planetary hour draws near?'

Carla frowned. 'I know nothing of astrology, Monna Livia.'

The woman gave a mysterious, self-satisfied smile. 'It is the hour of Venus. I shall soon light candles to the goddess and you will fashion my portrait after a statue of her that I have had copied. Together we shall perform magic, Carlo. A spell to attract my husband to me once again, and bring him to my bed.'

Her words made Carla feel uneasy. What if the spell failed, would she be blamed? But the lady rose from her bed and tripped over to a wall cupboard which she opened to reveal a small image, a *Venus Pudens* standing on a scallop shell. The alabaster figure stood on green silk with one hand over her pubic mound and the other at her breast, yet her seductive smile seemed more designed to bring attention to those areas than divert the onlooker's gaze.

'Isn't she beautiful?' Monna Livia said. 'I know I am no beauty, but I am sure your skill can make me look like her. And although I have borne three children I am still proud of my figure.'

She spent a few minutes muttering prayers to the goddess then pulled the shift over her head and dropped it carelessly over a nearby chair, presenting herself to Carla in the nude. Although she was far heavier in the bosom and hips than the slender figure in the cupboard she did have quite a pleasing shape. Smiling, she mimicked the pose of the statuette. 'Will this do?'

'I – I suppose so.'

'Then set up your easel and let us begin. I'm most

anxious that the work be done at the correct planetary hour.'

While Carla prepared her canvas and palette, setting her things out on the small folding table that had been provided for her use, Livia Bardarelli adorned the statue with a tiny gold necklace and lit candles which she placed on either side. A small pot of incense was ignited too, replacing the sweet scent of the flowers with the heavier aroma of sandalwood.

When she looked up from her preparations Carla saw her subject already posing, looking towards her easel with the same ambiguous expression as the statue. She knew that her success or failure would probably be reckoned in terms of her ability to reproduce that enigmatic smile, which somehow managed to be both shy and sly. She picked up her brush and began to sketch the woman's voluptuous figure in a sepia tint.

Although obviously not in the first flush of youth, with breasts that sagged slightly under their own weight and a stomach too fully rounded, Monna Livia was still a handsome woman. Carla worked to the cooing accompaniment of the doves, her nostrils filled with exotic perfume compounded of fresh flowers and smouldering bark. Soon she felt as if she were truly under a spell. Her eyes scarcely focused on the work before her, her hands acted of their own accord and the air seemed full of a ghostly presence that heightened her senses and induced a strange languor, in which nothing outside that room mattered. The portrait was taking shape in a kind of dream, and Carla began to believe that she truly was under the influence of magic.

When Monna Livia suddenly moved her arms Carla felt as shocked as if a statue had come to life. She dropped her brush on the floor and, as she bent to retrieve it, heard the woman say, 'I think that is enough for today. My arms and back are stiff, and so is my neck. I'm not used to posing for artists.'

Setting aside the disappointment she felt at returning to the mundane world, Carla rose from her easel while her model rubbed her aching parts with soft groans. She saw the work she had done through impartial eyes and realised that it was very promising, but before she could say anything Monna Livia was giving orders.

'Go over to that drawer, Carlo, and bring out the phial of oil you'll find inside. My apothecary prescribed it for aches and pains and I'm in sore need of it now.'

Carla did as she was told, although she resented the woman's peremptory tone. I am her portraitist, not her maid, she thought. But no sooner had she brought out the phial than further demands were made of her. 'Just give my neck a rub, will you? I'll lie on the bed.'

So she found herself cast in the rôle of masseuse. Sometimes she had rubbed Piero's back for him with a similar remedy so she knew what to do, but she hated being treated like a servant. It was no use complaining, however. She knew she was lucky to get this commission, and if she didn't perform to this woman's complete satisfaction then excuses might be made to wriggle out of the contract. She knew that sometimes happened to artists who failed to please, or where the price of a commission could not, after all, be met by the patron.

Kneeling astride the woman's pale legs, Carla poured some of the oil into her palm and began to apply it to her shoulders with gentle strokes.

'You can press harder than that,' she was told. 'And mind you go all the way down to my thighs and calves. I'm aching from top to bottom.'

It felt very strange to be stroking another woman's body, but Carla was fascinated by the meaty curves of her flesh and the soft texture of her skin. When she reached the springy mounds of the woman's buttocks Monna Livia parted her thighs with a moan, but Carla thought no more of it, continuing down her legs with long, firm strokes.

When she had done her calves Carla thought her work was at an end, but she turned over onto her back with a sigh, saying, 'My feet, you can do my poor feet that have been standing so long!'

Carla felt embarrassed to see the naked sex of another woman so shamelessly exposed. As she smoothed the fragrant oil from her heels to her toes she couldn't help glancing at the plump vulva, plainly visible beneath the sparse brown hairs. The thick lips were pink and moist, resembling an exotic fruit or smooth seashell. Her eyes travelled up beyond the furry mound of her sex and the greater mound of her belly to the twin globes of her breasts. The whole of that female body seemed to her like an undulating landscape, full of curves and planes, and she marvelled at its voluptuousness. By comparison her own slim figure really seemed more like a boy's.

Suddenly she realised that Monna Livia's eyes were open, watching her. She blushed and the woman laughed. 'What's the matter, Carlo – never seen a naked woman before?'

'Seen? Yes. But to touch . . .'

'Ah, so you *are* a virgin! I thought as much. How old are you, sixteen, seventeen? Perhaps I should improve your education a little. How about an anatomy lesson?'

To Carla's horror she opened her legs wide and displayed the deep pink contours that nestled between her thighs without the least embarrassment. Fascinated, Carla could not avert her gaze despite the hot tinge of shame that was creeping up from her neck to her cheeks.

'If you want to be a great artist you should know the form of everything,' Monna Livia continued. 'After all, I am as God made me. We women may vary in size proportion but we're all furnished by Mother Nature with the same basic equipment. And very useful equipment it is too, both for giving birth and for giving pleasure.'

Carla met her knowing gaze and blushed more deeply. The thought that perhaps this lady intended to seduce the young painter she had invited into her bedchamber struck her with terrifying force. If that was Monna Livia's intention her secret would soon be discovered.

'I – should really be leaving now,' she said, awkwardly.

But the woman caught hold of her wrist, forcing her to remain where she was on the bed. Slowly Carla's hand was guided towards the damp, pink chasm. Then a low, coaxing voice suggested, 'Why not feel me down there? If you've never handled a woman before it will be good to know what one feels like.'

Carla tried to protest, but she was struck dumb. Her fingers brushed the wiry pubic hair and then found the wet opening surrounded by folds of soft, luscious flesh. There was a hard bulge at the top and the rest was slippery, soaking her fingers with copious juices. She heard Monna Livia sigh loudly and lean back against her pillow. 'That's right,' she murmured, 'have a good feel, there's a dear. And don't stop until I tell you!'

Although a part of Carla was dismayed at having to go through the charade, another part was fascinated, led on by some voyeuristic urge to discover what other women were like beneath their clothes. She stroked the vulva at random, but every time she came near to the protruding nub at the top there would be cries of, 'Oh yes, there! Right there!' and she realised that was the organ that was giving its owner most pleasure. She could recall how she sometimes throbbed and burned in the same place herself, and she began rubbing it tentatively, feeling the fleshy bud grow beneath her fingertips like a miniature penis.

'Lick me now, right where you're touching me!' came the sudden, strange command.

Carla hesitated. Monna opened her eyes and stared at her with a look of desperation. 'Please!' she begged. 'You want to know how to give a woman pleasure, don't you Carlo? If you kiss a woman between the legs she will be so grateful to you. That way you may secure any woman's favour including mine, believe me!'

Despite the bizarre nature of the request Carla bent her head towards the musky quim. She had sucked Piero off many times before now, but it had never occurred to her that women might like the same treatment. She smiled, recalling how she had taken on this commission in order to further her art education. Now she was being educated in other ways too!

The first taste of another woman was alien, like sampling some strange fruit, but Carla persisted and found the love-juices growing sweet on her tongue like some musky delicacy from the sea. She first laved all over the swollen tissues with the flat of her tongue, then used the tip to stimulate the bulbous clitoris.

Monna Livia responded with ecstatic sighs and murmurs of encouragement that made Carla bolder and soon she was mouthing and licking her with abandon, her hands stroking the smooth thighs all the while. Every so often she glanced up between the full breasts to see the look of rapt concentration on the woman's face and her heartbeat raced in sympathy. She recognised the fever that often held her in thrall when she thought of Marco in her lonely bed at night and the light of comprehension dawned. Was this what happened to women when they were in love? Did this hectic fit torment all females from time to time, turning their bodies into fierce, craving beasts?

As she proceeded the wide hips began to lift and turn, almost smothering Carla as her nose was blocked by the downy mound. She buried her face in the folds of flesh and applied herself to the task with renewed determination, feeling her own body responding in sympathy to the woman's mounting libido. Where she was heading she had no idea. All she knew was that the same force that drove Monna Livia on was the one she had felt, time and again.

Although she had no idea how long she had inhabited that sensual world of musk and juice and swelling, throbbing flesh, Carla became aware that her neck was cricked and her tongue was aching. Just as she was wondering how much longer her services were required Monna Livia gave a loud cry that, at first, she feared was one of pain. The woman was bucking her hips, her breasts were heaving and a red flush was spreading over her face and chest. Carla was about to get help, thinking perhaps she was ill, when she realised that something different was happening. The shuddering spasms that racked Monna Livia's body were born not of suffering but of exquisite joy.

'Oh, oh, oh!' came the ecstatic cries. 'Oh, how wonderful!'

'Wonderful?'

Carla observed the trembling of her body with a strange detachment. Was she having one of those fits that Piero had when he spurted his seed? Her own body was hot and throbbing too, but she drew back not knowing quite what was expected of her and perched on the chest beside the bed once more.

Monna Livia flopped back onto the bed, utterly spent, and it was some time before her chest ceased to heave and her cheeks regained their normal pale hue. At last she opened her eyes and gave Carla a beatific smile.

'Thank you, young sir. That was more than welcome. If only you knew what pleasure you brought me just then!'

'I'm glad madonna is satisfied.'

'Satisfied? Oh yes! You satisfied me as much, if not more, than my dear husband used to when we were in the first flush of our youth. But pack up your things now and be gone. If anyone were to come in and see us like this it would be disastrous for both of us.'

'Am I to come again?'

Monna Livia gave a wicked chuckle, deep in her throat. 'You can make *me* come again, any time you like!' Seeing Carla's incomprehension her expression grew sober and she continued in a more businesslike tone, 'Yes, of course. I've arranged it with your master. The second sitting is in three days' time. Clear away now then off you go, there's a good lad.'

Carla left in a daze, hurrying back to Piero's with her half-finished painting strapped to the easel. Three of the lads were on an errand and Marco was helping Giovanni, so Carla went straight to the bedroom. She set up her portrait and lay on her bed considering it while she took stock of what had happened at the *Palazzo Bardarelli*. The plump figure of Monna Livia in her goddess-like pose seemed to mock her as she recalled what had passed between them.

Most confusing of all was the realisation that, in a strange way, Carla had enjoyed what she had been obliged to do. At first she was afraid that, living amongst men, she had somehow absorbed their sexual preferences by constant exposure to their talk, and become a lover of other women. But she had only to think of Marco to realise that it was not so. Given the choice she would far rather have a man do those things to her!

So she came to regard what had happened as a kind of mutual celebration of womanhood. Although Monna Livia had taken her for a boy, secretly Carla had been identifying with the other woman in her blissful transports. Perhaps the invocation to Venus had worked, after all. And the experience had been educational too. The idea that women could enjoy the same kind of climactic pleasure as men had come as a striking revelation to Carla. Now her vague yearnings and fruitless arousal no longer seemed insatiable but full of potential. One day a man would do to her what she had done to Monna Livia, making her feel those same rapturous feelings. Would that her first true lover could be Marco!

Chapter Seven

Carla attended the second sitting with Monna Livia with some apprehension. She was pleased with the way the portrait was going, but uncertain how she was going to be received. Would that frustrated lady require the same service as last time? When she entered the woman's bedchamber it was arranged as before, with the statue of Venus already garlanded and the room filled with the scent of roses and sandalwood.

'I am ready for you,' the lady smiled. Carla knew at once that she did not just mean ready to sit for her portrait. She had obviously been thinking about the last time. Her cheeks were already flushed and beneath the thin robe her dark nipples were stiffened into points. Carla felt her insides quail as she wondered whether Monna Livia would be content with more of the same, or whether she planned to go the whole way this time. If so, Carla would risk being exposed as a charlatan.

The sitting began with decorum, Monna Livia appearing to be the model of matronly dignity even though she was entirely naked. This time Carla endeavoured to present an idealised portrait of her patroness, disguising the marks of time and presenting her as a youthful goddess. She still had to be recognisable, however, and it took all Carla's skill to achieve the right balance between her two objectives.

At last she allowed her sitter to rest while she took a long, hard look at her own handiwork. 'I think I can put the finishing touches to my work on my own,' she announced. 'There is no need for you to model any longer, madonna.'

Carla was half hoping that she would be allowed to leave forthwith, but the noblewoman's eyes sparkled lasciviously. 'Oh good! Now we can have some fun!'

The moment Carla had been dreading was upon her. She put down her brush and walked over to the bed where Monna Livia was already arranging herself, patting the place beside her as she lay. 'You served me very well last time, young sir. I hope you can please me as well again. If you do, there will be extra reward for you. Just for you, understand? I don't want your master to hear of it.'

Carla hated the idea of being paid for her sexual services. It had already occurred to her that Piero was keeping her more as his whore than his apprentice, and the idea was distasteful. Now she was to be used in that way once again. Yet she was not in any position to object in either circumstance.

'Come, let's not be coy!' Monna Livia put a finger beneath her chin and raised her face so that their eyes met. 'You know what I am hungry for, and you know how to serve my appetite. Besides, I believe you enjoyed it last time. I saw how flushed your face was afterwards. No, don't deny it! This time you shall see more of the action, I can promise you.'

The woman pulled Carla towards her and began to kiss her rapaciously on the mouth. Panic struck deep within her as she contemplated her words. What on earth did she mean by "more of the action"? It sounded ominous.

'Rub my starving little pussy!' Monna Livia commanded. 'Make her sleek and happy, then you can slip more than just your finger inside me!'

Carla almost drew back in alarm at that, but stopped herself just in time. While she fingered the streaming wet vulva, feeling the nub that gave such pleasure grow hard and throbbing under her ministrations, her mind was racing to think of a way out of her dilemma. If she was expected to serve this woman as a man would serve her, then it was impossible.

'Oh, I long to be filled!' She heard her mistress moan. 'Fill me up, little one, give me a good, thorough shafting I beg of you!'

'I am shy,' Carla said, her mind racing in desperation to find a way out. 'And I hate others to see my organ. If you will agree to blindfold yourself I shall use it as you request.'

Monna Livia sat up in surprise. 'Silly boy! Do you imagine you're built differently from any other young man? I assure you I shall not be put off, whatever it looks like. My need is too great for me to be fussy. Besides, I'm sure yours is perfectly normal. Many men believe their organ to be small or mis-shapen through ignorance, when there is nothing wrong with it. Why don't you show me?' She grinned as she added, 'I've seen quite a few to compare it to.'

But Carla shrank back from contact. 'No, please! I – I will not be able to perform properly, and if you refuse to cover your eyes then I must decline to do you this service.'

The gentlewoman pouted. Evidently she was not used to being thwarted by servants. Suddenly Carla felt afraid. What if she ordered her to be whipped for some misdemeanour, or declared herself dissatisfied with the portrait out of spite? Aware of her own vulnerability, Carla desperately tried to think of another way out of her dilemma but no alternative plan came to mind.

'Well, if you insist,' Monna Livia said, suddenly. 'Come on, I haven't got all day. I'll go off the boil if you keep me hanging on much longer. Hand me a scarf from that chest and bind it round my eyes, if that will please you. Hurry now!'

Carla slid off the bed and found a silken swathe in the heavy oak chest which she proceeded to tie around Monna Livia's head. When she was convinced that she could no longer be seen she went over to the makeshift shrine of Venus and stole one of her candles.

'If this doesn't do the trick, nothing will!' she told herself with a smile.

Soon she was preparing the woman for penetration by licking and sucking her wet pussy, like last time. Monna Livia began to moan and groan, keeping up a continual noise as Carla went about her task. When she was convinced that her opening was large enough, she first put three of her bunched fingers inside and then straddled her thighs as if she were about to plunge her cock in.

'Now I will come into you!' she told her, trying to sound suitably enthusiastic. 'Oh, what a wonderful prospect! You do me great honour, lady, by granting me this favour!'

'No, it is *you* who are favouring me! Ooh, what a cold penis you have my dear! Never mind, I shall soon warm it up for you ... Ah! Now I have it inside me, your little treasure. How very hard it is! I shall squeeze it tight and that will please both of us.'

'Oh, oh yes!' Carla declared, trying not to giggle as she manipulated the candle in and out. To make sure she gave satisfaction she caressed her breasts with one hand and stroked the bulging clitoris with the other. Monna Livia's cries increased in frequency and intensity, her face growing quite pink as she approached her climax.

'I'm learning a lot,' Carla thought. 'Now I know how I might be satisfied myself, if ever I get a chance to put theory into practice!'

A few more twists and thrusts of the candle had the woman bucking and shaking like a fevered animal, and Carla knew she had achieved her goal. Hastily she pulled out the candle and, on the pretext of needing the privy, hurried over to replace it. When she returned to the bed Monna Livia was lying there panting, the scarf torn from eyes which were regarding her unorthodox lover with dreamy vagueness.

'You have nothing to worry about, my dear,' she smiled. 'Although your organ might not be as large as some, it is just as capable of bringing any woman pleasure I can promise you. You should be proud of the way God has made you, just as I am.'

'Then I hope your husband may return to your bed, madonna,' Carla said, humbly. 'Let me take away the portrait and finish it to the best of my ability. I shall bring it back in a week's time for your approval.'

'Excellent! But before you go, let me give you what I promised you.'

She retrieved her silken purse from under her pillow and drew out three silver coins which she placed in Carla's palm. 'There you are! But don't think I am paying you like a fancy boy.' She gave a grotesque wink. 'That is a little reward for the extra trouble you have taken over my portrait. It was all part of the spell, you understand.'

'Thank you, madonna.'

Carla was very anxious to leave before the situation became even more embarrassing. She hurried back to the house with her things and hoped to escape to the bedroom where she could work on the finishing touches, but Piero waylaid her.

'Carlo! How did the sitting go today? Will two sessions be enough, do you think?'

'Oh yes!' she replied, a shade too readily.

He gave a slight frown, and then broke into a grin. 'Bring your things up to my room and tell me all about it.'

Carla didn't want to tell him anything, but she had no choice. After he had examined her portrait and complimented her on the likeness, he went on, 'So you painted that trollop in the nude, did you? Her insistence, I suppose. Did she try to devour you? They say she has an insatiable appetite for young boys. I hope you managed to keep it up – your disguise, I mean!'

He laughed uproariously and Carla was afraid the others would hear. She was on tenterhooks all the time, wondering how much longer she could preserve her false identity in that place, and Piero had her just where he wanted her. Sometime she hated him for knowing the truth and taunting her with it.

Piero noticed her blushes and pulled her over to his bed. 'Come on, spill the beans!' he insisted. 'I want to know all the details. Did she seduce you at the first sitting? Who suggested she should model in the nude? Her, I bet!'

'She was posing as Venus.'

'Hm. Not got quite the face or figure for it, has she? But go on. What did she ask you to do?'

'It was to be a kind of magic. To rekindle her husband's desire.'

'And you believed her? That was just a ploy, to prepare you for the seduction scene. Her old man is just that, an old man. He's past it, hasn't been able to get it up for years. Once he did his duty by her and got her two sons his juice ran out.'

'How do you know that?'

'She makes no secret of it and neither does he. Her affairs are condoned by him. When Bardarelli asked me for a portrait of his wife I knew he was pimping for her.'

'What?' Fury raced through Carla's veins like hot wine. 'You mean you let me go there knowing she wanted my body? How could you make me go through that charade! What if she had found out my secret, what then?'

Piero laughed, his mocking brown eyes only making her more angry. 'I knew you would be discreet. More to the point, so would she. There's no way she would admit to having been duped. Besides I knew you'd come back with an amusing tale to tell so – out with it!'

'I did not go there for your entertainment!' Carla snapped. She felt incensed, ready to strike the man. 'I went because it was a chance to do some real work, to improve my skills.'

'Sure you did,' he said, soothingly. 'And you made an excellent job of it. But you can never be openly acclaimed as an artist. Face it, Carla, and learn to live with it. Meanwhile, we can have some sport. Come, I've locked the door and we shan't be disturbed. Tell me everything that went on between you and Monna Livia.'

Carla felt trapped. She owed Piero everything, yet she felt used by him. And she had become dependent on the dark sensuality of their lovemaking. He had become necessary to her, and she was starting to hate him for it. She knew, as soon as she began to describe her experiences with the noblewoman, where it would lead.

'The first time,' she began, 'after I had finished my work, she bade me examine her. She said an artist should be intimately acquainted with all kinds of physical form, including that of a woman.'

Piero chuckled. 'Little did she imagine! But go on. She didn't stop there, did she?'

'No, she wanted me to touch her. It felt very strange at first, like my own body and yet unlike. Her nether parts were softer and more open, I fancy, than my own.'

'That's because she's had plenty of traffic in there, not to mention three brats making their way through her sacred portal. But what happened next?'

'She wanted me to put my finger inside her, so I did. It felt very hot and wet in there.'

'Just like you!' Piero grinned. He fumbled beneath her tunic and found the top of her hose. Thrusting in his hand he was soon poking around in her pussy, making her tingle and melt. 'Now you know how it feels from both angles, don't you? Which do you prefer, doing or being done to?'

Carla hardly knew what to say, but in the end she told him what he wanted to hear and his grin spread wider. 'You like it when I do it to you, don't you? Well keep on telling me what you got up to with that woman and I'll soon have a hard-on like a wolf in heat. Then you'll get a thorough seeing-to.'

'She wasn't content with me just feeling her . . .'

'I'll bet she wasn't!'

'So she asked me to lick her.'

'Oh, the dirty cat! And you obliged, did you? What did her cunny taste of?'

'I don't remember.'

Piero brought his fingers to his nose and sniffed. 'It's not a thing I've a taste for, although I believe some men are mad for it. They liken it to all sorts but mostly sea creatures. No wonder Venus was supposed to have been born from the foamy waves. Anyway, get on with your story. I want you to finish before I get too randy to listen any more.'

'Well I went on licking and sucking her until she swelled up and then began to moan and thrash around. After that she seemed satisfied.'

'They say some women are easily satisfied, others more difficult to please. But I satisfy you, don't I puss?'

Carla avoided his gaze, murmuring her assent, but in her heart she knew he could never bring her to that exquisite peak of ecstasy that she believed she might experience with Marco. Mostly because she would not let him. No matter how eager her body might be for his stimulation, she kept her heart and soul intact.

'Go on then,' he urged her. 'What happened this afternoon: same scene as before or something different? Wait a bit, let's get you undressed properly.'

He pulled off her hose and tunic until she lay there naked and his hands roved all over her warm body, tweaking at her nipples and stroking her thighs until she found herself hungering for him despite herself. Sometimes she hated her body for acting of its own accord, responding to his caresses even when her heart was set against him.

Carla resumed her story, determined to get it over with as soon as possible. 'This time she wanted me to penetrate her but, having no proper equipment, I had to improvise.'

'Ha, ha! Let me guess – a brush handle. No, far too

thin! The leg of your easel? No, too square. Hm – well, what *did* you use, you saucy girl?'

Carla couldn't help giggling. 'A candle!'

'Ah, the time-honoured devotional aid of the virgin! But I'm sure you know all about that, don't you? So you satisfied her with a tallow tadger! But how could you possibly disguise the fact?'

'I told her I was shy and she was to use a blindfold.'

'Ho, a good one! And she believed you, the credulous fool! You'd have thought the smell would put her off.'

'The room was filled with flowers and incense.'

'Of course. And she didn't quibble over the size? I'm sure it was hard enough for her, at least.'

'It seemed to be. She was just as pleased with my efforts as before. In fact, she ... ' Carla was about to mention her reward but stopped herself just in time. 'Well, she told me that I'd satisfied her even better than her husband could.'

'That's no wonder, considering he's hardly up to doing it at all! Still, you did well my girl. I'm proud of you. And now you've got me in such a state that I can't wait to come inside you, so we'll dispense with the preliminaries if you don't mind.'

He heaved himself up on top of her and was soon working noisily towards his climax. Carla lay there wondering if Monna Livia felt good when her lovers were inside her, whether she thrashed and moaned as much as when a candle was doing the business. It was all strange to her. Although she could feel herself being stimulated, her pussy growing moist and her labia throbbing wildly, she knew she was not in the state that woman had been in. There had been something violent about it, something more intense. And all she felt as Piero pulled out of her and soiled the sheets with a long, loud groan was a kind of numbness.

'*Nome di Dio* girl, that was fucking great!' she heard him say as she lay there, exhausted. 'Talking about it gives you an appetite for it, don't you find? You were wet enough for fish to swim in there! Now get up, there's a good girl, and bring me some wine. I've a thirst on me like a summer drought.'

Carla rose from the bed and gave herself a perfunctory wash between the legs before putting on her man's attire and going downstairs. The kitchen was cool and empty in the late afternoon, with the apprentices taking a brief siesta in their beds while the master was otherwise occupied. If only they knew how! Carla thought wryly.

She was pouring wine from the barrel into a pitcher when the door opened and Marco entered. 'Oh there you are!' he said, cheerfully. 'I wanted to ask you how you were getting on with your portrait. May I see it?'

'Yes, of course,' she smiled happily. 'I just have to take this up to Piero.'

Marco put a solicitous hand on her arm. 'How is he treating you these days?'

'Not so badly. He means well, even if he is a bit rough at times. Mostly when he's been drinking.'

Marco's mouth set into a pout that was almost ugly. 'If he ever seriously harms you . . .'

'Don't worry, Marco, I'm far too quick for him. Now, are you coming upstairs? The portrait is on my easel.'

After she had given Piero his drink Marco surveyed her handiwork. 'He's damn good, isn't he?' he said to Piero. 'Are you going to put Carlo in my place when Giovanni or I leave? He deserves an apprenticeship, surely?'

'What a man deserves and what he gets in this life are two different things.'

'But surely merit should be rewarded. You won't find a keener or more talented young man than this in all Florence – nay, Tuscany. You'd be a fool to let him go elsewhere, Piero.'

Carla was embarrassed by their talk, and saddened too. Although Piero pretended to go along with it they both knew it was all empty chatter. But she couldn't help wondering what would happen when either Giovanni or Marco left to become journeymen in their own right. Would Piero take on a new apprentice, or manage with the ones he had left? Either way, the others might regard her scornfully when it became obvious that she'd been overlooked for promotion.

Marco continued to examine the portrait, exclaiming over the delicate portrayal of the eyes and the fine fleshiness of the body. 'You've made the woman look almost beddable,' he declared, to which Piero gave a hearty guffaw.

'She'd have you if she could Marco, and Piero here too. At the same time, probably. The woman's a voracious bitch, everyone knows that. Some of those noblewomen can't get enough of it, you know. They read lewd poems and sing rude songs, joking with the men just as if they were their equals in love and lust. I can't make them out at all.'

'You'd have your women chaste and modest then, eh?' Marco asked, a twinkle in his eye.

'I'll take an honest whore any day, but you'd think those high born women would have more decorum. They'll seduce anything in breeches, or so I've heard.'

Marco gave Carla a wink, making her feel even more uncomfortable. She longed to be alone with him again, but the way she was feeling, that could be far too dangerous. With every day that passed she longed to reveal her secret identity to him, to throw herself on his mercy and declare her love for him, but she feared the consequences: not just for her but for him too.

After a week of careful attention to detail, the portrait was finished and Carla was summoned to the *Palazzo Bardarelli* where the nobleman and his wife were expecting to view it. She was ushered into the great hall on the first floor, and gasped when she saw its splendour. There were windows covered with oiled cloth through which the sunlight was filtered like old gold, and the walls and ceilings were covered with ornate paintings and tapestries. A long table with fruit carved on the legs was laden with pitchers of wine and sweetmeats whilst the noble couple sat on high-backed chairs covered with silken cloth embroidered with silver, as if they were king and queen.

'Please, put your portrait on the easel where we may peruse it,' Messer Bardarelli told her.

She obeyed then stood back, watching the man's face anxiously for signs of reaction. For a while his wily eyes moved all over the picture, his expression inscrutable. Then he sat back in his seat with a smile. 'Excellent! You have favoured my wife, but not excessively. She makes a tolerable Venus, does she not?'

Carla bowed. 'Certainly, *Signore,* if it pleases you.'

'It does please me, certainly.' She saw the ironic cast to his eye as he bade her rise with a wave of his hand. 'Has the young man pleased you, wife? With his portrait, I mean.'

'Oh yes, husband. Very much so!' Monna Livia was smiling broadly, making Carla quail. The pair of them seemed to be playing some game in which she felt like an innocent pawn. Perhaps not quite so innocent, however.

'My wife would like to thank you personally,' Messer Bardarelli continued. 'She has a reward for you in her bedchamber. Shall we adjourn?'

Carla's heart sank at the thought that she must return to the scene of the crime. She had expected to be given her bag of money right there, and then to leave the house of her shame once and for all. But it seemed her ordeal was to be prolonged.

Once they arrived in Monna Livia's bedchamber she made no attempt to hasten the process. Her husband sat down heavily in a chair and began to sip from the goblet of wine poured for him by a servant. He then dismissed the servant and bade him close the door behind him.

'So, wife, you found this young man's labours entirely satisfactory, did you?'

Monna Livia smiled. 'Oh yes! In every way!'

He turned to Carla, his eyes sharply focused beneath the beetling grey brows. 'I should like to see you service my wife, as you have done before. Have no fear, sirrah. I know all about it.'

Carla thought she would faint, she was so horrified and shocked by his proposal. Her mind raced ahead, selecting and rejecting excuses as soon as they came into her head. There was no way she could think of to escape discovery this time. With the husband watching she could make no substitute for the organ she so obviously lacked.

But the woman unexpectedly came to her rescue. 'The young man is shy, and last time he would only take me if my eyes were hidden. I fear we shall embarrass him if he is obliged to perform before a witness so awesome as yourself, dear husband. He will never be erect enough to carry it off.'

'Then what do you suggest?' the man asked, peevishly. 'You promised me a show, Livia. Something to get my pecker up so I can at least have a wank, and now you're telling me the show's off. What are you playing at?'

She hastened to his side, caressing his brow and making soothing noises. 'Don't fret, dear, you shall have your show. Here's what I propose. The lad shall lick me, as he did before. Then, if you can manage to get hard enough, you may come into me at the crucial moment and we may ride the waves of bliss together. How does that strike you?'

'Very well indeed!' he beamed. 'Got that, boy? You're to make my wife ready, and get me going at the same time, then you're to stand back and let me dive in there. I'm sorry to deprive you of your prize at the last knockings, but you'll get well paid for your pains.'

Carla almost laughed out loud. Unwittingly the couple had let her off the hook, and she was very grateful to Monna Livia for her ingenious solution to the problem. She even gave the woman a conspiratorial smile as they walked, hand in hand, over to the bed.

'You see?' the noblewoman whispered in Carla's ear. 'We shall get him back into my bed with or without the help of Venus. Now make sure you get me thoroughly aroused, give it all you've got, and I'll play my part to perfection too.'

With a voluptuous sigh, the woman lay down on the bed and loosened the girdle securing her gown. Carla knelt beside her, gently stroking the soft golden hair and trying hard to look as if she really lusted after her. She was acutely aware of the hungry eyes of the old man as he watched from his vantage point and hoped that her antics would have the desired effect.

Taking her time, Carla first bared the large breasts and began to lick at them with her tongue fully extended, so her husband could get a good view. She heard him groan and knew that her first move had been a good one. She pushed the heavy globes together and licked down the cleft between them, moaning herself as if she were in the throes of unrequited passion for the woman.

'Isn't she a beauty, my Livia?' the old man said. 'Don't you just love her jugs, boy? Bet you'd love to put your little cockie between them and roll those fat titties around it until you shoot your spunk, but you're not going to. This is my bed and my wife, young whipper-snapper, and I won't let you use anything but your mouth on her. Get down between her legs as soon as you like, and make sure I can see you licking her lovely pussy.'

Carla obeyed at once, anxious to get her part in this bizarre show over with as soon as possible. She tasted the familiar flavour of pussy once again and, this time, found it more arousing. Since she had told Piero all about making love to this woman it seemed less strange, and now she was almost enjoying it as she felt the hot flesh pulsate beneath her tongue.

'Oh, he's making me feel so good!' Monna Livia cried.

Her husband answered with a wicked chortle. 'Me too! This is doing me a power of good, and no mistake! I can't imagine why we didn't think of this before.'

'Desperate ills seek desperate remedies,' Carla thought, and almost laughed out loud.

The juices running out of Monna Livia's cunny now

110

tasted sweet and fresh, her pouting sex lips were thick and swollen with desire and Carla sensed that it would not be long before the paroxysms would shake through her as they had before. But was her husband ready for her? She looked back over her shoulder and saw the old man sitting astride his chair and manipulating his penis. He grinned sheepishly at her and she saw his semi-flaccid organ rear a little. He nodded urgently and waved his hand at her, encouraging her to continue.

Carla bent her head to the fragrant quim and at the same time reached up to caress the voluminous breasts with their hard, lust-ripened nipples. Monna Livia gave a deep, guttural groan and her hips shook so wildly that it seemed to be all over for her, but when Carla took her mouth away from the streaming vulva she cried out for more.

'Go on, lad, don't stop!' she heard Bardarelli say behind her. 'This is the strongest my plonker has been in a long while.'

Carla bent her head again and licked delicately at the swollen clitoral bud, making Monna Livia sigh with heightened pleasure. She arched her back and lifted her hips, moving them in an abandoned way which had her husband groaning too. He got up off his chair and came towards the bed, grunting rhythmically while he gave his cock a good rubbing.

'Are you ready for me, wife?' he said at last. 'Because I reckon I'm about ready for you. Get out the way, boy, and let your elders and betters show you how to do it. There may be snow upon the roof but there's still a fire in the chimney!'

Carla was glad to make way for him even though a part of her had been really into what she was doing, relishing the tastes and odours that were now growing familiar to her. She retreated to the chair where he had been sitting, slightly embarrassed to be forced into the rôle of voyeur, but then Bardarelli called her back. 'Hey, I need your help lad. Quick, come here!' When Carla was kneeling on the chest beside the bed he told her to take hold of the root of his penis and help guide it into his wife's vagina.

'Hold fast, give it a good squeeze and that will keep it stiff,' he said, wincing as his aged knees strained to take his weight. Once he was in she took her hand away and then he began to thrust with surprising vigour, as if his life depended on it.

'Oh husband, how wonderfully virile you are!' Monna Livia exclaimed. 'You'll make me come in no time.'

'Better not take too long,' Bardarelli muttered. 'I can't keep it up all night, like I used to.'

Less than a minute later Monna Livia was climaxing with histrionic sounds and gestures, making Carla wonder whether it was a genuine experience or she was putting it on for Bardarelli's benefit. At any rate it was too much for her poor husband, who spent himself in a wild flurry of gasps and groans then collapsed between her thighs.

There – my – dear!' he gasped. 'Perhaps – we have gotten – another son this day.'

'I should not be surprised,' she said, winking at Carla who was dazed by all the sudden excitement. 'You are so much of a man, my love, that only a sturdy boy could come from all that excessive virility.'

Bardarelli chuckled and settled his head comfortably on his wife's bosom. Carla felt awkward, not knowing whether she should go or stay, but eventually he remembered she was there. He felt beneath the pillow and brought out a bag of silver which he tossed carelessly at her.

'That's for your pains, sirrah. You've made my Livia look lovelier – so my plonker could get a stonker and bonk her!' He gave a joyous chuckle. 'Ha, did you get that, wife? Best joke I've made in years! Best fuck I've made in years too, what?'

'Yes, dearest,' she smiled, with a wink at Carla.

The couple seemed happy and, as she left them together, Carla was almost envious. It must be good to have a companion, to go through good times and bad with them. She found herself wishing blessings on them, perhaps another lusty son to carry on their line. For herself, she had a bag of silver that would no doubt help her in the months ahead, months that she feared she might have to face alone. As she walked through the empty streets Florence had a melancholy air in the afternoon sun with everyone indoors, out of the blazing heat. Carla couldn't help wondering what would become of her when Marco left Piero's employ and she was left behind.

'Oh Marco!' she murmured, kicking her way through the dusty streets with her worn leather boots. 'If only you and I could be together as lovers, how contented I would be!'

Chapter Eight

*P*iero was very pleased with the money he got for Monna Livia's portrait. He was even more delighted when it was hung in Bardarelli's office for all the visiting bankers and merchants to see. Of course he got all the credit for it, since Carla was thought to be only his apprentice and it was presumed that the fine detail had been added by the master himself.

Amongst the people who saw the portrait was a priest called Father Giacomo. He had come to the Bardarelli mansion on business, seeking to commission some fine wool tapestries for the new chapel in his church, and some quality in the painting struck him forcefully. He called at Piero's workshop one morning asking to see more of his work.

'I am impressed,' he said, after seeing work-in-progress on the Saint Sebastian and a small painting of St John the Baptist that was being made for a Dominican monastery. 'Tell me, how long would it take you to make a Madonna for a private chapel?'

Piero's eyes flicked towards Carla for an instant and she knew what he was thinking. If the priest had been drawn to them by her handiwork then she should be the one to take on this commission. Although it piqued her to be deprived of any real recognition, she was willing enough to take on a new project.

'A month at most,' Piero replied. 'Provided you were not wanting anything too complicated, of course.'

'Oh no, it is to be quite a small work. An Annunciation, but I lay more emphasis on skill than on gilt and ultramarine. I want particular attention paid to the Virgin's features. She should be portrayed in the first stage of Disquiet, but not as I have seen some other artists represent our Holy Mother. You would think, in some cases, that she was about to sock the angel Gabriel on the jaw or push him out of the window, so violent was her attitude!'

Carla stifled a giggle, unsure whether it would be seemly to laugh at the irreverent image presented by the priest. He seemed to have definite ideas of what he wanted, and went on to describe her robes.

'I want her clad in charitable red and humble black with just a hint of pure white, and dignified by a faint golden halo. You can leave out the blue, except for a few touches on Gabriel's wings. She's to have a prayer book open on her lap and there's to be a view through the window of the Tuscan hills.' The priest smiled at Piero, then reeled off the dimensions. 'Got all that? I leave it to you to calculate for labour and materials. When we agree a price you can make a start on the cartoon and I shall come to inspect it in a few days' time.'

Just as Father Giacomo was turning to go he seemed to notice Carla for the first time. His dark eyes were fixed on her face with a questioning look. Then he said, 'This lad, here, could be your model. There is something innocent and charming in his expression that would not look amiss in the face of Our Lady.'

Piero gave a dry laugh. 'Innocent, eh? Well they say even the devil is not so black as he is painted!'

Once the priest had gone, Piero sat down and made his calculations. He came up with a sum that he thought was reasonable, then added another fifty per cent.

'The Church can stand the cost,' he explained. 'They're

115

spending a fortune on that new chapel so I don't see why we shouldn't get our share. But if you're to sit as the model I don't know how you're going to contribute to the work.'

'Why don't I paint myself by looking in a mirror?' Carla suggested.

'What an absurd idea!'

'I can think of no other way.'

Piero frowned. 'Neither can I. All right, I shall find one for you to use. You must do the lion's share of the work, Carla. It is your style that attracted the old fool and he might not be so happy with mine.'

The implication was incredible. Was her master really suggesting that her work was superior to his, even though she was so inexperienced?

He seemed to read her mind and gave a short laugh. 'I'm not saying your work is better than mine. Only that some people, that priest included, seem to prefer a more naive style like yours. Best give him what he wants, then we'll all be happy.'

The work was not as satisfying as Carla had hoped. She was allowed to paint only the Madonna's face, modelled on her own, and the background scenery. Piero found he had the time to paint the angel himself, and she had to admit he made a good job of it too.

'Angels are my speciality,' he told her. 'I once did a whole heavenly host for the ceiling of a private chapel.'

Marco saw the painting when it was nearly finished. He recognised Carla's face at once. 'What a convincing woman you make!' he laughed. 'Just like at the Carnival. If I didn't know you were male I should start to have my doubts about you!'

Carla just smiled wanly, taking care not to catch Piero's eye. Their master found it all hugely amusing and she was afraid that, one day, he would take the joke too far.

In August, on the Feast of the Assumption, the apprentices were allowed out on the town. At Piero's suggestion they took advantage of the fact that all the churches were open to visit the masterpieces of famous artists and learn from them. They crossed the butchers' bridge and walked along the riverside until they came to the church of *Santa Maria del Carmine.*

In the dark interior, heavy with incense and illuminated by hundreds of flower-ringed candles, they made their way to the Brancacci chapel. There Carla was enchanted by the moving frescoes of Masaccio. She particularly liked the expulsion of Adam and Eve, which showed Adam covering his face in shameful despair and Eve sobbing aloud at her own weakness. The figures struck her as intensely life-like and human. For several minutes she stood gazing at the exquisite study in light and form, wishing that she could paint as well.

'He was the first to show light coming from one source,' Marco told her. 'It seems obvious now, since all light comes from the sun. But that one development gives his paintings a new reality, making everything seem so natural. I'm proud to belong to the same guild as such a master!'

After their stint of serious study, the small gang of youths went back out into the bright sunshine. There was a holiday atmosphere everywhere, with stalls and street vendors selling all kinds of food and drink, strolling players, musicians and entertainers, spectacles such as bear baiting and tourneys in the main squares. Although not such an important feast as St John the Baptist's, there were processions of girls bearing garlands and after the church services some of the young girls gave their guardians the slip and went to mingle with the lads, chatting and flirting with them for as long as they could before they were found by their elders and scolded.

Carla found herself with Marco when one of the pretty young wenches, her hair wreathed with daisies, came up and greeted him. 'Haven't I seen you at the apothecary's?' she asked, by way of an opening.

'Possibly,' he grinned. 'I go there to buy pigments sometimes, for my master. But what were you doing there? You look the picture of health, and surely your beauty needs no enhancement?'

He was regarding the girl with strong interest, standing casually with his weight on one leg and his hand on his hip as if he were assessing the goods. Carla felt queasy as she realised that he was attracted to her, and the wine she had drunk lay heavily on her stomach. Her heart was fluttering like a trapped butterfly and there was a dull, jealous anger stuck in her chest like an indigestible lump.

'I go to buy perfumes, and combs for my hair,' the girl smiled, turning her head for him to see her elaborate coiffure. Then she leaned forward and presented him with her pale, slim neck. 'Can you smell my jasmine?'

'I smell your jasmine and your rose too,' Marco said, his voice low and seductive. 'What is your name, fair creature?'

'Elena if it pleases you, sir.' She simpered at him and Carla had a terrible urge to strike her across the cheek, leaving an ugly red weal. She could hardly bear to continue eavesdropping on their conversation yet she felt compelled to stand there like a ninny, even though Marco was completely ignoring her.

'It does please me, very much.' Marco's voice dropped to little more than a whisper but Carla, attuned to the movements of his lips, picked up his words. 'And you may please me even more, charming Elena, if you will meet me in Saint Margaret's garden, at moonrise.'

The girl giggled and nodded, turning the knife in Carla's already throbbing wound. She knew that the public gardens, across the river in the *Oltrarno* district, were a favourite rendez-vous for lovers. Elena melted into the crowd with a longing glance, her fingers lingering in Marco's until the very last moment, and Carla felt sick with envy. Oh, her fate was too cruel! It should be *her* exchanging loving looks with Marco and arranging a lovers' tryst. She loved him far more than that little flirt ever could!

On the way back home Carla was so sullen and withdrawn that even Marco noticed.

'What's the matter, Carlo?' he asked.

Giovanni, overhearing, piped up. 'He's envious, because you've got yourself a fuck for the night and he has none.'

'That's not true!' Carla protested in desperation, but Giovanni only laughed at her.

'Why don't you come to the stews with me? I'll find you a tasty piece. I've tried them all out so you just let me know what you fancy and I'll recommend the best one.'

Carla shrugged, not knowing what to say. Marco came to her rescue. 'Leave the boy alone, Giovanni. He'll get into girls when he's good and ready. Not all men are randy bastards like you, you know!'

Giovanni spat contemptuously and hurried forward to walk with Luigi, Antonio and Matteo, snubbing them. Marco gave Carla a rueful smile. 'The sooner he leaves Piero's employ the better, if you ask me. He should be setting up on his own. It irks him that he's still with the rest of us. But he needs money for new premises and he spends it like water, drinking and whoring. I think he's still deep in debt.'

'What about you?' Carla asked, trying not to betray her secret fear that he would leave her. 'What are your plans for the future?'

Marco's face softened, his eyes growing dark and dreamy while his mouth relaxed into a half-smile. 'I want my own business too, more than anything. But I'm prepared to wait until the right opening comes along.' He paused, as if wondering whether he could trust her. Then he said in a low voice, 'Promise not to tell anyone?' She nodded fervently. 'All right, I'll tell you. I've heard of a place that would do me very well, but it's a bit more than I can afford right now. I'm trying to arrange a loan, and if I succeed I doubt I'll be spending many more nights under Piero's roof. But you mustn't breathe a word of it, mind, in case it all falls through.'

Flattered as she was that Marco trusted her with the information, it was a heavy blow to Carla's heart. The prospect of remaining in the house without Marco was hateful to her. She would rather run away, seek her fortune elsewhere, than remain where Giovanni could torment her mercilessly and Piero use her as he pleased, with no one to speak up for her or brighten her day with thoughts of love.

'I hope you don't go too soon,' she ventured, her voice sounding weak and pathetic.

Marco laughed at her with gentle indulgence. 'I warned you not to rely on me too much, little Carlo. You must learn to stand on your own two feet. It's a harsh world out there. Still, you never know, you might come and work for me. I shall need an apprentice or two.'

He spoke casually, as if the idea meant nothing to him, but it gave Carla hope. Now she had a dream, a real dream that might come true one day. She vowed to hold on to it, to mentally take it out and polish it like a treasured object whenever she felt downhearted.

The five of them dined at a tavern that evening, surrounded by bawdy singing and drunken foolery. Carla didn't much care for the atmosphere and she was relieved when Marco rose from the bench. But her relief was short-lived when she remembered that he had an appointment with pretty Elena.

'I'll leave you chaps now then,' he told them, swaying slightly on his feet since his belly was full of wine. 'See you in the morning, if not before.'

'Give her one for me!' Matteo called with a grin.

Luigi made an obscene gesture with his forearm and Giovanni got up too. 'I'm off to the stews!' he declared. 'Who's coming?'

After Marco had disappeared, Luigi and Matteo went off in the direction of the market telling Carla to take Antonio, 'the baby', home. She did so sadly, but once she was there in the house with the young apprentice tucked up in his bed and Piero snoring loudly in his chair she felt unbearably restless and decided to venture out again. She took a lamp and made for the bridge across the Arno, knowing that she was only storing up more pain for herself but unable to resist the urge that led her feet on a straight path towards Saint Margaret's garden.

The walled garden had belonged to a convent that had been destroyed by fire. When the nuns moved to a more spacious building they gave the land to the *Signoria*, for the people of Florence to enjoy. Now, in the moonlight, it was a pretty wilderness of roses and herbs that scented the night air, a place of winding mossy paths and overgrown shrubs. Carla peered through the wrought-iron gate but could see no one. She pushed gently and, with a slight protesting groan, the gate swung open on rusty hinges. Taking a deep breath she extinguished her torch and entered the garden.

It didn't take her long to find where they were. In the middle of the tangled undergrowth was a small grotto with a stone statue of the Virgin standing on a higgledy-piggledy pile of rocks. Water gushed feebly from the dank ferns behind, but in the cave to one side of it she could make out two prostrate forms. There were sounds too: heavy breaths and whispers, the occasional giggle. Carla felt her pulses racing and was filled with guilt, but she couldn't resist waiting to see what happened.

Slowly her eyes became more accustomed to the darkness, and when the moon suddenly came out from behind a cloud and illuminated the mouth of the cave with its eerie light she almost gasped aloud at what she saw. Marco was kneeling between the upraised knees of the girl, his mouth obviously in contact with her private parts. Carla felt such an intense pang in her guts at the thought of him giving another girl that special pleasure that she doubled up as if she had a cramp, and her eyes filled with tears.

'This is stupid!' she told herself. 'I'm just torturing myself by being here.'

Yet she could not bring herself to leave. The horrible jealousy was just a part of everything she felt about

121

Marco, as legitimate as her desire, her love, her friend-ship. She felt a perverse urge to explore even the darker side of her feelings, to watch him making love to another woman even though she was suffering horribly.

Elena was wriggling about and making louder noises, her skirt about her waist. Carla saw the back of Marco's head rise and then his lips sought the swelling of her breast while his fingers played with her down below. There were muttered words from her, pleading with him, and soon he was grappling with his own clothes. For a few seconds Carla witnessed the proud appearance of his cock, stiff and thick in readiness for the job in hand, and she felt sick to her stomach but she could not tear her eyes away.

Without hesitation he resumed his position between Elena's legs and thrust straight into her, making her give the loudest cry yet. The envy that filled Carla's whole being was so bitter she could almost taste it, like bile. Elena settled into the jogging rhythm easily, proving she was practised at this game, and her panting words of encouragement drifted out of the cave and into the silent night: 'Mm, that's the way, *caro*! Good and strong, that's how I like it! Push, push harder now!'

The girl was shameless in asking for what she wanted, making him do it to her, and Carla was shocked. It seemed only a short time ago that she had been com-pletely ignorant about sexual matters, and what she had learned recently had astonished her. How could that girl bring herself to behave in such an immodest manner within a few feet of the Virgin's image? She glanced at the statue and saw it, for the first time, as something alien and forbidding, instead of the warm and comfort-ing figure she'd been taught to believe in. Mother Mary and her faithful followers denied that women had urges like men, pretended they were as cold as stone when it came to sex. But Carla knew different, and so did Elena.

With that thought, her jealousy was subtly trans-formed into a kind of sisterly understanding. If she had to choose between being like one of the chaste nuns who used to frequent these gardens and being like hot-blooded Elena, she knew which she wanted to be.

The couple reached their consummation with much gasping and panting, then lay quiet like two racing horses after a chase. Carla decided it was time to slip away. She hurried back along the hidden pathways feeling exhilarated, as if something had been freed in her.

When she got home Piero was awake and seemed to have recovered from his drunken stupor. He greeted her with lustful eyes and for once she was not averse to obliging him. Seeing Marco and his whore had awoken her appetite, and she could feel that her body was hot and ready for the same sport.

'Come upstairs!' he grunted hoarsely, slapping her behind as she went up before him.

The instant they were alone in the garret he fell upon her with slobbering kisses. Carla hated the smell of stale wine on his breath, so she manoeuvred herself round and presented her posterior to him, knowing that he liked taking her from behind just as well as in front. It didn't take him long to uncover her tight, round buttocks which he proceeded to bite softly and kiss while his hands travelled round to play with her engorged nipples and slippery pussy.

'You like it like this, don't you?' he murmured in her ear as he pushed his thick tool into her. 'You're getting quite a taste for it altogether. What if I made you my wife and got some fine sons by you? I dare say you'd like that. I'm a good catch, I am, with my thriving business and all. Maybe I won't pull out tonight, and we'll see if we hit the target, eh? Wouldn't you like that, my little pretender?'

Carla felt a pang of despair travel through her, chilling her to the bone. If he got her with child she would have little option but to wed him, and her dream of some day loving Marco would be shattered. She said nothing, but fervently hoped she could manage to avoid such a fate. Piero was banging away lustily, pulling her hips towards him at every thrust so that her buttocks pushed against his stomach, and she knew it wouldn't be long before he shot his load.

Wiggling her hips to feel the hard length of him more keenly, Carla listened to his heavy gasps until they seemed to reach a crescendo. Then, just as she thought he would be able to hold out no longer, she lunged forward onto the bed and he slipped out of her. There was a dribbling sensation over the back of her thighs and knees accompanied by a curse and she knew that she had timed it accurately.

Piero slapped her hard on the behind, making her flesh smart. 'Thought you could give me the slip, did you girl?' he grunted. 'Well, there'll be another chance don't you worry. I'll get you with child yet and then you'll be mine or take the consequences. I fancy you won't take long to choose between a roof over your head and a life on the streets.'

But Carla privately vowed that, if it came to it, she would find somewhere else to go. She had money now, stashed under the floorboards beneath her bed where no one knew about it. Not a fortune, but enough to give her a start. Perhaps she would leave Piero's when Marco went. The idea of becoming Marco's apprentice was very appealing, especially since the only other option Piero now seemed to be offering was motherhood.

Next morning she joined the other apprentices at their meal and found them discussing the night's business. Giovanni was loudly proclaiming the virtues of one Simonetta, a particularly buxom whore who enjoyed her work immensely.

'She's particularly good at cock-sucking,' he was saying. 'She has a big mouth, for one thing, and a tongue that's long, thick and very agile. She'll bring you off that way first, then get you ready again in no time at all. Then once you get inside her she's as tight as a cat's arse. She knows plenty of good tricks, like squeezing you with her pussy until she milks you of everything you've got. And the tits on her are good for a wank, if that's your

124

inclination. She'll let you stick your cock in her mouth at the same time, and she loves drinking your spunk. Can't get enough of it.'

While he spoke, Giovanni kept giving Carla covert glances as if he wanted to impress her. She mistrusted the way he seemed to be always getting at her, in one way or the other. But then he turned his attention to Marco. 'How did you get on? Was she experienced, that girl, or just an amateur? Did you have to pay her?'

Marco laughed. 'No, it didn't cost me a penny! I reckon she was just hot for it, and she liked me. It wasn't the first time she'd done it, either, although she didn't know any fancy tricks like your Simonetta. Sometimes it's more refreshing to have a girl like her, though. She seems more sincere, and she enjoys it more than a woman you have to pay.'

'Give me a whore any time,' Luigi piped up. 'They know what they're doing, they don't get involved, and they know how to dose themselves if they get a disease. If you just pick up a girl on the street you don't know what you're getting yourself into.'

'Remember Lodovico?' Matteo said. 'He had an affair with a woman who turned out to be a man. It took him three months to find out because he wouldn't let him fuck her – him!'

'What happened when he found out?' Giovanni asked.

'You don't want to know!'

Carla, listening in to their frank discussion, suddenly realised that she was privy to things most women would not even dream of. Through their acceptance of her as a boy artist she had won their confidence and now they talked about anything under the sun in her presence. But what if they should discover she was a woman, what then? Would they be outraged that she had eavesdropped on their male secrets, been treated as 'one of the lads'? Perhaps even Marco would be disgusted to think that she had heard him talking in detail about his sexual exploits. She gave a big sigh, so loud that everyone noticed.

Giovanni turned to her with a grin. 'What's up, greenhorn? Tired of hearing us talk about sex when you've not had a go at it yet? I did offer to take you to a whore, remember, but you turned me down.'

'Leave him be,' Marco said.

But Giovanni would not give up. He came close to Carla and looked straight into her eyes with a searching, mocking expression. 'What is it, then?' he asked softly. 'You're not one of those queer types, are you? The sort that would rather have a man's dick in their arse than stick his own cock in a woman?'

'He shares a room with Piero,' Matteo reminded them all, with a grin. 'And we all know what a randy bugger he is. He'd stick it in anything, provided it was warm and wet!'

'Well?' Giovanni's tone was insistent, menacing. 'What do you have to say for yourself, pretty boy? Are you and the master having it away up there every night or what?'

Carla shrank from him in terror, not knowing what to say. His eyes gleamed wickedly at her and she was terribly afraid that he would do something physical. But then Marco pulled him back with a laugh, 'Come on, Giovanni! In my opinion a man's sex life is his own business. What harm has Carlo ever done you?'

The man growled. 'It's queers – I can't stand them. If I knew for sure I was living under the same roof as one I'd . . .'

'What would you do, Giovanni?'

All eyes turned to the door where Piero was standing, hands on hips. He had evidently overheard the last few seconds of conversation, but Carla could see Giovanni running the last minute or so back in his memory and turning pale as he recalled what he had been saying.

Piero came up close to his oldest apprentice, very close, his belligerent jaw thrust into Giovanni's white face. 'N – nothing,' he stammered, retreating until his back was against the wall. 'I – I didn't mean anything. It was – just a joke!'

'I never did like your sense of humour! You know, if

you're not happy here Giovanni you could always leave. You've finished your apprenticeship and you're only here by my grace and favour. You do understand that, don't you?'

'Yes,' he replied sullenly, his eyes downcast.

'Good. Well my conditions are that you work twice as hard as anyone else and make half the noise. Is that clear? Otherwise you're out on your ear.'

Carla had never seen Piero pull rank so forcefully and she was impressed. He had come to her rescue, in a roundabout way, and for that she was grateful. Yet one look at Giovanni told her that she was still in danger from the man. She suspected that if she gave him the slightest opportunity to do her down he would take full advantage of it. From now on she would be especially wary of him.

The work on the Annunciation continued through the week, with Carla learning a great deal as she watched Piero fashion the angel into an ethereal beauty with birdlike wings and an exquisitely sensitive face. Her own efforts were acclaimed too, not only by Piero but by the other apprentices when they were invited to take a look, since their master encouraged them to learn from each other.

'You have painted Our Lady in your own likeness!' Matteo exclaimed, at once. 'How extraordinary!'

'It was what Father Giacomo wanted,' Carla explained, modestly. 'I had to do it by looking in a mirror.'

After that, self-portraits became all the rage. The mirror was passed around and each of the younger apprentices had his turn at gazing at his blurred image and trying his hand at reproducing it. Suddenly there was a familiarity about the faces of the saints, angels, classical figures and bystanders in all the paintings that issued from Piero's workshop.

'Enough is enough!' the master announced at last. 'We shall flatter our patrons more by reproducing their likeness than our own.'

Carla had almost forgotten about pretty Elena, so she

was shocked to find her hanging around outside the door one day, asking for Marco. Luigi conveyed the message with a wink.

'Your girl's outside,' he said, twisting the knife in Carla's already tormented heart. 'Better find out what she wants, Marco. It could be good news – or bad!'

The others waited with their ears cocked, obviously wondering if he had got her with child. But it seemed that she was only after another assignation.

'You want to watch her!' Giovanni sneered. 'If she's got her claws into you there's no telling where it will end. You don't want to get saddled with a woman at this stage in your career.'

'It's not like that,' Marco said. 'She just wants a bit of fun, that's all. And I know how to give it to her.'

'Well mind you pull out in time, that's all.'

Carla was staring wistfully at him and caught his eye. Marco smiled and came over to put his hand on her shoulder. 'Maybe I'll see if she has a friend for you, Carlo. Would you like that?'

She shook her head, but had to suffer Giovanni's taunts once again. Feeling that her situation was becoming unbearable, Carla went upstairs to put the finishing touches to her Madonna. Piero was out, so she had the attic room to herself and she soon settled into the dreamy state where she became totally immersed in her work. This was what she loved best, this almost mystical communion with her muse. She could forget about everything else: nothing in the world mattered except her art, and for that she would put up with a great deal.

Chapter Nine

*F*ather Giacomo sent word that the 'little model' for
the Madonna should bring the painting to his house
himself when it was done because he wished to 'congrat-
ulate him on his handiwork in person'. Carla heard the
news with a sense of foreboding. Piero insisted on Luigi
accompanying her as far as his door. With such a
valuable painting she needed a bodyguard, and Luigi
was the burliest of the apprentices.

'Once you're inside, you watch your back,' he warned,
echoing her own unspoken fears, when Carla set out
with the panel wrapped in cloth under her arm. 'Some
of those priests have a reputation for liking young boys.
If you sense that he wants something more from you
than your artistic skill make a quick excuse and run for
it, that's my advice.'

So it was with some trepidation that Carla rang the
bell of the priest's house. He lived alongside his church
and a pretty servant boy opened the door doing nothing to allay Carla's fears. She was shown into Father
Giacomo's study, a pleasant room overlooking cloisters.
In a few minutes the priest arrived, already beaming.

'Ah, the young *maestro*!' he began, stretching out his
fleshy hands towards the painting. 'I can hardly wait to
see what your master has made of my request to fashion

the Virgin's features after your own. Unveil your handiwork, child, and let the dog see the rabbit for I'm raring
to go!'

Carla found his enthusiasm strangely unsettling. She
was half afraid he would be disappointed when he saw
her efforts, but there was more to it than that. The gleam
in his eye was almost lascivious and she guessed that he
had some hidden motive for wanting to have his 'Virgin'
modelled on a boy.

Her fears redoubled as she drew back the cloth and
set the painting on a stool for him to see. Father Giacomo
gave a guttural groan and pressed his hands together as
if in prayer, his brown eyes filled with an unnatural
light. 'Oh, superb!' he murmured, raptly. 'What an aid
to devotion this work shall prove! I cannot wait to see it
in the chapel with a votive light before it. Such innocence! Such subtle charm! Tell me, which parts of the
painting did you execute yourself?'

When the priest heard that she had done her own self-
portrait his admiration knew no bounds. He flung his
chubby arms into the air exclaiming, 'What immoderate
talent in one so young! Tell me, child, has Cortoni taught
you everything you know?'

'He has taught me a great deal, but I have always
loved to draw. Painting I could not do until I joined
Piero's workshop, but I enjoy it greatly now.'

The priest's round, flabby jowls came close to Carla's
face, making her cringe inwardly.

'And what else has your master taught you, eh boy?
Come, you can speak frankly to me. Imagine you are in
the confessional. Does he lie with you at night and bid
you perform dark deeds for him?'

'I don't know what you mean, Father!' Carla said, but
her blushes betrayed her.

The priest's fat finger tickled beneath her chin as he
continued, 'Oh, I think you do! But never mind, that is
your own business. I would like to show you our church
and the chapel where your painting shall hang. Will you
come this way?'

Carla followed through a side door and found herself in the cloisters. They were cool and pleasant in the heat of the day with a shady cypress in the middle of herb gardens, and she began to feel more relaxed. The priest led the way into the church which was almost empty, except for a few old women praying in the side chapels.

It was a long time since Carla had entered a church that was not thronged with people and the peaceful atmosphere stirred her soul. Since she had left home so much had happened that her old devotions had been almost neglected and now she felt pangs of guilt. Perhaps she should make her confession to this priest after all. But the thought of telling him about her life with Piero made her quail, and how could she confess her greatest secret, that of her gender, without getting into real trouble?

Following Father Giacomo's confident stride Carla reached a small chapel with family tombs and an altar which had a plain reredos. He gestured towards it with a smile.

'Your masterpiece shall be displayed right there behind the altar. What do you think of that, eh? Everyone will see it when they kneel and pray.'

'I am very honoured, and I am sure my master will be too.'

'Come, I wish to show you the other works of art we have here in our church.'

First he showed her a Madonna and Child, which he claimed was far inferior to her own work although Carla found it quite charming and well-executed. There was an elaborate altarpiece with Christ in Majesty and the saints ranged behind; statues of the Virgin with Saint Jerome and Saint Paula; an attractive painting of Saint Martin dividing his cloak for the beggar, and a large fresco showing a group of flagellants in procession. It was before this last picture that the priest lingered, with a wistful expression on his face.

'You see how those men in black are atoning for their

131

sins?' he said. 'One of them is me. Can you recognise which one?'

Carla peered at each face in turn until she found the unmistakably pudgy features of the priest. She pointed to it and he smiled. 'That's right,' he sighed. 'I was a member of that order until my hands were stricken. Now I can only just manage to grip the chalice and perform other sacred tasks. God sends such afflictions to try us, child, but sometimes it is hard to fathom why He should deprive me of the means to serve and honour Him.'

Father Giacomo led the way back through the cloister to his study. He went to a small cupboard and brought out a long box of carved cedar wood which he laid on the table. 'In here is my most prized possession,' he smiled, opening the lid.

Carla was amazed when he brought out a leather multi-thonged whip, with a beautifully decorated handle inlaid with coral and mother of pearl. The tip of each thong was threaded with a turquoise bead and he caressed them thoughtfully as he spoke in a dreamy, distant tone.

'Those who have never experienced it cannot imagine the purifying power of the scourge, the immense relief that follows a vigorous self-cleansing. I tell you, boy, it is a mystery every bit as sacred as that of the Holy Mass. To feel the flesh chastened and subdued beneath the flying lash, to have one's sins purged through suffering just as Our Lord made atonement for the sins of mankind – oh, it is a consummation most devoutly to be desired, and I bitterly regret its absence in my miserable life.'

To Carla's horror he tried to give her the leather handle around which he had bound the thongs. She shrank back, unwilling to believe what her mind was beginning to suspect. The priest gave a horrible smile, a wheedling look coming over his face as he took her right hand and pressed the whip into it, closing her fingers over the thick, stubby handle.

'There, you now hold in your hand the instrument of my greatest bliss,' he murmured, his eyes staring at her

with the fevered intensity of a fanatic. 'Just a few strokes
will suffice to satisfy my soul, child. You need not
attempt more than your strength will permit or your
soul can take. I understand that, to a tender spirit, the
very idea of afflicting pain is distasteful, but consider
my need more than your squeamishness, I beg of you.'

Carla felt the horrid thongs untwine from the handle
and hang down, as if ready for service. She stared at it
in horror. 'I – cannot, forgive me!'

'No, it is I who needs forgiveness. And I know it will
not be granted to me until I have atoned for my sin. For
me, there is only one way. If I could administer the
flogging myself I would gladly do so but, as I explained
to you, I am unable on account of my infirmity.'

'But why me?' Carla was near to tears. She was
trembling all over at the thought of what she was being
asked to do, wondering how on earth she could get out
of it.

Father Giacomo's face softened as he gazed into her
face with a look of blind adoration. 'Because you have
the face of a Madonna, my child. No matter that you are
not a woman. Sometimes boys have a purity that women
lack. That is why we choose their sweet voices for our
choirs, and imagine them as little angels when they walk
up the aisle in procession carrying their candles.'

'But I am no angel.'

He put his finger to his lips, shaking his head. 'Indulge
me, child, let me keep my illusions. If I can believe that I
have been chastised by an avenging angel how much
more complete will my purification seem. Now see, I get
down on my aching knees to plead with you!'

To Carla's horror he lifted up his black skirt and fell
with a groan onto the stone slabs. She felt mesmerised
by his strange passion. Although she recalled Piero's
advice to make excuses and run she was rooted to the
spot and could no more flee than she could speak. Her
embarrassment increased as the priest hitched his robe
into the cord at his waist and revealed his withered
genitalia.

133

Before she could recover her wits he was bending over on all fours, displaying the sagging cheeks of his naked buttocks. 'Now, strike!' he commanded her. 'As many as you can manage, sweet angel of holy retribution, for I have grievously sinned!'

She heard him muttering his prayers over and over in the silence that followed. At first she simply stood there dumbfounded, not knowing what to do, but the sight of his prostrate flesh was oddly tempting and soon she found herself raising the scourge aloft. The leather felt warm in her palm and she shook it experimentally to see the fronds dance in the air. There was a soft clinking of the little stones as they clashed together.

'Ah, divine sound!' the priest exclaimed, without looking round. 'It is the music of the ancient sistrum that the Egyptians used in the worship of Isis. Sweet Virgin Mother, I now consecrate this instrument to thee! May my pain bring me closer to thy dear Son, whose agonies have ransomed the soul of every Christian.'

Carla was disturbed by his talk, and grew impatient. If the only way to shut the old fool up was to whip him then she would do it. Hesitating no longer, she brought her hand down sharply and the thongs cracked as the stones buffeted against his pale backside.

'Ah, bliss!' the man exclaimed. 'At last my miserable flesh is being healed!'

Carla found the sight of him ridiculous, his words absurd. She remembered the village priest who had last heard her confession and a wave of irritation spread through her. What did those stupid priests know of life and love, cloistered in their make-believe world of sin and atonement? She raised her hand again, and this time the whip fell with more assurance upon the quivering flesh beneath.

'Here's one for Father Andrea!' she thought. 'Here's for making me feel guilty when I was a willing partner and had no cause to feel shame!'

The priest groaned as the little stones made their

smarting impact on the soft cushions of his behind. His prayer became more fervent, taking on a grovelling tone.

Carla smiled, lifting the instrument on high for another stroke. She thought, 'This one is dedicated to you, dear cousin Stefano. For first seducing me, then thinking you had me in your power forever more!'

This time the leather bit into the priest's backside along with the stones, making red marks. He gave a long, shuddering moan and bent forward so that his chin was on the ground and his posterior raised even higher in the air. Looking down, Carla could see his balls swinging beneath his thighs in their flaccid sac.

'Another?' she enquired.

'Yes – please, dear angel!'

This time the blow would fall on Piero's behalf, she decided. For keeping her in thrall to him in exchange for his silence, and for using her body without regard to her own feelings. The whip snaked down viciously and Father Giacomo shrieked with the pain, but now she was inured to the priest's cries. He had become symbolic of all the men who had abused her in any way. This one was for Giovanni and his spiteful remarks. It proved to be the unkindest cut of all and it left the man prostrate and gasping, his buttocks a red lattice of weals.

'I can do no more,' Carla said flinging down the whip, her arm aching.

The priest eventually managed to turn his head on his creaky neck and gave her a wan smile. 'Thank you, thank you, blessed boy!'

'May I go now?'

'Yes, yes. I am duly shriven and my soul rejoices, even as my body suffers. Help me up, child, so that I may give you your just reward.'

He staggered to his feet, leaning heavily upon Carla's shoulder, then went over to a drawer and withdrew a small purse on a thong. 'Here, your wages. You are to take these back to your master, and he will know what share you are to have. Let me fasten the purse on to your belt, for safe keeping.'

Carla felt decidedly uncomfortable as the groping hands felt under the fold of her tunic for her belt. She was afraid he had other intentions and all the time that he was trying to tie on the purse she was expecting his hands to wander. Much to her relief, they did not. Once the money was secured he stepped back, smiling broadly.

'You may tell your master I am well pleased with you – with your painting, I mean. If he will come to our church this Sunday he may see it fixed to the altar in the chapel I showed you. If it pleases him to bring you I shall be glad to see you both, and perhaps we may take wine together afterwards? That would please me greatly. Yes, greatly.'

His manner was obsequious now, and Carla could not get out of his oily presence fast enough. She hurried back to the workshop with her hand over the bulge in her tunic where the purse was, and it was with great relief that she finally set foot through Piero's door once again.

They were very busy, as usual, and the minute Carla appeared there were cries for help from all sides, making her flustered.

'Can you put some gesso on for me, Carlo?'

'Where are those brushes you made yesterday? I've been looking all over for them.'

'Do you know where there's some more ochre and umber? We're running out fast here.'

She sighed, realising that until there was another commission she must go back to being a dogsbody again. Still she accepted her fate. In theory her status was less than even young Antonio's, since he was a proper articled apprentice and she was not. So far she had been extremely lucky to be given the kind of work she had.

Lucky? Nonsense! Carla corrected her thoughts as she bustled about the workshop. It was her talent that had brought her those opportunities. If only some day she could be fully recognised as an artist she would live and die happy.

That evening Piero showed his usual curiosity about

how she was received by their patron. His eyes gleamed at her in the twilight as he sat on the bed, pulling off his boots, and she knew that he was having lascivious thoughts about her.

'What did that old bugger of a priest want from you?' he asked, slyly. 'More than just the painting, I'll be bound. Tell me everything, Carla, and don't spare any details. I'm in the mood for a bit of titillating fun!'

She smiled at him, not averse to the idea herself, and settled down beside him on the bed. At first she described their visit to the church to see the altar where their work would hang.

'Yes, yes, we shall go there on Sunday and see it for ourselves,' Piero promised. 'But what happened when you went back to his quarters. Did he make a grab for you, or what?'

'No, nothing like that. It seems that he is one of those weird *flagellantes* who beat themselves cruelly to atone for their sins.'

'I've seen them processing around from time to time, and a gruesome sight it is too.'

'Well, he told me he couldn't do it to himself any more because of his afflicted hands.'

'Ha, that's a good one! I must remember that next time a pretty girl is reluctant to wank me off! So, did you oblige?'

'Yes. He brought out his whip, a rather beautiful one adorned with coloured stones, and asked me to lash his bare behind. I felt sorry for him, he pleaded with me so strongly. At first I was reluctant to inflict pain on him, but he entreated me and at last I knew that was really what he wanted.'

Piero chuckled. 'So you went ahead and beat the shit out of him? Good for you! There are a few more of those priests I wouldn't mind giving a thrashing to myself. Not all of them, mind you. Like any profession the Church contains some pious and sincere men. But the ones I'm thinking of are those who preach hellfire and damnation, filling people's heads with all sorts of non-sense just to keep them under their unholy thumbs.'

Lazily, he lifted up Carla's tunic so he could reach her small breasts and fondle them while she talked. 'Tell me more,' he went on. 'Like I said, every detail.'

'I was very nervous at first, afraid of hurting him too much,' Carla confessed. 'But the harder I hit him the more he seemed to like it. He called me his "avenging angel", and praised our Lord and Holy Mother at every stroke.'

'Ha! And how did his fat bottom look when you had finished with it?'

'Very red and sore, but he didn't seem to mind. On the contrary, at the end he looked well pleased both with me and with himself. It was very strange. I could not understand it at all.'

'Well I don't know about going to extremes. I don't think I'd like that either. But a little friction where it stimulates at a crucial moment can be extremely pleasant, and it's given me an idea. Here's how I want it to be tonight. First you will lick and suck me to the best of your ability so that my cock is strong and raring to go, but you will stop short of a climax. When you judge I'm teetering on the edge and about to come, I want you to turn me over and spank my bare backside until I shoot my load. Do you think you could manage that?'

She told herself that at least she would be safe from getting pregnant that way. 'I'll try.'

'Good girl. Take your clothes off then, I want to see your luscious little body in all its naked glory before we start. Madonna indeed! You'd be a better model for the Magdalene – before her conversion!'

Carla stripped and knelt before him as he lay on the bed with his arms above his head and an expression of pleasant anticipation on his face. She felt a brief pang of disgust, seeing herself about to perform an act which she had come to regard as commonplace even though she knew nothing about it a few months ago. How far she had come since then: or was it a case of how low she had sunk?

A priest would certainly tell her so, even that same priest that she had given such a beating earlier that day. Men! They were such hypocrites!

Once she saw Piero's thick member rise up to greet her, however, all such thoughts were banished as she applied herself enthusiastically to the task. She turned herself round, at her master's request, so that he could fondle her genitals while she licked him and it wasn't long before she felt the fire within and began to enjoy it as much as he. While she lapped at his glans with her little tongue she fondled his balls, feeling their hardness within the soft sac.

What was it like to have a cock and balls, she wondered, not for the first time. Living amongst men as she did, she felt as if she had forfeited a part of her womanhood, for everything that made her a woman was hidden most of the time and she had no one with whom to share her feminine preoccupations. She did not have the time to be lonely, yet sometimes there was a wistful yearning for her gentle mother, her sister and village playmates. Men were coarse and vulgar, thought nothing of teasing each other to the point of cruelty, or turning their petty squabbles into fist-fights. Many times Carla had been obliged to dodge when someone threw a punch in her direction over some imagined misdemeanour.

'Careful!' Piero admonished her when she squeezed his scrotum rather too hard, a timely reminder that men could be sensitive creatures too.

She licked the length of his shaft and he groaned in delight when she sucked at the slit in his glans which had just begun to ooze. Her hands caressed his stomach and thighs, feeling the furry layer of hair that made him a man and different from her. There was already a hollow ache inside her like a hungry wound, a craving to be filled. Now she could understand what desire was and how hard it could be to resist. The knowledge that Piero had no intention of penetrating her this time only made her want it more.

'Mind you don't go too far now,' Piero warned her.

His voice was strained and she knew he was on the verge, so she slowed the pace, licking his bollocks instead of his dick and avoiding the swollen red tip entirely. She would make him wait for his satisfaction, the pig! Her own satisfaction would come when she took her hand to his bare backside and gave him a good walloping!

His mouth moved to her pussy, gobbling hungrily, and the throbbing of her clitoris increased almost unbearably. She could feel the juices running out of her and trickling over her hairy lips, mingling with his saliva to bathe the whole region with musky secretions. She thought of Marco, imagined him coming in and finding them like that, and her imagination took it even further.

What if he should join in, entering her from behind while she was thrashing the master? Her insides seemed to take a somersault at the very idea and she gave an involuntary moan. Piero grinned up at her. 'What is it – are you getting excited too? Little minx, you've grown more and more randy since you've been living here. I've taught you a thing or two, haven't I? You've got a lot to thank me for.'

Yes, she thought, for without you I should never have been able to live here under the same roof as my beloved Marco. But her thoughts threatened to turn melancholy, and that would never do. Resolutely she applied herself to licking the tumid shaft once more and when it was practically bursting at the seams with unfulfilled lust she finished with a flourish of her tongue across his glans.

'There you are – now turn yourself over and let's have a look at those buttocks of yours!' He obeyed with a groan, rearranging his tackle as he sank back onto the mattress. 'Not like that, up on all fours!' she told him. 'Then I can feel your posterior nice and hard when I slap it.'

'Oh, you are a little harridan!'

'I'll be whatever you want me to be, you know that,'

she said, but her tone was cynical as she added, 'I'm Piero's dog: you whistle, and I'll jump.'

He grunted, lost in a world of sensual suspense, and she braced herself to give him what he wanted. Raising her hand high she looked down at the two pale moons of his buttocks. They were plumper and firmer than the thin, sagging buns of the priest, and when she brought the flat of her hand down on them the flesh felt pleasantly cushiony so that her hand bounced a little. She giggled, enjoying the slight sting on her palm, raised her hand and repeated the action. Faster and faster she slapped until she had a noisy rhythm going, but then she grew afraid that it could be heard downstairs.

'What's the matter?' Piero grunted peevishly. 'I was just getting off on it. Why have you stopped?'

'I thought the others might hear . . .'

'Let 'em! I'll tell them I was giving *you* a good thrashing. They'll never believe it was the other way around!'

He chortled in delight, which only increased her determination to give him a good seeing-to. This time she began a relentless series of stinging slaps that had him wriggling in the sheets like an eel as he strove to achieve his climax. Again and again she brought her hand down on the reddening cheeks, first the right then the left, feeling the muscles grow taut in an attempt to fend off the blows.

Piero was groaning almost continuously and quite loudly now, so she wanted it to be over. At last his moans reached a crescendo and from the way he shuddered and swore she guessed that he was soaking the bed with his ejaculation. It seemed to go on for ages, accompanied by constant shaking and noise, so she was sure that if anyone had been listening at the keyhole they would have known exactly what was going on in the master's bedroom.

After his orgasm Piero lay inert, breathing heavily, and Carla went over to her own bed where she could lie more comfortably. Her own body was still full of unrequited desire, but she did not expect any more attention from Piero that night. He was clearly exhausted and would soon fall asleep, even though she had done all of the work.

'Oh Marco!' she breathed into the night air, her cheek wet with tears. 'How much longer must I keep my secret from you?'

Again she thought of him coming to make love to her in that room, like a ghost, invisible to everyone but her. This time she imagined him taking her in his arms and kissing her fervently, his lips passing down to her breasts where they licked and suckled like a hungry child. Even at the thought of it her womb leapt for tortured joy and the aching void intensified.

Then she imagined his warm, sweet lips traversing her tense stomach, playing teasingly around her navel while she tingled and moistened down below. She could almost smell the musky, aphrodisiac aroma of his sweat that she had often breathed in the workshop driving her wild with desire. How wonderful it would be to grab a handful of those dark, glossy curls and stroke the creamy skin of his nape while he mouthed his way down to heaven!

When his lips finally reached those hidden folds they would be tenderly swollen and slick with her own essential oils, testament to how much she wanted him. Carla sighed aloud, then paused in her fantasy, afraid of waking Piero. But by now he was snoring at full blast and she knew nothing short of a thunderstorm would rouse him. Carefully she parted her labia with her fingers and felt the smooth, inner lips that guarded her most precious sanctuary. If only she could have saved herself for Marco! But it was too late to regret her loss of virginity. All she could hope for was that, some day, he would bring her the total fulfilment which had so far evaded her. That would really be worth waiting for.

Slowly Carla introduced her forefinger into her own pussy, feeling the velvet walls close around it as she moved further in towards her womb. Imagining it to be Marco's penis she gave it a loving squeeze. Her secre-

142

tions started flowing more strongly and soon her hand was so covered in her own wetness that she dared not move it in and out too fast in case it made too much noise. Her thumb was pressed against the pulsating button of flesh at the top of her vulva, and the hot, tingling sensations were spreading through her, filling all her lower body with wonderful warmth and vitality.

She wanted to go on pretending, to make believe that she really had Marco as her lover, but although her body craved further stimulation her mind would not continue. It seemed such an empty pastime to be day-dreaming about the man who lay sleeping on the floor below. Perhaps he was engaged in similar activity. If so, she guessed he would not be thinking about her, but about pretty Elena, whose body he already knew intimately.

The thought depressed Carla, making it impossible for her to gain any more satisfaction from her self-pleasuring. With another sigh – this time more frustrated than voluptuous – she turned over on to her side, curled one arm protectively around her head and prepared for sleep.

Chapter Ten

The workshop had been a pleasant place that morning until the news broke that Piero had given Carla the chance to work with him on another important commission: a fresco in one of the family chapels in *Santa Maria Immacolata*. Now Giovanni's jet-black eyes had that hard expression in them that Carla had come to fear.

He spat venomously as he complained, 'That job should be mine, Piero! I am the senior artist here and yet you have overlooked me once again in favour of an upstart who's not even apprenticed. What the hell is going on here? Is he your fancy boy, that you give him such preferment?'

Piero tried to soothe him, placing a hand on Giovanni's arm that was rudely pulled away. 'Now don't fret, Giovanni, there's a good reason for my decision and you've a right to know it. You are working on the Belloni portrait and that must be finished for the wedding. I can see what an excellent job you're making of it, and when the couple see it you may be sure that they will commission more work from you. By the time that happens I expect you'll have set up on your own. But in the meantime this fresco must take priority and there's no one else I can give the job to except Carlo.'

'What about Marco and Luigi?' Giovanni persisted, sulkily.

'They are both busy with the Ciari project, while Antonio and Matteo lack experience. I didn't make this decision lightly, I assure you. If you'd been free you would have been my first choice for this fresco. But it will be good for Carlo to have the experience too.'

Giovanni muttered something under his breath that sounded obscene, but the wind had been taken out of his sails by Piero's tactful response and there was little more he could say. Even so, Carla could tell he was still riled and she feared the consequences. Much as she was looking forward to working on the new fresco with Piero she knew that this was just one more black mark against her in Giovanni's Book of Grievances.

The fresco in the Verazzi chapel was to be scenes in the life of the Virgin, starting with the Immaculate Conception and leading through the Annunciation and the Madonna of the Milk, to the Stabat Mater and the Pietà. A tall scaffold was erected in front of the wall to be decorated, and after they had applied a thin coat of lime the cartoon was pricked out in charcoal by Piero whilst Carla prepared more plaster for the area they would work on that day. She then hastily ground the pigments and mixed them with water bound with egg white for the painting. They had to work very quickly, before the plaster set, so only a small area could be done at a time. While Piero re-drew his outline, Carla applied red and yellow ochre where it was needed and soon the glowing colours began to take on a life of their own.

It was wonderful working by candlelight in the peace of the chapel, with only the occasional murmur of a prayer or rustle of a priest's robes to disturb their peace. Piero worked in silent concentration on the wet plaster, gesturing his wishes rather than uttering them, and soon a kind of unspoken communication developed between them. By the end of the day the scene with Saint Anne was completed. It took up just a sixth of the wall.

'Well done!' Piero smiled as they descended from the

scaffold together. 'I've seldom had a fresco go so smoothly on the first day.'

'Will I be able to do more tomorrow? I mean, not just mix paints and apply them broadly but put in some of the detail?'

He smiled at her, his expression kindly. 'I don't see why not. I trust you to do the job properly, and it will be good practice for you. But you'll soon find out that wet plaster is an unforgiving medium. You must work with broad strokes, not fine ones, and the effect must look good from a distance. Still, I'm prepared to let you experiment, since it's only by trial and error that you will succeed.'

Carla felt honoured. She was getting a full apprentice's training without having to go through all the formalities and preliminaries. No doubt if Giovanni's suspicions were confirmed and he discovered that she and the master really were lovers he would call it favouritism, but she believed it was because of her innate skill.

When they returned to the house there was an excited atmosphere amongst the others which puzzled Carla at first, but she soon found out what it was all about. Marco came up to them, glowing-eyed, and announced that he had acquired his own premises just round the corner in the *Via Calimala* and would soon be leaving to start up his own business.

Carla's heart instantly sank like a stone, although she put on a brave face and pretended to be glad for his sake. But the moment she had been dreading had arrived. Marco would be leaving her alone: what would become of her dreams, and her secret identity then? Who would protect her when Giovanni's spite expressed itself physically, as it surely would when she had no one to take her part?

Piero took it badly too. 'You gave me no warning,' he grumbled. 'How am I going to find a replacement for you at such short notice?'

'Well, there's always Carlo here.'

'He's not a candidate right now,' Piero said brusquely,

dashing her hopes. 'I need someone who can pay the fees.'

'So you're using him as slave labour meanwhile, isn't that it?'

'How dare you!'

Piero went to strike at Marco but then stayed his hand, probably realising that the lad was beyond his control now. Carla listened to their exchange in despair. Her position in that household would be even more like drudgery from now on. She knew that she could never be accepted into the Guild while Piero knew she was a girl, but she longed to have more status as an artist all the same.

The lads wanted to have a bit of a party, to give Marco a good send-off, and although Piero protested at first when they offered to chip in he could hardly refuse. Carla wondered how she could bear to attend. They would expect her to be jolly and wish him well, not one of them suspecting what heartbreak she was secretly experiencing at the thought of him leaving. It was an ordeal she dreaded.

Yet, on Marco's last morning, he took her aside before she went off to the church with Piero, and said something that made her heart sing. 'I mentioned that I'll be needing an apprentice or two, didn't I? Well, if you want a job I'll consider taking you on. It will take me a few weeks to get settled, mind.'

'Oh Marco, do you really mean it?'

Carla looked straight into his lustrous brown eyes, elated at the thought of working in close proximity with the man she loved, of sharing his house and table.

He put a friendly arm around her and gave her a hug. 'Of course I mean it! You're wasted here on that buffoon Piero. I could train you up properly, give you some jobs to really show off your particular skills. And I wouldn't take all the credit for it either, like he does.'

It sounded like a dream come true, but like most of her dreams Carla did not quite trust it. She resolved not to brood upon it, though. Marco had said he wanted her, and that was enough. She could enjoy the party now.

When she and Piero returned from their labours at *Santa Maria Immacolata*, preparations were already under way. The lads had festooned the downstairs workshop with anything they could find in the way of ribbons, flags, rosettes and banners. It looked a riotous mess, but who cared? It was obvious to anyone who walked in the door that a celebration was in progress and that was all that mattered.

They had bought several flagons of Tuscan wine, great cartwheels of bread, crocks of olives and balls of fresh goats' cheese wrapped in vine leaves. There were other apprentices there too, friends and neighbours, but Carla was disconcerted to find a few women amongst them. She had become unused to female company over the past few months and their presence disturbed her. A superstitious voice told her they might detect that she was one of them and expose her as an impostor. It was a recurring nightmare for her.

Once the party got under way, however, she forgot her fears as each of the lads took it on themselves to entertain the rest with bawdy jokes, songs and dances that soon had her in fits of laughter. Marco was the chief butt of all their jokes: Marco, who would soon no longer be one of the lads but a journeyman, a master with others working for him.

By rights Giovanni should have attained that status first but he was poor and in debt, while Marco's family were able to pay the Guild's matriculation fee. It was no surprise to Carla to see Giovanni get more drunk, more quickly, than anyone else. It was his way of coping with the ignominy of the situation. He sang a vicious song about the devil raping an old maid and Carla shrank from his fiery, lustful eyes as he bellowed out the obscenities.

Then, around midnight, the door opened and three whores entered, including the pretty Elena. A great cheer went up from the men and some of the women guests discreetly disappeared. Carla was tempted to leave too, but Piero was barring the way to the stairs and she didn't feel like pushing past him so she stayed in her corner, trying not to look too conspicuous.

'Dance for us, ladies!' Marco called, holding his beaker aloft. 'Show us your fine bodies in action! Dance like the Three Graces before Hermes, and let your movements speak of love!'

They obeyed, casting off their jewel-bright satin dresses and performing in their flimsy shifts so that the nipples on their round breasts and even the dark vee between their thighs was clearly visible. Carla watched their slow, weaving dance with fascination. They moved to the sound of Luigi's flute and Antonio's little drum, bending and swaying in an ever-changing circle that sometimes turned itself inside out when they pirouetted under each others' arms.

'It is a very old dance,' Marco told her, his voice slurred with alcohol. 'Old as the hills.'

He began to laugh in an odd, almost hysterical way that Carla disliked. His eyes grew dim and his head nodded to one side as his neck could no longer support it. Suddenly he slumped against her, throwing his arm around her neck, and she felt a surge of such violent longing that she could hardly control herself.

Elena came to her rescue. She broke from her sensual dance and came over to pull him into her arms. 'Come on, sweetie, it's me you want not him!' she said softly, kissing his cheek. 'Why don't I put you to bed? You look like you've had enough for tonight.'

Carla wanted to fight her off, to claim him as her own, but she knew that would spoil everything. It was so hard to have to sit there and smile, to watch Marco being carted off upstairs by Elena and Luigi and to know that the other girl would be sharing his bed that night. She gazed wistfully after him until she realised that Piero was watching her, and then she blushed. He came over to where she was sitting and tapped her on the shoulder.

'Let's go upstairs too. This party will go on all night if someone doesn't make a move.'

She looked up, hating him in that moment since she knew very well what he wanted of her. All she wanted was to weep for her Marco, to savour the promise of working for him after she had endured the misery of his going. Not that she could say anything to the master, of course, not yet. Glumly she followed him towards the door but as she went she was aware of Giovanni's hard, taunting eyes on her all the while. Could he possibly have guessed about her attachment to Marco? Or was he just relishing the fact that he would soon be able to taunt and torment her without hindrance?

Once they were in the topmost room Piero practically tore the clothes off her in his eagerness to explore her tired body. Carla let him paw and mouth her as he wished, she was far too drained either to resist or to take an active part in the proceedings. She lay on his bed with her legs spread while he worked up his erection, struggling to make it hard enough to get inside her. At last he managed to push it in and Carla, detached and remote as she felt from him, was aware that her body was responding in the way it was now used to, becoming soft and wet for him even though the rest of her was indifferent.

As he pumped away she marvelled at how routine it had all become for her, how soon she had become used to these nocturnal practices. Soon, though, everything would change. Marco would send for her and she would go to live under his roof, become his apprentice. What would happen after that she had no idea. She simply did not want to think about the choice she might one day have to make: whether to keep her secret along with her apprenticeship, or whether to confess her secret in the hope of winning his love. If she took the latter course it would almost certainly cost her the chance of becoming an artist.

Piero's labours came to an end in a volley of shuddering groans and his cock shrank almost instantly, flopping out of her vagina. Carla hoped that meant she stood less chance of becoming pregnant. It was the other great fear in her life that if she grew big with child Piero would forget about making her his wife and she would be cast out onto the streets and left to fend for herself. There would be few options for her then.

She pushed Piero's head away from hers, hating the stench of his wine-sodden breath, and he fell over onto his back. There was a noise at the door and she sat up in alarm, wondering if a rat had entered the room, but she could hear nothing more. Gently she extricated herself from her master's grasp and managed to get up from his bed without disturbing him. She then sought her own bed with a need that was deep and urgent. She had to be alone with her thoughts and feelings, to examine just how she felt about Marco on the eve of his departure, when he was spending the night in the arms of another woman.

Of course Carla was jealous, but she was also optimistic. He loved to make love, that much was obvious, and if one day she revealed her true nature and feelings to him then they might enjoy their love-making all the more because they were both experienced. How wonderful it would be to have the crude act that she had repeated with Piero transformed into an act of love! How much more meaningful would even a simple kiss be when it was performed with sincere love!

Despite her racing brain and restless body, exhaustion battled with Carla's need to think and feel and eventually sleep won. In the morning she awoke with a sore head, like almost everyone else in the house, and her first thought was of Marco. Had he left already? She knew he was planning to go first thing in the morning because, as he said, he hated prolonged farewells. Creeping from her bed she dressed hastily and went down the creaking stairs to see if anyone was about.

The kitchen was empty, but as she raked the sullen embers she heard someone come into the room behind her. Sure that it must be Marco, she turned with a welcoming smile that froze on her face when she encountered the dour face of Giovanni. He was unshaven and his night-shirt was open to the waist, showing the thick mat of dark hair on his chest. Despite his obvious weariness, his eyes looked at her with a cunning expression and his mouth was curved into a sardonic grin. 'Up early then, little trickster? What mischief are you about now, sirrah – or should I say, *madonna*?'

Carla stared at him in consternation. Was he simply mocking her portrayal as the Virgin, or had he – horror of horrors! – somehow discovered her secret?

She decided to assume he meant the former. 'It was not my idea to sit for the Holy Mother. I would not have presumed so far.'

Giovanni's smile widened, striking terror into her. 'Oh I think you have presumed very far, very far indeed! You presumed that we would not notice the lack of hair upon your cheek or the fact that you had too much up top and not enough down below. You presumed we would take you for a shy young lad, who is scared of girls. Shame on you for your presumption!'

He knew! God preserve her, she was in deep trouble now! The smug look on his saturnine face told her that he would take full advantage of his new-found power over her, and she dreaded what might follow.

'H – how did you find out?' she stammered.

He came close to her, putting his hand on the wall beside her head so that he leant over her, emphasising his superior height. Carla shrank back, terrified, as his voice became low, almost seductive. 'Last night I saw something in the way Piero treated you. It wasn't the first time I'd noticed it. I've had my suspicions for some time so I was determined to test them once and for all. It wasn't difficult. Piero was so drunk he forgot to lock the door.'

'You saw – that!'

Carla's voice was weak with dismay as she realised that her coupling with the master had been witnessed. Giovanni gave a sardonic nod. 'Yes, my little whore, I saw everything! You didn't seem to be enjoying it much, I must say. What were you thinking about as you lay there with dreamy eyes? Perhaps there is someone else under this roof that you would prefer to fuck – that's it, isn't it?'

For a moment she was afraid he knew about her feelings for Marco, but she shook her head, trembling all over. To her surprise, his expression softened a little and he stroked her hair with a smile that was almost friendly. 'It's all right, little one, I know you fancy me something rotten. That's why you're always pretending to hate me. But I can tell you've really got the hots for me, it's written all over your face.'

Carla was dumbfounded. Part of her was relieved that he had guessed wrongly, but another part of her realised that she would be in even worse trouble if she denied it.

'Don't be scared,' Giovanni whispered, his face very near hers. 'I'll be a far better lover to you than him upstairs, you'll see. We'll keep it a secret, of course, but then you're very good at that, aren't you? I'm the only one who guessed the truth out of all of us, but then you know what they say: the truth will out!'

His mouth came down full on hers, depriving her of words and breath in one long, rapacious kiss that left her senses reeling. She had not experienced such strong passion before. He was kissing her with a crushing fierceness that verged on the cruel, making any opposition impossible and it was obvious that there was no use trying to resist. She might as well play along with him.

At last he broke away abruptly and began to pull her across the room. 'Come on, we can't stay here or we'll be discovered. I know just the place for us.'

Then Carla knew he meant to sate his lust right away and a pang of despair went through her. Would she ever be free of the marauding instincts of men? Now she was in two men's power, and the one man who might protect her was no longer around. The impact upon her was devastating. As she staggered from the kitchen her knees felt weak and her head spun.

He took her down to the cellar which was used as a storeroom. It was damp and smelly, the abode of rats and stray cats. As they descended into darkness there was a horrid scurrying of warm, furry bodies accompanied by squeaks and hisses. Carla shuddered and felt bile rise in her throat. What kind of place was that to make love in?

You cannot call it love, she reminded herself bitterly. This would be an animal coupling, a bestial act of intercourse, no more, and for that it was as good a place as any. Giovanni lit the candle he'd picked up in passing, then lit the two sconces on the wall in turn. The place was filled with barrels and bundles, some containing artists' materials, others household goods. Some of the stuff was covered in cobwebs, giving it a dismal air.

'I'm sorry, this is not very congenial surroundings for an amorous encounter.' Giovanni's grin was ironic. 'But it's the best I can do at short notice.'

Carla braced herself, expecting him to fall upon her like a rabid beast, but he did no such thing. Throwing down some sacking to form a makeshift bed, he pulled her down on to it and gently proceeded to remove her clothes until her small breasts and downy vee were exposed. His smile widened as he brushed his hand lightly across her pubic mound.

'To think all this was hidden beneath your dowdy men's clothes. You should be clad in silk, satin and velvet my dear, to show off your exquisite form.'

This was not at all what Carla had expected and she was nonplussed. The cruel Giovanni, whose looks and curses had held her terror for so long, was now behaving quite out of character. Yet she had a horrid suspicion that it could not last. His hand went towards his own body and he parted the folds and openings of his clothes with deft fingers until he produced his own naked member, which sprang forth in a lively fashion making her gasp with surprise.

The penis which he possessed was the largest and thickest she had ever seen. It was impossible to imagine it entering her without wincing at the thought. He noted her shock with pleasure, stroking his cock as if it were a pet animal.

'Many girls have been astonished by the size of my organ. Some have fallen over themselves to pay homage to it in most delightful ways and you, I'm sure, will be no exception. There is no need to be coy. I know you have serviced the feeble member of Piero our master, now you may pay lip service to my superior tool. Come, I have waited long enough. Put your delicious young lips to the task, and get that tongue working, too.'

He pushed her head towards his rearing erection but it was all she could do to stretch her lips around the glans. The bulbous organ tasted salty and strong, making her gag, but she persevered, afraid of the consequences if she refused. Her tongue became very active, making up for not being able to get much of the rigid flesh into her mouth, and she worked it up and down the shaft rapidly, attempting to cover as much of it as she could in as short a time.

For a while this seemed to satisfy him. He gave a series of contented grunts and stroked Carla's hair from time to time, which gratified her and soothed her fear. If this is all he wants from me I can bear it, she thought, willing him to come quickly. But he was evidently used to holding out, and no matter how expertly she tongued him he resisted the urge to ejaculate.

'Enough!' he said at last, lifting her head away from his genitals. She stared straight into his black eyes and found his expression inscrutable. 'Now my dear, I want you to straddle me and let me play with your pussy. Little puss has to be as wet and slippery as possible if she's to let big brother rat come in to play!'

Carla was terrified. That huge prong looked as if it would split her in two, but she could see no way out now. She still feared Giovanni, despite his sweet words and docile manner. He was like a big wild animal, pleasant and easy-going until his path was crossed, when he would unleash a furious and destructive force from within himself. She did not trust him at all.

'Come, let me help you.'

He pulled her, open-legged, on to his broad flat stomach and made her sit there while his long, thick finger dabbled in her vulva. At first she resisted, clinging to some futile hope that if she did not moisten and seem ready he would not try to enter her. Soon, though, she felt her body responding as it had done to Stefano and to Piero. There was something degrading in the idea that anyone could produce that effect in her, making her wet and throbbing, yet it was exciting too. Before a minute had passed Carla was wanting that big, fleshy cock inside her, yearning to be filled with its sweet meat and ready to open up and receive it.

Giovanni reached up and rubbed across her small breasts, tweaking the nipples playfully. 'Oh you are a randy little thing, aren't you?' he said, in an almost affectionate tone. 'The others felt sorry for you, having to submit to Piero's buggery, as they thought. But all this time you've been enjoying him in a different way, haven't you? Well, if you aren't the sauciest minx I've ever come across! Now get up onto your knees and we'll see how much of my giant member we can feed into your ravenous maw, shall we?'

She did as she was told, positioning her sex over the shiny ball of his glans, which was now the colour of a ripe fig and oozing a little white juice. Giovanni seized it firmly and began to prod into her vulva, opening her up. When she flinched he told her to relax or it would hurt her all the more, so she made an effort to loosen up and soon she felt the viscous glans lodged at her entrance.

'Easy does it!' he murmured, and the domed head pushed a little further in, making the surrounding skin stretch to accommodate it. At first it was uncomfortable, verging on pain, but it was remarkable how soon she was able to take more and more of the gigantic prick into her elastic quim.

156

The sense of being completely filled was novel, and Carla realised for the first time how different men's dimensions could be in that department. Yet she felt disappointed that she could take in no more than a few inches. Giovanni allowed her to set the pace, rising and falling in a rhythm and speed she felt happy with, but it was a mechanical coupling that lacked some special dimension of the imagination. No matter how hard she concentrated on the feeling of being thoroughly filled she could not remove from her mind the image of a brood mare being serviced by a stallion.

'What are you thinking about?' he demanded at one point.

'Oh – you, of course.'

'My dick, you mean. That's the only part of me that matters to women. Oh, don't try to pretend otherwise. I'm used to it, and it is of no consequence to me. If it means I get regularly laid that's all I care about.'

So it was to be just a bestial coupling, she thought. Suddenly she felt sorry for the man. Giovanni had no idea about love between a man and a woman. All he knew was this empty ritual of fucking. He wanted her to worship his large cock, just as he believed other women did and he had no idea how much they all despised him. His view of women was demeaning, suggesting that all they wanted was filling up like so many hungry babes.

'It would be so different with Marco,' Carla thought and the tears rolled down her cheeks of their own accord. Too frightened to wipe them away she allowed them to roll down her cheeks and chin until they plopped onto her chest, praying that Giovanni would not notice.

Fortunately he had begun his rapid ascent towards orgasm, and she clenched her vaginal lips over his glans to hasten the climax, just wanting it to be over. She hoped to see him lose control, wanted to see that coolly handsome face grow distorted in the throes of the love-agony, but she was disappointed. At the moment of release all she saw was an intensification of the dark, savage light in his eye and heard a brief sigh exhaled.

And all she felt was a profound relief that, for the moment at least, it was over.

Carla rolled off him but instead of pulling her into his arms he stood up, steadying himself against the clammy wall of the cellar. He looked down at her, his cock semi-flaccid but still dripping. 'Aren't I the best?' he grinned. 'Some people say size doesn't matter, but you know different now, don't you?'

She nodded, afraid to gainsay him, but in her heart she despised his pathetic egotism. What really mattered was how you felt about your lover, she was quite sure of that. Giovanni might get her worked up physically, but he could never affect her heart. As he continued with his gloating display of dominance she smiled to herself, realising that he was making himself ridiculous. The Giovanni who strutted and crowed had no power over her now, not now she had the measure of him. He was a fool, who had let his big dick go to his head, thinking that was all that mattered in the world. But there were other ways to a woman's heart, ways that the likes of Giovanni, blinded by their own arrogance, would never know.

Chapter Eleven

Marco had gone by the time Carla went back upstairs – separately from Giovanni, to avoid suspicion. She saw his empty place at the table with a sinking heart, and when Piero appeared and announced that a new apprentice would be arriving straight away her sense of foreboding increased.

'What's his name?' Luigi asked. 'How old is he?'

'He's called Domenico and he's thirteen. A promising lad, from a good family. I'm sure he'll fit in very well.'

'Where will he sleep?' Luigi asked, winking at Matteo.

'Ah, yes!' Piero turned to Carla with a placatory smile. 'He'll be taking your place upstairs. I shall have to keep a close eye on him, make sure he settles in and does his work properly.'

She was aghast. 'But where will I sleep?'

'With the others, of course. You can have Marco's bed. And you'll have to go back to routine jobs again. I just haven't the time to supervise two of you closely. Besides, Matteo and Luigi need the experience. Once Giovanni goes they'll be the senior apprentices and will have to take on more advanced work.'

Every word seemed to sound the death knell to her hopes and dreams. Carla bit her lip, knowing it was useless to protest. Her day as 'favoured newcomer' was over and she must go back to being the charity child once again. Only this time she would have Giovanni to contend with instead of Piero.

Giovanni avoided her eye most of the morning but she was acutely aware of his presence as she ground the colours with pestle and mortar or prepared the painting surfaces with gesso. Whenever he had dealings with her he was scrupulously polite, but she saw the knowing look in his eye and felt his hand linger a second too long whenever he took a brush from her fingers. His new attitude towards her was enigmatic, and she wondered just what was going on behind that bland, indifferent gaze.

Once she had performed her tasks to the satisfaction of the others she decided to go out for some air. She had no wish to be there when the new boy, Domenico, arrived. It would be humiliating to have to play second fiddle to him, although he was much younger. Her few things had already been moved out of the attic room and brought down to the chest next to Marco's old bed. She was dreading the night, when she must lie in it.

Carla walked briskly through the town until she came to the river, then she continued along its bank where the path led towards open fields. There was a feeling of oppression in her breast that she could hardly bear, and she needed to think about her new situation. With long strides she walked through reed-beds and marshy ground, hardly aware of what was around her. What are my choices? she kept asking herself. What is best for me to do?

One thing was certain: she could not bear to stay in Piero's household if she must go back to drudgery and give up her pleasure in fine work. The church fresco had been completed, and to see it in the mellow light of candles with the gold highlights gleaming amongst the other jewel-bright colours filled her heart with pride and joy. To have to stand by and see others get the best work would be unbearable now.

Yet if she stayed there was no telling what Giovanni

might do or say. He was unpredictable, quixotic. He might tell her secret to the others, and then what would become of her? She might turn into a plaything for them all, to be handed from bed to bed like a whore should they have another night of drunken revelry like the last one. She had sensed their envy of her when she was Piero's favourite. Now they might well have their revenge.

But then there was Marco. He had said he wanted her as his apprentice, yet if she accepted his offer how could she then tell him about her true gender? There was no knowing how he might react. She might win his love, but then she would have to give up her work. Or, if she kept her secret from him, she must suffer the torture of being near him every minute of the day but unable to touch him, or talk to him about her feelings. Neither option seemed possible.

There was a third possibility; that she should strike out on her own and make a fresh start. It was a prospect that appalled her, yet she had done it once and could no doubt do it again. She thought of the artists in the *loggia*, of the street life she had been so glad to leave behind, and her soul shrank from exchanging her present ease for such hardship.

First, she decided, she would visit Marco in his new abode and see what transpired. Filled with hope, she returned to the city centre and made her way to the *Via Calimala*. It was very quiet, since the noonday sun had forced everyone indoors, and when she reached the new premises she found them shuttered. She tried the door and it opened, so she crept in.

The room was dark and at first she was unable to see anything, but after a few seconds vague shapes came into view. There were bundles and baskets piled high on one side of the room, evidently waiting to be sorted. Then she saw a makeshift bed in the far corner where Marco lay naked. Carla had a brief impression of his beautiful lean body, his chest smattered with just a few dark hairs and his pale cock hanging from within a bush of black curls. Seeing him lying there so innocent and lovely, made her tears well up and a huge lump stuck in her throat.

But he was not alone. Beside him lay Elena, equally naked, her plump round breasts crested with flaccid pink nipples. One of her legs was entwined with his and the wispy hairs of her pubis were just visible beneath her raised thigh. It was obvious that they had been enjoying each other just a few minutes ago. The air was still perfumed with musk and sweat from their coupling and the sheet bore a wet mark.

Elena stirred and gave a low moan in her sleep, frightening Carla into retreat. She closed the door quietly behind her, the tears coursing helplessly down her face. There was no room for her there, not in any capacity. She could not bear to work as Marco's apprentice, to see him flirting and kissing his girl in front of her eyes with no thought for how it might be hurting her. Neither could she risk revealing all, and then being rejected in favour of Elena.

'At least I know what I must do now', she told herself as she returned to Piero's house with a determined stride.

Domenico, the new boy, had already arrived. He was small and thin, but with an eager, bright-eyed expression which suggested a will to succeed. Piero was making a show of being kind to him, but Carla couldn't help wondering if he would be abused by his master the same way all the other apprentices had been. She had no reason to think otherwise.

For the rest of the day she kept a low profile, unwilling to attract attention to herself. Whilst she ground pigments and fashioned brushes for the new recruit her mind was working hard, planning her escape. She knew now that she had to leave as soon as possible.

In the late afternoon she found herself alone in the workshop with Giovanni for a few minutes. He couldn't resist coming up behind her, clasping his hands on her breasts beneath the concealing tunic. His voice giggled softly in her ear and she could feel his hard cock thrusting between her buttocks as she stood working the pestle in the mortar.

'That's right, grind away!' he murmured. 'You and I will be engaged in similar work soon enough. In fact, why not come down into the cellar with me now? We won't be missed for ten minutes. I've been hot for you all day.'

She shook her head, trembling. 'I have to finish this job for Domenico.'

The door opened then and Luigi entered. Instead of springing back from her in alarm, as she would have expected, Giovanni gave her a playful slap on the rump saying, 'He's got a woman's arse on him this one, don't you think?'

Luigi sniggered. 'Maybe that's because Piero's used him as a woman once too often.'

'I could use a woman too, couldn't you? Maybe we'll get hold of one tonight and share her. You can have her cunt and I'll have her arse, how about that?'

Carla glanced up in alarm, and saw Giovanni's dark eyes flicker in mocking confirmation of her fear. Her hand shook so much that she dropped the mortar and the red powder spilt on the floor. Fortunately it was only burnt ochre, not a more precious colour. She wiped it up, acutely conscious of the men's eyes upon her, but when the rag was soiled she thought of her period and felt her cheeks redden too. How on earth would she manage to conceal her monthlies from the others now that she was no longer secluded in the garret? One more reason for getting out of there as quickly as she could.

From then on she was just biding her time, waiting for the opportunity to slip away without so much as a by-your-leave. When they all sat down together for their evening meal she looked round at the familiar faces and felt a pang of regret, wondering if she was being too hasty. After all, these people had become like a second family to her. But the predatory look in Giovanni's eye when he met hers across the table confirmed her decision.

It would not be easy fleeing in the dark, but at least she had a full belly. Carla slipped upstairs on the pretext of going to the privy and gathered up her small bundle of money and possessions. Most precious amongst them were her three brushes, her chalks and the small packets of pigment she had managed to squirrel away. She went back downstairs and out through the side door, near the steps that led down to the cellar.

Once she was out of the house Carla scurried along in the dark, expecting at any moment to hear a shout and running footsteps behind her. She only slowed down once she had hurried through the warren of side streets leading past the *duomo* towards the Church of the Most Holy Annunciation, with its miraculous shrine to the Virgin. There was no moon and it was hard going, her feet sliding in unspeakable sludge and stumbling over hidden obstacles. At first only the occasional beam of candlelight from a building lit her way, but then she heard the distant rumble of thunder and the sky became illuminated with flashes of lightning as the first drops of rain fell.

Carla sought shelter in the porch of a church on the road to San Domenico. Shivering and exhausted, she fell into a fitful sleep and awoke in the early hours of the morning with an ache in her bones that provided a physical correlate to the misery she felt in her heart. Tempted as she was to retrace her steps and seek the warm comfort of Marco's old bed, she forced herself to carry on into the unknown.

The city was waking up, its outskirts filled with the crowing of cockerels and bleating of goats. As the urban streets slowly turned into country lanes Carla felt her spirits lifting for she was, after all, a country girl at heart. Her stride became jauntier and when she found some ripe figs on a wayside tree she breakfasted on them hungrily, relishing their juice as well as their stringy flesh.

'Hey!' a woman called from a nearby hovel. Carla paused in her thieving, ready to run, but the woman shouted, 'I have bread and milk if you're hungry.'

Eagerly she went over and was soon sitting at the woman's board, wolfing down a mug of warm goats' milk into which she'd dipped a hunk of bread.

'How long have you been on the road?' she was asked.

'Only since last night.'

'You look like a boy, but you talk like a girl,' the peasant woman observed, bluntly. 'Which are you?'

Carla smiled. 'I'm a girl. I dress like this on the road for protection.'

'Very wise. But why aren't you with your family?'

'It's a long story. I'm looking for work. Any idea where I might find some?'

The woman frowned. 'You're better off trying at Fiesole, up the hill. There are a few big villas there where they might need a kitchen maid. I take it that's what you have in mind?'

Carla nodded, knowing there were few other possibilities for a new girl in a strange town. 'I wouldn't mind getting hold of some women's clothes, though,' she added. 'I'm willing to pay. I'll pay for my food, too. Here . . .'

She began to rummage in her bundle but the woman held up her hand. 'Don't bother. I can feed a stranger at my door without going bankrupt. And I may have a few old clothes for you too, things that my daughter's outgrown. Give me a few minutes.'

She disappeared into a back room and eventually came out with a plain dark green dress with a square neck and long sleeves. 'Will this do? I'm afraid there's no underskirt.'

'Marvellous!' Carla held it against her. The sleeves were a bit long and the bodice would be too full, but what did it matter? She would look like a woman again and that gave her a huge sense of relief. She hadn't realised how much tension had been involved in her cross-dressing, in living with the constant fear of discovery.

Outside was a pump, and Carla gave herself a good washing before putting on her new clothes. She was very pleased to be wearing a skirt again. 'Please let me give you something for it,' she said, but the woman was adamant. Then Carla had an idea. 'Wait, I know what I can give you!'

She took out her chalks and looked about her for a suitable surface on which to draw. There was a clear piece of whitewashed wall in the corner, so she took her stool and sat by it to make a portrait of her benefactor. The woman giggled when she discovered what Carla was doing, but she seemed pleased and sat still with a half-smile on her face. While she worked, Carla thought that this peasant woman had been a more generous patron to her than any nobleman could have been. She had helped her in a time of greatest need.

The hastily executed portrait was quite a good likeness, and the woman was delighted. 'Imagine, you a mere girl with such a talent! What a shame you weren't born a boy. You would go far.'

The words were kindly meant, but they struck despair into Carla's heart. How many times must she be told that she could not succeed as an artist because she was the wrong sex? As if she could help how nature had made her! But she swallowed her pride and thanked the woman once again before setting out on the road to Fiesole.

The sun was up by now, bathing the verdant landscape in soft gold. Beside the dusty road grew a profusion of wild flowers and herbs, their scent bringing medicine to the soul, and beyond were vineyards and olive groves already weighed down with ripening fruit. Tall cypresses and spreading umbrella pines punctuated the hills, while above the birds were already circling, singing their morning hymn to Phoebus. It was impossible to feel downcast in such a beautiful setting and before long optimism surged back into Carla's heart.

The town of Fiesole stood on a hilltop, and on the slopes below there were many fine villas. When Carla came across the first of these she paused at the ornate iron gate set into the high wall. There was a bell-rope, and she hesitated while she peered through the gate at the garden beyond. Low hedges marked out square beds with geometrical precision, and she could just glimpse brilliant blooms, lush foliage and, in the centre, the glitter of a fountain.

'Oh, I should love to live here!' she sighed, pulling on the rope.

After several tugs a gruff servant appeared, puffing down the gravel path towards her. He seemed annoyed at being disturbed and Carla had little hope of finding employment, but she greeted him politely then enquired anyway.

To her surprise he did not reject her outright. 'We might need someone in the kitchen,' he said thoughtfully. 'Have you had any experience?'

'I worked for some artists in Florence,' she replied. 'And I often prepared their meals and cleared up after them.'

It was the truth, more or less. The man examined her up and down, evidently finding her clean and respectable-looking. He unlocked the gate and let her in. 'Follow me!'

The door they went through led to a spacious kitchen where several servants were already hard at work. A fat, red-faced woman was stirring something in a huge vat over the fire, and the man called to her. 'Hey, Marta, here's a girl looking for work. Could you do with an extra pair of hands?'

'I'll say!' the woman grinned, pushing back a strand of her greasy grey hair. 'What with the feasting coming up, and two laid off sick. I can't say whether it will be permanent, of course, but she's welcome to stay for a month or so.'

Carla grinned delightedly, but she was allowed no time for pleasantries. 'Put your bundle in that corner and help Lisa at the table,' she was told at once. 'She'll show you what to do.'

The girl called Lisa was short and pretty, with lustrous dark hair and eyes. She gave Carla a wry grin, handing her a paring knife and a bundle of green beans. 'What do you want to work here for?' she mumbled, so the old woman couldn't hear. 'It's a madhouse, I can tell you!'

'It's better than being on the streets though, isn't it?'

Lisa nodded. 'I'll give you that. But don't let anyone take advantage of you. If anyone gives you any stick come to me, and I'll sort them out.'

Carla appreciated the friendly overture, and soon warmed to her companion as they sliced away together. Despite what Lisa had said, she was sure she had fallen on her feet. This was a grand household which held feasts and employed countless servants. A great new adventure had begun. Perhaps it would take her mind off Marco and the others, easing the pain of the past.

Over the next few days Carla found out a lot about the household of the Panzani family, where she was now living. Her chief informant was Lisa, with whom she shared a bed. Lisa seemed to see herself as her protector, and advised her about many things including her appearance.

'You should rinse your hair in centaury, to make it fair,' she said. 'Then you'd look really pretty.'

Carla took her advice and saw herself transformed. The blonde look made her brown eyes appear more friendly and lent warmth to her skin tone. She gratefully accepted scraps of braid and tiny strips of lace that Lisa had gleaned from the ladies of the house, sewing them on to her plain clothes to make them look prettier. Soon she was attracting male glances.

There were men a-plenty coming and going in that household. The head of the family, old Giorgio, was a widower and his mistress was living under his roof with her two small children, his bastards. In addition there were his legitimate heirs, two bachelor sons and two

168

married daughters. Carla gathered that they rubbed along pretty well under the same roof, all having their own private quarters.

The feast was to celebrate the coming-of-age of Giorgio's elder son, Tommaso, but of the two young men Carla much preferred Bruno, the younger one. It was his bright, intelligent eye that caught hers with a look of keen interest whenever she was about some business above stairs, and she often saw him watching through a window while she was walking in the garden.

It was at the birthday feast that they became better acquainted as Carla was one of those chosen to wait on the guests. She washed her one dress until most of the stains were faded, did her hair up in a pretty braid sewn with beads that Lisa gave her, splashed herself with lavender water, pinched her cheeks and bit her lips to make them red, before presenting herself in the great dining hall.

At first it was confusing to see so many strangers and hear the deafening noise of chatter, the clatter of silver dishes and the background tinkle of music. The fifty or so guests sat round a long table covered with a damask cloth with matching napkins. In the middle was a silver model of a ship, bearing the condiments, and there were silver bowls containing fruit and sweets too. Garlands of fresh flowers decorated the room, filling the air with their delicate scent, and beneath the table the dogs were lurking, waiting for scraps.

Carla followed Lisa straight to a long sideboard where they were to lay out the dishes for serving. 'You take the far end with the silver eel paste and I'll take this end with the gilded trout,' Lisa suggested. 'Then we'll go round with the finger bowls.'

When it was Bruno's turn to be served he threw Carla a dazzling smile and put his hand on her wrist. She looked right into his dark brown eyes, set beneath nobly arched brows, and felt her knees weakening. He was one of the most handsome men in the room, his black curly hair falling to his shoulders in a riot of glossy curls. He wore a scarlet silk jacket, exquisitely embroidered in gold and sewn with pearls.

'Not too much of the eel paste,' he said, with a wry smile. 'Eels have a reputation for heating the blood and mine's quite hot enough already.'

Carla blushed as she heaped a small spoonful onto his plate. Looking at her all the time, he picked up a piece of bread, dipped it in then popped it into his mouth. 'Mm, delicious!' he said. 'I wish you could taste my eel, pretty thing, but perhaps another time. What is your name?' She bobbed a curtsey as she told him. 'Well, Carla, bring me a finger bowl if you please.'

She hurried to obey him, and when she presented him with the porcelain bowl filled with rose-scented water he splashed a little onto her wrist. 'Oh, I have sprinkled you! How careless of me.'

'It doesn't matter, sir,' she said, backing away.

'Wait, let me wipe your wrist.' He took his napkin and gently dried the spot whilst he held her fingers with his other hand. Carla's cheeks were hot and her pulse was racing so fast she was sure he must be able to feel it beneath the cloth. He patted her fingers before she drew them away, and his smile was knowing as he spoke in a deep, low voice.

'Run along and attend to your duties, Carla. But be sure and bring me some tasty delicacy again soon, selected by your own sweet hand.'

When she met up with Lisa again she found her dalliance with Bruno had not gone unnoticed. 'He fancies you!' Lisa whispered, giggling. 'Better give him a wide berth if you don't want things to go too far.'

'Nonsense, he was just being kind that's all.'

'When men like Bruno are kind to women there's always an ulterior motive, believe me. You're new in this house, Carla, and you'd do well to listen to what others tell you. Some of us have been here long enough to know what goes on, and I could tell you some stories about that one!'

'Please do!' Carla grinned. 'Tonight, when our duties are over. I'd love to know more!'

Lisa gave her a reproving look, but she didn't say no. Carla went about serving the other guests with a light heart. Now she had something to look forward to, some tasty gossip. She had been missing the light-hearted banter which had always gone on in Piero's house, realising that she wasn't yet fully accepted by the other Panzani servants. Lisa was the only one who had been really friendly to her, so she would make the most of it.

Carla watched Bruno out of the corner of her eye for most of the evening. He was flirting continually with the two ladies opposite, making them laugh and blush, and she felt a confused mixture of emotions. Although it was obvious that he was not the constant kind, she did find him terribly attractive, and after being without a partner of any kind for over a week she was starting to hunger for sex. It surprised her, since she had not thought of herself as enjoying her encounters with Piero and Giovanni. Yet the rough-and-tumble had been exhilarating, even if she had ended up more frustrated than satisfied.

There were two more chances to get near to Bruno and she made the most of them both. When the bowls of fruit were passed around she selected a particularly fine apricot and handed it to him on a small silver salver. He took it with a grin and beckoned her close. She bent her ear to his lips and he whispered, 'You've chosen well. The bloom on this fruit is like the bloom on your cheeks, and it bears the same rosy blush. I shall make you blush even more, Carla, before the night is out. Will you then find me a ripe strawberry?'

She giggled, feeling the heat rise in her cheeks again which made him laugh out loud and sink his white teeth into the succulent flesh of the fruit. The juice ran down his chin and he licked all around his mouth with his pink tongue, his black eyes twinkling at her, then wiped off the rest with his napkin which he gave to her.

'Fetch me a clean one, Carla. And another finger bowl.'

She did as she was told, and watched as he dabbled

the fingers in the scented water. He was so near that she could feel the sensual heat emanating from him and smell the spicy perfume mixed with his own musk. Her senses reeling, she returned to the kitchen before she did or said something that would get her into trouble.

'Carla, you look like a bitch on heat. What have you been up to?' Lisa asked at once. 'Was it something that Bruno said to you? Go on, you can tell me!'

'He is such a flirt, Lisa! It's not so much what he says as how he looks at you. As if his eyes could burn holes in your clothes and see what's underneath.'

'It's his hands you want to watch. They'll grope and wander wherever they like if you give them half a chance.'

'Has he done anything to you?'

Lisa looked sly. 'Maybe.'

'You will tell me, won't you? Tonight, when we're in bed.'

'Maybe.'

Lisa's green eyes were dancing teasingly at her, but Carla knew she would tell her all about Bruno soon. She was the sort who never could keep a secret, but she enjoyed teasing anyone who was as full of curiosity as Carla was, especially where men were concerned.

It was disappointing to hear the footmen clearing the tables for dancing and the musicians striking up with their loud, rhythmic strains whilst she and Lisa had to do the washing up. Carla longed to catch a glimpse of Bruno dancing. She was sure he would look really elegant and sophisticated as he steered one or other of the beautiful ladies around the polished floor. It wasn't long before she was in a dream, her hands slowing as her concentration wavered, and only the sharp reproof of old Marta brought her back to earth with a thud.

The night seemed endless, the sounds of music and laughter wafting down to the kitchen while piles of dishes, cutlery and saucepans had to be washed, dried and polished. By the time the two girls were allowed to go up to their bedroom Carla was afraid Lisa would be too exhausted to talk. But as soon as they scrambled into their shared bed, dressed only in their shifts, Lisa put her arm around her and pulled her close.

'You wanted to know about Bruno,' she began. 'Let me tell you quickly, before the others come up to bed.'

'Yes, please!' Carla cuddled up to her friend's warm body with a sigh. 'I want to know *everything*!'

'I'll tell you all I know. When I first came here Bruno started behaving towards me exactly as he is now acting towards you, flirting and teasing, staring at me wherever I went.'

'And how did you respond?' Carla asked eagerly.

'Oh, I played hard to get! I'm not the sort to throw myself at any man, you know. Besides, I have a sweetheart. His name is Federico and he's a *condottiere*, fighting for the Duke of Milan. When he comes back from his campaign he's going to marry me. He promised.'

'Oh Lisa, you never said!'

'Well you never asked. Anyway, I'll tell you about Federico another time. It's Bruno who interests you most, isn't it?'

'Yes. So you resisted his advances?'

'I led him on a bit first. It was fun. Once he kissed me in the orchard and I slapped his face. You should have seen his expression! I fancy not many girls refuse him. He's far too handsome for his own good. I know for a fact that he's got at least three girls in the family way.'

'*Three*? All servant girls like us, were they?'

'By no means! One was a servant, a pretty Neapolitan girl. He tupped her one afternoon in the pantry – she told me herself, and I saw her belly swell a few months later. As soon as old Giorgio noticed she was dismissed.'

'What happened to her?'

Lisa shrugged. 'I don't know, we lost touch. Another of his lovers was the wife of a nobleman, with whom he carried on an affair for almost a year. She bore a son and passed it off as her husband's even though the poor old sod was past it.'

'How did they manage to keep the affair secret?'

'They first met at a banquet at her husband's villa. She told her husband the doctor had ordered her to take walks in the countryside three times a week, and she used to meet Bruno at an old barn. We all knew about it. Sometimes some of us would go and spy on them.'

'Did you go?'

'A couple of times. I saw her on all fours like a dog, with Bruno taking her from behind. He went on and on for ages before he came, and I think she came two or three times as well. They were horny as goats for it.'

Carla felt a ridiculous stab of jealousy. She knew it made no sense. Bruno should mean nothing to her and she didn't even know the anonymous noblewoman. But the thought of her enjoying him with such abandon made her horribly envious. She had never really enjoyed a man completely like that, and the more she heard about what pleasure some women experienced the more she wanted it for herself.

'You said there was a third,' she reminded Lisa, quietly.

'Ah yes. That was a wench from the village. He found her when he was out hunting and got detached from the other men. She showed him where he could water his horse and, while his horse was drinking, he seduced her.'

'There and then?'

'Yes, it was just the once. Nobody would have known about it if the girl hadn't come to the door with a belly you could carve meat on. Of course he denied it and the girl was sent away, poor thing. But I'm pretty sure it was him. She'd never have dared to come here if she wasn't sure of the identity of her lover.'

'How terrible! Left to fend for herself, with no help?'

'Not exactly. I have a cousin who lives near the girl and she said that a mysterious bundle of florins was left at her door a few weeks later.'

Carla sniffed. 'He has a conscience, then.'

'To a degree. But you see it's as well to give him a wide berth. Not only is he the sort who can't help

174

following his cock, but he also seems to be extremely virile. Some of the girls here believe they can get pregnant just by looking him in the eye!'

'Well he is extremely good-looking . . .'

Carla sounded more wistful than she had intended. To her surprise, Lisa propped herself up on her elbow and stared at her in earnest. 'Now look here, don't you start getting any ideas about that man, will you? I like you too much to see you come to harm.'

'I'll only flirt with him a little.'

'That's too dangerous. If you give him the least encouragement he'll take advantage. Mind you, if you can get him to make mouth music for you he'll take you to seventh heaven.'

'You mean, to sing for me?'

Lisa giggled. 'No, silly! Mouth music is what we call pussy-licking. You know, when a man kisses your privates. He's expert at that, so they say. I saw him do it to his lady-friend for ages once and she had three paroxysms, each stronger than the last.'

Carla wanted to tell her that she had never been brought to orgasm that way, but she was still shy of discussing such matters. Her longings were secret and she was half ashamed of them, believing them to be a weakness that she should hide rather than give into. Yet they were growing stronger every day, and these stories about Bruno made it even harder to resist his allure.

When she settled for sleep, with Lisa's back turned against her, Carla was still thinking of the handsome nobleman, remembering how his eyes had pierced hers with bold assurance and how gentle his fingers had been when they touched her wrist. 'I must avoid him whenever I can,' she told herself primly.

But another voice inside her said, 'What if he seeks *you* out, what then?'

Chapter Twelve

*B*runo did seek Carla out, not long after the birthday feast. She was sitting on a stone bench in the garden in the cool of the evening, resting her legs after a hard day in the kitchen, when she saw him coming towards her through the maze of low hedges. Blushing, she took up her sewing again and pretended she hadn't seen him, but he came straight up and boldly asked if he could sit beside her.

'Whatever pleases you, sir,' she replied, unable to look him in the eye. Her fingers trembled as she tried in vain to continue with her task.

'I'll tell you what pleases me,' he said in a low seductive voice as he sat down beside her, too close for comfort. 'The sight of your pretty face and figure. It's a long time since such a beauty has joined our household.'

Carla knew false flattery when she heard it. She regarded him archly. 'I am no beauty, sir, and you know it.'

He was undaunted. 'Perhaps not in the classical sense, but you certainly have charm. Besides, you know what they say about beauty. Tell me, Carla, where did you work before you came here?'

'In Florence.'

'Which household? I probably know the family.'

'I doubt it, sir. I worked for a painter and his apprentices, keeping their house in order.'

Bruno's dark brows arched in surprise but he said nothing, which disconcerted her. The silence that fell between them was broken only by the distant bustle of the kitchen and the trilling of birds. Carla continued with her sewing, aware of the devastating effect the man was having on her. Although her eyes were downcast she could see the taut strength of his thigh in the black hose, smell the evocative scent of his perfume which failed to mask completely his masculine body odours. She could feel the sexual heat emanating from him and, although she dared not look too closely, she was sure that he was aroused by sitting so close to her.

At last he said, 'You look so demure, sitting there with your sewing, but I have a feeling that a wanton heart beats beneath those delightful breasts. And I mean to discover it, soon.'

To her astonishment he rose abruptly and strode off, leaving her confused and embarrassed. He had declared his intention in so bold a manner that it left no doubt in her mind that he intended to seduce her whenever the opportunity presented itself. His arrogance amazed her. Presumably he had done it so many times that he thought nothing of it. She had never felt so helpless, even at Piero's. What disturbed her most was the irresistible attraction that such an obvious lecher had for her.

Bruno had made it plain that he knew about her previous experience, that somehow he sensed she was not a virgin. That probably meant he would make love to her without preliminaries if he caught her alone. The prospect both excited and alarmed her. It was a situation she could either submit to or manage to her advantage, and she was determined to take the latter course. 'Mouth music', that was the key. She might show him that she could give as good as she got in that department!

After that she was always on her guard. A kind of sixth sense told her when Bruno was near, and then she

177

felt herself becoming keyed up, her pulse racing and a flush rising in her cheeks. Even Lisa noticed it.

'You've got the hots for him, haven't you?' she commented, dryly. 'Well, don't say I didn't warn you!'

When they met in company he would sometimes wink at her, or find some legitimate way of making fleeting contact. Their fingers would touch if he asked her to hand him something, or if they met each other on the stairs when no one was looking he would pinch her bottom or even steal a brief kiss. His advances grew bolder with every passing day so that Carla found herself in a state of almost constant arousal. He was the first person she thought about when she awoke, and the last before she slept at night.

But beneath all the excitement of this new attraction lay an old hurt, the pain of deprivation. Carla missed her art. She sometimes took out her crayons and tried to sketch the view from her bedroom window on a piece of old sheet stretched tight or some board she had rescued from the yard, but it was not the same as the old days when she had the finest materials at her disposal.

One day Lisa came into the room while she was drawing and looked over her shoulder.

'That's really good, you know. I wish I had a talent like that.'

'Much good would it do you!' Carla replied gloomily. 'You could only amuse yourself and maybe your friends with it.'

'What's wrong with that? You know how we often sing while we work to keep our spirits up, and tell stories for the fun of it. You could do portraits of me and the others too, just for our entertainment.'

'Entertainment!' Carla scoffed. She continued, passionately, 'Why is it that men are allowed to make a living from their talents, while women are only expected to go into service or else have babies? It's so unfair!'

Lisa stared at her blankly. 'But if both men and women were allowed into the professions everything would break down! There's men's work and women's work, everyone knows that!'

'Only because the Guilds have ordained it. Take painting, for instance. There's nothing an artist has to do that a woman can't manage. I know, I've watched them at work. If you can draw and colour as well as a man, why should you be banned from earning money at it just because you're a woman?'

Lisa shrugged. 'Why can't men have babies? It's how the Good Lord arranged things.'

'It's not the same and you know it. I can see that women wouldn't be strong enough to do some jobs, but painting is not hard physically. It's just that men don't want women to invade their territory, and that's the truth.'

Lisa giggled. 'They're probably afraid we'd turn out to be better at it than they are!'

'Ah, now you're talking!'

'They're happy enough to have us wash and cook and clean and mend for them. Which reminds me, you're wanted down below.'

With a sigh, Carla put away her drawing and smoothed down her apron. She didn't mind working in the kitchen too much, but it came a poor second after her work as a painter. When she remembered how she had worked on the fresco with Piero a tear came into her eye and she brushed it away impatiently. She could not afford to be harbouring false hopes of being able to paint properly again. The best thing was to forget all about the past. Perhaps she should not even use her chalks again. Although it gave her pleasure for a few minutes, it would only make her miserable and discontented in the long run.

It proved impossible to stop drawing altogether, however. One fine autumn day the garden was looking so mellow and lovely in the late afternoon sun that during her break Carla hurried to find her chalks and some waste paper she had scrounged from the kindling pile in the kitchen. She then went downstairs to the stone seat.

She began to sketch the statue of Venus and Cupid that stood surrounded by myrtle bushes, and she soon became so absorbed in her work that she failed to hear footsteps approaching.

'Ah, the budding artist!' came Bruno's ironic tone. She tried to hide her work but he pulled her arm away and gave a low whistle. 'Whew – not so budding! Where the devil did you learn to draw like this?'

'I – I have always done a little drawing, sir.'

He took the paper off her and sat down on the bench, scrutinising it. 'I can't believe this wasn't done by a trained hand. Someone must have shown you. Come clean, little one, who was it? Your father, perhaps, or a brother?'

'No, really, I learnt by myself. I just draw what I see, for my own amusement, that's all.'

'May I keep this?'

Carla didn't really want him to, but she couldn't refuse. He folded it up and put it in his purse, then took her hand and raised it to his lips. With his eyes surveying her face closely he kissed each of her fingertips in turn. 'The hand of a genius,' he smiled afterwards. 'I wonder what else this little hand can do, my dear. Shall we find out?'

He pulled Carla to her feet and almost dragged her over to the myrtle grove. There was a hollow centre to the thicket where grass grew, and he drew her down beside him. She knew that they were completely concealed from the path, since the place was filled with shadow at that time of day, and her heart began thudding painfully in her chest as she realised he might do whatever he liked to her there.

'I told you I would find out just how experienced you were!' he said with a grin, placing her hand on his bulging hose. 'See how ready for you I am. You may bring him out into the open if you wish, and have a good look at him.'

Carla hesitated. A part of her hated the thought of more rough-and-ready sex with a man she scarcely knew. Especially when her heart still belonged to Marco. Yet another part of her found it exhilarating – and that part was winning. She glanced shyly into Bruno's darkly handsome face, saw the devilish glint in his eye and knew she could not resist. Slowly she reached into the steamy depths of his hose and felt warm rampant flesh.

'Ah! Such cool fingers!' he sighed when she took firm hold of his thick shaft.

Carla extricated his member and stroked it gently, watching it expand and flush like a creature emerging from a chrysalis. Soon his erection was strong, the purplish glans shiny and rearing up in proud defiance. Cupping his balls with her other hand Carla began to caress the glans with her thumb, feeling the sticky liquid emerge in oozing drops from its single eye. Bruno groaned voluptuously and reached down the neck of her dress for her breasts, which he caressed with frantic fingers. They fastened on her nipples and proceeded to pinch and pull them into shape, making Carla cry out as hot desire streamed through her like lava, overcoming all resistance.

'You want it too, don't you?' he said, his lips nipping at her earlobe, making her shiver.

She gulped and nodded. He put his hand up her skirt and felt the wetness of her sex, testimony to her lust. His red lips curved into a knowing smile and approached hers where his tongue played slowly along the seam of her mouth, forcing it open, then pushed in to duel with hers. His saliva tasted cool and fresh, slightly lemon-scented, and she felt her last defences against him crumble.

Bruno laid her down and held her close, his fingers where she most wanted them. While she continued to caress the hard shaft of his penis he whispered in her ear, 'I want you to tell me all about your first time. Who did it to you, where and when?'

She looked at him in surprise, but his fingers slowed on her and she knew that if she wanted the stimulation to continue she must do as he said.

'I – it was with my cousin Stefano, when I was sixteen. We were out in the countryside and he first gave me a spanking.'

'On your bare behind?' Bruno asked, his eyes gleaming hotly at her. She nodded. 'How did it feel?'

'Sort of tingly and nice.'

'Just like this?'

Bruno gave her clitoris a rapid frotting that had her gasping and moaning, then his tormenting fingers slowed again as he murmured, 'Go on.'

'Then he kissed me. I'd never been kissed by a boy before.'

'But you liked it. Did he deep-tongue you, like this?'

She felt Bruno's hot, wet tongue invade her mouth with brutal force, choking the breath out of her. At the same time he plunged into her with his forefinger, making her squirm with a confusing mixture of alarm and delight. Before she got used to the dual assault on her senses, however, he withdrew and questioned her again. 'What happened next?'

'He – he wanted to see my breasts.'

'I'm not surprised.' Bruno pulled down her sleeves abruptly and she felt the material rip at the seams. 'Don't worry,' he said carelessly,' I'll get you a new dress.'

Within the inadequate covering of her chemise Carla felt her breasts harden with desire, the nipples stiffening as soon as they were exposed to the air and to Bruno's lustful gaze. He took one in his mouth and chewed it softly, as if it were an exquisite delicacy, sending seismic waves of erotic energy pulsing through her. Caught up in the new sensations Carla let go of his penis, but he replaced her hand at once.

'Don't stop what you're doing, it's too nice. But tell me what happened after he got to your breasts. Don't spare any of the details, mind!'

'He – he touched me, where you're touching me now.'

'Ah!' His eyes were like black gleaming coals. 'Did he take your maidenhead with his finger or his prick?'

Carla was amazed at the frank way he was talking.

She'd heard the apprentices talk like that so she wasn't shocked, but she had thought noblemen spared women such verbal crudity. To her surprise, she found the rude words arousing and lost her own inhibitions. 'His finger, I think. I'm not sure.'

'But he did penetrate you?'

'Yes.'

'And it felt good?' Two fingers entered her this time. Bruno rolled them around, his knuckle against her clitoris, intensifying the friction until it became almost intolerable. 'How big was his dick? Did it feel the same as this, or thicker?'

'A bit thicker, I think.'

'He was pretty well hung, then.' For a moment Bruno withdrew his hand, leaving her gasping with frustration, but then she felt a thicker bunch of fingers enter her. 'A three-finger sized cock, was it?'

She nodded, unable to speak, her body a mass of quivering desire. To have her pussy filled again was wonderful. She hadn't realised how much she had been missing it, this feeling of completeness and warm gratification.

'How did he fuck you, fast or slow?'

Carla strained to remember but her mind was growing fuzzy, overwhelmed by the pleasurable signals from her body. 'Both, I think. He did it in a kind of rhythm, fast and slow.'

'It wasn't his first time, then.'

'I don't think so. He seemed to know exactly what to do. And he promised me he would pull out in time.'

Carla flushed as she recalled what Lisa had said about Bruno, how he'd fathered several children. Would he be annoyed at the reference?

But his grin only widened and he chuckled softly. 'Sounds like he had his feathers singed once or twice, like me. How did you feel when he put his cock in you for the very first time?'

'Wonderful, I couldn't believe anything could feel so good. There was a melting feeling deep inside me, and something was tingling down there too. I'd had some feelings like that but nothing so strong before. Then he started to move and I soon learned how to move with him so it felt even better.'

'In and out, in and out,' Bruno grinned, making his hand work like a thrusting penis. 'Come on, don't forget that my prick needs rubbing too.'

It was huge now, taut and active against her palm. Carla did her best to stimulate him while the relentless finger-fucking went on in her quim, making her almost faint with the hunger of wanting him. Although she would have loved to feel the girth of his sturdy tool inside her she knew it was better this way. Evidently Bruno had learnt his lesson – or else he had been severely reprimanded for his profligacy by his father – and did not wish to risk another illegitimacy.

'And did he make you – come, that first time?'

Bruno's voice was breathy and strained so Carla knew he was close to a climax himself. She intensified her efforts, moving the supple skin of his shaft more rapidly over the hot, throbbing flesh beneath.

'Mm . . . ' she said non-committally, unwilling to break the spell they were both under. His excitement was leading her on into a maelstrom of wonderful sensuality where her pussy felt like an overflowing fountain of bliss.

Then they heard voices. After a few seconds of conversation Carla recognised Bruno's elder brother, Tommaso, walking in the garden with two of his friends. She glanced fearfully at Bruno, who winked and put his finger to his lips. She grasped his cock tightly in alarm and was taken completely by surprise when it began to pulsate and spew in her hand.

'Fuck!' she heard him exclaim, then he continued in a low whisper, 'I was hoping to continue after they'd gone. You stay here and lie low.'

Before she realised what was happening, Bruno had got to his feet and was emerging from the myrtle grove into the path of the other young men. She heard Tom-

184

maso exclaim, 'Bruno! What were you doing, hiding in those bushes?'

'Just taking a leak,' he replied. Carla marvelled that he could play it so cool seconds after ejaculating. It was obvious that he was practised in the art of snatching his sexual satisfaction wherever he could, and getting away with it.

The sounds of the men's voices died away and she guessed they were walking towards the flat, sandy area at the end of the garden for a game of bowls. Cautiously she crept out of her hiding-place and dusted herself down. She soon discovered that the sleeve of her dress was gaping, showing the shift beneath, and she hurried back indoors hoping no one would see her before she could get to her needle and thread.

But Lisa was there, waiting for her. She took one look at her friend's dishevelled state and a sly grin crept over her face. 'He caught you, didn't he? I knew you were out in the garden, so when I saw him go I guessed he was after you. Well it's all your own fault. If you will go sneaking off by yourself . . .'

'Lisa!' Carla's tone was curt. 'It's none of your business what I do.'

'So it's *Signorina Pudica* now, is it? Don't you put on airs with me. I know you better than anyone here. You just couldn't wait to throw yourself at that rake, could you?'

Carla was angry. She flounced past and went upstairs to find her sewing things, slamming the bedroom door behind her. She lay down on her bed shaking, but soon recovered and went to the window which overlooked the garden. There in the distance were the four men playing bowls. She stared at Bruno, laughing and joking with the others, and wondered if he was telling them about his most recent conquest. A bitter pain seized her heart.

'Oh Marco!' she sighed. 'It's you I want to be making love with, not the likes of him! Yet when my blood is hot I can't help myself. Is there any hope for me?'

When she had hastily mended her sleeve Carla took out her sketching things and consoled herself by making a quick study of the men at play. While she was drawing Lisa entered. For a while Carla ignored her, but then the other girl came up with a placatory smile.

'I'm sorry, Carla, that was mean of me. Will you forgive me?'

'All right. But why did you say it – are you jealous?'

'I suppose I must be,' Lisa sighed. 'With Federico so far away I can't help lusting after other men, but I want to be faithful to him, really I do!'

'Have you – you know, with him?' Carla asked, coyly.

To her surprise, Lisa shook her head. 'No, he thinks I'm chaste. Well I am still a virgin, technically speaking. But he doesn't know about Tommaso. You can't afford to let a man know about your past if you hope to marry him.'

'*Tommaso!*' Carla stared, astonished. 'This is the first I've heard about him!'

'Oh, it was a long time ago. Soon after I came here. Tommaso flirted with me first, you see. I think that's what got his brother interested. But I wasn't having Bruno think that just because I'd dallied with his brother I'd do the same with him.'

Carla held her fingers to her temples, her eyes wide with mock disbelief. 'You are a devious one, Lisa. But now I've told you all about what I did with Bruno you just have to spill the beans about Tommaso. That's only fair.'

They settled down on the bed, side by side. 'I was a naive young girl when I came here,' Lisa began. 'When Tommaso started paying court to me I thought he wanted to be my sweetheart – you know, serious. So I encouraged him, fool that I was. He knew exactly how to woo me, too. Flattered me by saying I had the looks of a lady, that my mother must have had noble blood in her, all that rubbish. And he was always touching me, on the arm or shoulder. Sometimes he would run his fingers through my hair and sigh, like a lovesick youth.'

186

'What did he do when he got you alone?'

'You are impatient, aren't you? Well the first time he caught me I was in his bedroom. I was a maid-of-all-work in those days and if we weren't busy in the kitchen they'd set me cleaning. I was just smoothing down the sheet on his bed when he came in and locked the door behind him, just like that. I froze, I was terrified. But he came towards me with such a sweet smile on his face that I stopped being so frightened. He can be really nice at times.'

'But in his bedroom! What did you do?'

'I did nothing, I was like a scared rabbit before a fox. Anyway, he asked me to sit down on the chest by the bed and he told me there was something he wanted me to do for him. Something special.'

'Oh, yes?'

'At first it seemed innocent, hardly anything. He gave me some lengths of cord and asked me to tie him to the bedpost.'

'Tie him up? How extraordinary! Why should he want you to do that?'

'I didn't know at first, but there seemed no harm in it. I tied his wrists together, like he told me, and fastened them over the bedpost. Then he asked me to do the same with his legs, so I secured them to the post at the bottom of the bed.'

'You made him a prisoner on his own bed? Strange!'

Lisa giggled at the memory. 'It gave me a sense of power, I can tell you. When you've had people order you around all day – "Do this, do that!" – it makes a nice change to be the one in control.'

'I can imagine. But was that all he wanted you to do?'

'No. He asked me to take off my dress. I heard alarm bells then, as you can imagine, but he pointed out that if I'd tied him securely then nothing bad could happen. Still I resisted, but he said it would make him so happy that he would give me a present of a pretty pair of sleeves, so I agreed. I couldn't see any wrong in it.'

'When you took your dress off, what happened then?'

'He asked me to pull up my shift and bend over, so he could see my bare arse. I protested again, as you can imagine. It didn't seem – well, proper. And, to tell you the truth, no man had seen that part of me naked before. But I thought of those pretty sleeves – green ones, embroidered, he said – and did as he told me to.'

Carla giggled. 'You showed him your bum?'

'Yes. He asked me to pull my cheeks apart too, so he could see my "pretty pink rose" as he called it. He meant my anus. By now I was convinced that he was insane. Anyway, I kept my thighs close together so he couldn't glimpse my front bottom, and bent over just like he said. When I looked back at him over my shoulder I saw his eyes boring into me, staring so hard. I felt uncomfortable and pulled my shift down, but he told me to lie down on the chest beside the bed and pull up my shift in front.'

'He did? But weren't you close to him there?'

'Very close. But remember he was still tightly tied up so I felt safe. I lay down just inches from his cock and pulled up my shift. I had only sparse hair on my mound then, as I was quite young. He could see my pussy lips very clearly.'

'Did he get excited?'

'Yes, though he tried to hide it. I could see his hose bulging where his dick was rearing up. I lay there trembling, wondering what he would ask me to do next. He stared for quite a while at my sex and then asked me to part my legs. Now I really was ashamed, but extremely excited too. My love-button (of course, I didn't know what it was then) was pulsing wildly.'

Carla was trying to understand what was going on in Tommaso's twisted mind. 'He just wanted to look at you, then. I suppose he asked you to tie him up so he couldn't get into trouble. Still, it seems peculiar.'

'I thought so too, at the time. Now I know a lot more about what men like to do. Federico told me many things. Being a soldier, he gets to witness and hear about lots of things that other men don't.'

'Was that it, then? Was Tommaso satisfied with just being a Peeping Tom?'

Lisa shook her head. 'No, he wanted to see some action. Not his – mine! He told me to put my finger into my pussy and rub myself the way it felt good. I'd never done it before, you understand, so it seemed strange at first. And until I'd got the hang of it my poor pussy felt quite sore. But when I discovered the right angle to stimulate my love-button I found I couldn't stop. I was rubbing away, getting hotter and hotter, with his lewd eyes on me all the time. It didn't take me long to come, I can tell you.'

'You made yourself climax?'

'Yes. Like I said, it was my first time. When I told Tommaso he seemed even more pleased, as if he'd been present at my de-flowering. He didn't ask me to do anything for him though, despite the fact that he had a hard-on like a rolling pin. When I'd calmed down and put my dress back on he just asked me to release him from his bonds.'

'Is that all?'

'Yes. He kept his word, too. Next day he gave me these. But he warned me not to talk about what had happened in his bedroom, or he'd say I stole them.'

Lisa opened her chest and drew out a linen parcel which she opened to reveal an exquisite pair of emerald green velvet sleeves, embroidered with gold thread. Carla gasped. 'How beautiful! He really gave you those?'

'Yes. I've no idea whether he bought them or if they were hand-me-downs, but I didn't care. Not that I ever have occasion to wear them, of course. I'm saving them for my wedding day.' She chuckled. 'I'll never tell Federico how I came by them. If he asks, I'll say they were left to me by a rich relative!'

'But tell me more about Tommaso: did he ever trouble you again?'

'Now that's the funny part. He became quite distant with me after that. You won't tell anyone about all this though, will you? I trust you, that's why I told you, but

I'd get into terrible trouble if rumours went round about it and the news came to his ears.'

Carla squeezed her friend's hand. 'I won't tell, I promise. But you mustn't tell about me and Bruno, either. Promise?'

Lisa nodded and they hugged each other, giggling, their earlier quarrel quite forgotten.

Downstairs the household was waking up after the heat of the day and the clatter that floated up from the kitchen proclaimed that preparations for the evening meal were under way.

'I must go,' Lisa said, jumping from the bed. 'It's my turn to prepare the sauces. Coming?'

'Can't you say I've got a headache?' Carla pleaded. 'I want to mend my dress a bit more.'

'All right, but you'll have to come down eventually. We're short-handed tonight because Mario is visiting his sick mother.'

But once Lisa had left the room Carla remained on the bed, looking wistfully out of the window. The news that her friend had a lover that she was hoping to wed had filled her with a secret envy, and now her mood was melancholy once again. Not that she begrudged her, but although the one she loved was not so far away geographically as Federico was, he was light years away in practical terms. She thought of Marco and Elena: would he marry her eventually, too? The idea that he might wed another girl without ever knowing how much she cared for him was wormwood to her soul.

The sky was beautiful in its evening gown of purple, rose and gold. Carla gave a loud sigh and stretched voluptuously. Her body, still awakened after her encounter with Bruno and further roused by the spicy talk between her and Lisa, was making its need insistently felt. Idly she stroked her breast beneath her clothes, feeling the nipple swell with tingling warmth. The spot between her thighs began to vibrate too, and with a low moan she let her right hand find the hard button at the apex of her pussy.

Even through two layers of clothing she could feel the throbbing of her clitoris and impatiently she thrust her hand beneath her skirts, determined to gain satisfaction this time. Her cleft was filled with moisture, the sticky juices clinging to her forefinger as she parted her vaginal lips and found herself already melting with desire.

Only the thought of Marco could have produced such wanton lubricity. With her mind fixed on him Carla proceeded to rub herself, gently at first then with increasing pressure. She conjured up an image of his friendly, handsome face and saw his eyes looking straight into hers as she murmured 'Oh, Marco!' reverently, as if the mere repetition of his name could work some potent magic to carry it across the air to Florence and in through his window to his soul.

Now her libido was rampant as, in desperation, she applied more friction to her bulging clitoris. Soaked with love dew her fingers slid easily back and forth over the throbbing nub, dipping occasionally into the moist entrance to bring new sensations of delight. Carla removed her left hand from her breast and thrust it deep inside her quim while she continued to stimulate her clitoris. 'Ah, now!' she breathed, imagining that she was filled with Marco's penis. She could almost taste his lips on hers as she felt her body straining towards a climax.

All the lovers she had experienced were now fused into one lusty male in her fantasy, and that man was Marco. His phantom spirit was inside her, filling her completely and satisfying her beyond all expectation as she clenched in wild rhythm at her own fingers with her inner walls and told herself she was feeling his stout cock. The soft sighing of the wind outside became his loving murmurs, and the touch of the bedcover upon her overheated flesh became his caress. Entranced by the illusion, Carla felt something trigger inside her at last and knew that her first orgasm was approaching.

It crept up on her, starting with a deliciously warm tingle and accelerating into a wild rush of feeling so vivid that it made her gasp. The spasms gripped her over and over, taking her into realms of ecstasy that she could not have imagined, and letting her float there in a state of utter peace until the gentle throbbing began to fade and she was led back down again, like an airborne leaf floating down to the surface of a lake.

It had been so beautiful, so strange, that feeling of being completely possessed by something overwhelmingly personal, yet alien. Carla lay in a trance, trying to recapture the feeling, but after a while it evaded her. Then came a rush of pain, a feeling of abandonment that led her to cry out Marco's name once more, but this time in torment. It had all been a fiction. There was no Marco to take her in his arms and tell her he loved her. She had conjured a ghost and now she was alone, as she would always be alone. Marco loved Elena, not her.

Chapter Thirteen

*F*or the next few days, Carla was like a mouse stalked by a cat. She kept looking over her shoulder whenever she went into the garden or a remote part of the villa expecting Bruno to jump out at her, but he never did. Whenever she did see him he ignored her, but that only made her want him all the more.

'If I cannot have Marco, then at least I might have some fun!' she told herself, petulantly. But there was no one else in the Panzani household who made her pulse race so fast or filled her heart with hope and longing. She could not help remembering how he had waylaid her in the garden then dragged her off into the bushes, their lewd talk accompanying the most wonderful foreplay. She'd had the distinct impression that if they hadn't been prematurely interrupted he would have kissed her nether mouth and brought her to the height of bliss, heights that she had already begun to explore by herself. Surely he realised they had unfinished business!

For a whole week she suffered the ignominious frustration of 'look but don't touch' while Bruno strutted with his friends and flirted with any woman who came within his orbit – except Carla. Then on Sunday morning, when the rest of the family were at church, Carla was startled to find him suddenly appear before her as she threw out the slops.

'What have we here?' he grinned. 'Little Carla, all hot and bothered. Why not take a break and come with me? I know somewhere we can relax together. It's quite private, no one will find us.'

'I cannot. I have my duties in the kitchen,' she protested. His sudden appearance had thrown her and her indignation at being ignored had surfaced, making her manner off-hand.

'You should not allow your kitchen duties to override your duties to me,' he smiled. 'Don't worry, I'll make it all right. I shall tell Marta that I had some urgent needlework to be done and you just happened to be at hand.'

His smile was tempting, wickedly suggestive, and Carla knew that if she agreed to go with him she would be in for more dalliance. The temptation was too great. Already her heart was vaulting like a street-tumbler and she could feel her breasts swelling in anticipation of his touch. This time, with no chance of being interrupted, he would surely lead her to heaven.

He led her by the back stairs up to his bedroom and once she was inside he locked the door behind them. The situation was beginning to seem so much like the one that Lisa had got into with Tommaso that Carla began to wonder whether Bruno was of similar inclination. Or did he have some even more bizarre preference? Realising that she was now trapped with him for better or worse, she felt a wild flicker of fear run through her.

'You're probably wondering why I've been ignoring you,' Bruno began, taking her face between his hands and gazing deep into her eyes. 'If I told you the truth I doubt you'd believe it.'

'Try me,' she murmured.

'Then I shall come clean and confess. I haven't approached you because I feared my own recklessness as much as I feared the ridicule of others, but now I can

194

contain myself no longer. I admit that I've been totally smitten by you. I thought I was immune to the charms of women, that I could use and discard them at will, but your sweet face and lovely body have obsessed me from the moment we met.' His eyes brightened, shining with the light of sincerity. 'I admit it, Carla: scorn me if you will, but I have fallen head over heels in love with you!'

She drew back in shock, quite unprepared for such an admission. At the same time that she registered his words she heard another voice in her head say, *but I don't love him!*

'You look upset, my darling,' he said, disappointment obvious in his face. 'Am I to suppose that you have no such feelings for me? Is my devotion to be in vain?'

'I – I don't know what to say.'

'Then say nothing, only look on me and smile. I lay my heart at your feet, sweet Carla, *carissima*. Just tell me your heart holds no passion for me and I shall trouble you no more. Only say the word.'

'I – cannot deny that I feel *passion* for you, sir. How could I not, after what passed between us last week? But as for love, I know not.'

He seized her, his eyes staring so importunately into hers that she felt all of a flutter within. 'Passion? You feel passion for me?' She nodded, unsure what to make of this sudden turnaround. 'Then passion shall suffice!'

Bruno was staring so indecently at her that she thought him quite mad. Overriding her disquiet, however, was an overwhelming urge to throw herself into his arms and feel the heat of his body suffuse hers, to have his lips and hands explore her ravenously while she returned the compliment. Carla wanted him to take her without mercy, to force himself upon her and plunge deep into her secret heart. She knew it could only lead to disaster but right then she didn't care. It was extra-ordinary: she had never felt quite like it in her life.

'Take me, then!' she whispered, her whole body trembling with anticipation.

He lifted her and carried her over to the big bed where

he dumped her unceremoniously. Unbuckling his belt he threw it aside and pulled off his jacket, then rolled down his hose. His cock sprang up with self-confident lust, causing her insides to swoop and clench with desire, making her moan with longing.

Bruno wasted no time in undressing her. When she was fully naked, and he clad only in his shirt, he fell upon her and began to ravish her with his mouth. First his tongue plunged in between her lips like a marauding pirate, sucking the fresh saliva from her mouth and biting at her until her lips felt raw and swollen and she gasped for breath. Then he moved to her neck where he sucked the flesh strongly, sending tickles down her spine. Carla felt her stiff nipples brush against the hairs of his chest where they peeked through his shirt and longed for full, naked contact. She pulled at the fine lawn until it ripped and he chuckled with perverse glee at her desperation.

'Wait, impatient woman! I shall remove it, so!'

He pulled it summarily over his head and she fell to kissing the broad expanse of his chest with its fleshy planes, small hard nipples and exciting furriness. There was something animal about him that unleashed a similar bestiality in her. Heedless of everything except her own appetite, she licked and bit her way about his body until her mouth found the rearing prong of his erection.

'Yes, sweet temptress, oh yes, indeed!' she heard him cry, as her mouth closed over the viscid ball of his glans.

Carla thought she would swallow him whole, so great was her appetite for that fleshy organ. She took the whole of his shaft into her mouth, letting him poke her in the throat whilst she held her breath so as not to gag. Delighting in his blind, relentless quest for orgasm she felt her insides melt and quiver in sympathy as she encouraged him with licks and sucks to move nearer to his goal.

But Bruno was not content with satisfying only himself. 'Shift yourself around!' he growled. 'I want to suck you too.'

She swivelled her naked behind until her quim was near his mouth and sighed with rapture as his cool tongue pressed itself against the torrid, swollen tissues of her vulva. 'Ah!' she exclaimed, her legs spreading wide to allow him more access. She could feel his tongue darting right inside her, his lips sucking the delicate flesh of her labia right into his mouth and soon her pussy was swimming with the mingled juices of his saliva and her secretions.

Carla felt the unstoppable rise towards orgasm begin and knew that this time it would be all the more satisfying because her lover was initiating it. She continued to lick at the tumid shaft while she caressed Bruno's taut scrotum, and yet her attention was divided between the object of her lust and her own exquisite delight. Her tongue grew lazy as the cunnilingus increased her sensations until she was entirely focused on her own imminent release.

Suddenly Bruno's hand brushed across the tips of her nipples and she gave a gulping cry as her climax was finally triggered. The swirling ecstasy filled her consciousness as her body vibrated on a higher plane of sensual bliss, scarcely aware that he was thrusting hard into her mouth in a desperate bid to join her. Only when the hot stream filled her throat did she realise that he had reached his zenith too.

Afterwards she lay in his arms, limp and still throbbing, while he murmured endearments into her hair. Dazed by the intensity of the experience she hardly heard him at first, but then scraps of his speech began to penetrate her erotic stupor, filling her with amazement.

'. . . only one I ever truly loved . . . be mine forever . . . adore you . . .'

Carla couldn't believe her ears. She blinked and stared up into his dark eyes, sure he must be making fun of her, but he seemed in deadly earnest. It was then she grew afraid. No man of noble birth said such things to a serving maid! What mad devil had seized his brain? What did he want of her?

'I – I have to return downstairs,' she told him, wriggling from his arms. 'They will be missing me.'

'I miss you!' he sighed, lugubriously. 'Every minute of the day that you are absent from my sight. And when you are within view I can scarcely bear to see you. What cruel torment you cause me, my pretty one!'

'I cannot help it, sir,' she said, struggling into her clothes. 'I never asked for this. It is all of your own making.'

Bruno wagged his forefinger at her. 'But you encouraged me, you minx!'

'I'm sorry, sir. I meant no harm.'

'Harm? How can such bliss be harm? That is the paradox, is it not, that love can be so painful and yet so blissful, all at once.'

Carla thought of Marco and her heart warmed in sympathy. But she merely shrugged and made for the door. He leapt from the bed and caught her in his arms before she could escape.

'Stay, lovely girl! Let me kiss those sweet red lips one more time, I beg of you.'

She struggled, but his insistent mouth crushed hers and for a few seconds she gave herself up to the sensual contact once again. As soon as his grip slackened, however, she eluded him and hurried through the door, genuinely concerned that they might be looking for her down below. The minute she entered the kitchen Lisa gave her a sly smile as if to say, 'I know exactly what *you've* been up to!'

Something prevented Carla from confiding in her friend, however. She felt uneasy about the relationship that was developing between her and Bruno, unsure of where it would lead. It was one thing to enjoy a romp with a lusty young man, but quite another to find him emotionally entangled when his station was so far above hers. Carla was unsure exactly what the consequences might be but, knowing something of his amorous history, she was quite sure that it could not turn out well for her.

She tried to avoid Bruno as much as she could after that, but he lay in wait for her round every corner. Sometimes he snatched a kiss in a dark corner, sometimes he pushed her into an empty room and gave her a quick grope, but that was what Carla had come to expect. It was the usual treatment meted out to young female servants by lecherous noblemen, and generally it went no further than mild sexual harassment.

What disturbed her more were the gifts and notes that she found under her pillow almost every night. First it was a pretty silver necklace. Then she found a ring set with a cornelian. A perfumed handkerchief with a delicate lace border came next. His love letters swore eternal fidelity, talked of 'overcoming all obstacles'. This theme was continued with a pink silk square on which was an embroidered heart bearing the legend: *amor vincit omnia*. It was when he began writing poetry to her that she really became alarmed.

He was not even very good at it! The first verse that he addressed to her read:

> *Goddesses in human form*
> *Do not often grace our world,*
> *You descended from above*
> *And now my song is 'Love unfurled'!*

Carla did not mention these covert gifts to anyone, but it was becoming increasingly difficult to find hiding-places for them. She never felt under her pillow until she was alone in the bedroom, but she was constantly afraid of discovery. Then, one day, Bruno encountered her in the garden and dragged her off to a quiet corner, his expression radiant.

'I have told my father of my love for you!' he proclaimed, exultantly.

'Oh no!'

Carla clasped her hand to her mouth, but he gently pulled it away and kissed her fingers.

'Don't fret, dearest. I am sure he will allow us to marry. Of course he is upset now, but that will change when he realises how sincerely I adore you.'

She wriggled free of his grasp and ran headlong, back through the ordered serenity of the garden with her heart hammering in her ears. Knowing that Bruno's infatuation could lead to nothing but trouble for her, she still couldn't quite dismiss the spark of hope that his words had caused in her. What if she were to marry and be accepted into the Panzani family? She would become a lady! For a few brief seconds her heart soared with pride.

But no sooner had the thought taken hold than it was scornfully dismissed. More likely old Giorgio would blame her for seducing his son and stealing his affection. She might be allowed to become his mistress, but no more. And what of her love for Marco? It upset her that, for several days, she had given him no thought at all being so bound up with Bruno's courtship of her. What a fickle temperament she must have!

For several days Carla tried to avoid Bruno, but at last he caught up with her on the stairs.

'Come to my room!' he begged in a low voice. 'I must speak to you.'

'I cannot . . .' she began.

But he caught hold of her wrist and began to drag her up to his bedroom on the next floor. Carla was terrified. If she resisted him there might be a scene and then everyone would know what was going on. She agreed to come quietly, but insisted that his door remained unlocked. Sitting primly on the edge of a stool she listened while he paced up and down, gesticulating, as he spoke his mind.

'My father is not keen on the idea of me marrying you,' he began. 'So here is what I intend. There is a full moon in three days' time. I shall meet you in the garden at midnight and we shall make our escape. I have some money, and I shall take jewels that we can sell. When we are far from here we can find a priest to marry us, then I hope father will accept you as one of the family. If he does not, I shall stick by you all the same.' To Carla's dismay he flung himself onto his knees in front of her. 'I love you, sweet girl, and am determined that nothing and no one shall come between us.'

She took pity on him then, stroking his dark hair back from his brow as she said, 'Bruno, listen to me. What you feel is not true love but only calf love. You will grow out of it if I go away and let you recover, as if you'd had a sickness. I think that would be best for both of us.'

'No!' he cried, distraught. 'You must not leave without me! We'll go together – right now, if you wish. I cannot live without you, Carla. You must understand that.'

He began kissing her pussy rapturously, through her skirt. She felt his head pressed to her mound of Venus and there were tremulous stirrings within, but she resisted them and stepped back from him. 'Bruno, I'm going now,' she said, firmly. 'And I advise you to put me out of your mind. Goodbye.'

'No-o-o!'

His agonised cry echoed in her ears as she hurried downstairs, full of disquiet. The situation was getting out of control and there was only one way she could think to put an end to it. She must leave the Panzani house, leave poor Bruno to his melancholy love and let him slowly forget her. But just as she entered the kitchen Lisa rushed up to her.

'Have you heard?' she said, excitedly. 'A betrothal has just been announced and there's to be a big feast.'

'Who? Tommaso?'

'No, Bruno! The master's hired a marriage broker, and he's to wed Lady Isabella Salviati.'

'*What*? Does Bruno know of this?'

Lisa looked at her quizzically. 'That's a funny question! Why should he not know?'

'Nothing.'

'Nonsense, you're hiding something. What is it, Carla? What are you not telling me?'

'It's just that I saw him only five minutes ago and he said nothing about it.'

'Hm. Perhaps he meant to keep you dangling on a string, Carla, to have his cake and eat it. Men are like that, you know.'

Carla thought of the desperate way he had tried to get her to agree to an elopement and realised that he probably had known about his father's plan to get him married off. Old Giorgio must have been desperate to put a stop to the romance if he was prepared to see his younger son wed before the elder one. But now her position seemed all the more insecure.

'Why are you frowning so?' Lisa asked, scenting secrets. 'You're not sweet on the man, are you? If so, you're more of a fool than I thought you.'

'Thanks!'

Carla went over to the bench and began helping to shell peas. She was still in a state of shock and needed time to absorb the news and make plans. Perhaps she would be safe if Bruno were betrothed. At least she could more legitimately object if he approached her. But the situation was confused, and she thought again about simply leaving while the going was good. Upstairs she had quite a cache of jewels and money that would tide her over for a while until she could find a new position.

But she was forestalled. That very night she was summoned to the downstairs study and there stood the formidable figure of Tommaso. He was standing in front of the large desk with his stout legs astride and his hands behind his back, looking the very model of masculine power and authority. She shrank from him the minute she entered the room, guessing from his stern expression that he was standing in for his father who, so rumour had it, disliked dealing with the servants directly.

'Carla, I will come straight to the point,' he began. 'You have formed an unnatural alliance with my brother

202

Bruno, and my father wishes to have you dismissed from this household.'

Carla's blood boiled at the injustice of it. She knew it was unwise to protest but she couldn't help herself. 'It was not my fault! He approached me, seduced me, then said he had fallen in love with me. What could I do?'

Tommaso's tone dropped to the level of dark insinuation. 'I know you girls. I know what you are capable of. You are a wicked hussy who bewitches men's souls and holds them in thrall. You would have done the same to me, had I not had the strength of will to resist you.'

'It isn't true! A girl in my position has little option when a man like you approaches her. Not if she wants to keep her job and her reputation. Bruno has taken callous advantage of me, and now you will cast me out. Shame on you both!'

Tommaso came up very close and placed his hand beneath her chin. He stared down insolently into her eyes. 'Hush, woman! I know your sort. You are lascivious and wilful, you will do anything to get a man into your power. My brother is sorely smitten, and I admit that I am not immune to your charms either. It's best you leave this house before you lead us both into perdition.'

'What nonsense you do talk! It's yourselves you are leading into perdition. I have very little to do with it!'

His eyes flared with outrage. 'How dare you address me so! Do you realise I could have you denounced as a wily witch?'

'You would have a hard time proving it!'

'Would I, indeed?'

He took a hank of her dyed hair and yanked her head back so that she couldn't help but look him in the eye. She flinched, but remained outwardly cool. He was bluffing, but there was no telling what he might do next. She must appear as composed as possible.

'I'd say you bound me with magic cords, more secure than the strongest chains. I'd tell the court that you tormented me with lewd visions of yourself, that you appeared naked before me and taunted me with your sex. Would that be so far from the truth, little one? I think not.'

Carla was trembling now, afraid of the manic glint in his eye. She knew he might twist the truth convincingly, that his testimony might well stand up in court, and she was terrified. Two witches had been publicly hanged in the town hall square just a month ago, and Carla had heard gory tales of how they danced in the air as the rope tightened around their windpipe, and how their blood-curdling screams were cut off and a terrible silence ensued.

'I am no witch, as well you know,' she said quietly, sounding far more calm than she felt.

'Perhaps not, but you have thrown our family into turmoil and I cannot forgive you for that. As the firstborn I should have been married off before Bruno, but our father is afraid that my brother will go raving mad if he is not stabilised by marriage. And it's all your doing! He dotes on you, I can't think why. It would not be difficult to convince people that you dosed him with a love-philtre when you waited at table.'

Carla felt the blood drain from her cheeks. So he was serious about branding her as a witch! This time she was unable to hide her consternation and Tommaso laughed to see her looking so scared.

'That's got you really worried, hasn't it? But if you do exactly what I say you'll come to no harm, I can promise you. Just agree to follow my instructions to the letter and you have my word that no one will denounce you as a witch.'

'Your – instructions?' she said, faintly.

'Yes. You must do me one last service before you leave our employ. Kneel down!'

Her knees were trembling as she sank down on them, wondering what on earth she would be obliged to do now. She thought of telling him that she knew what he had made Lisa do to him, but decided only to use that information as a last resort. Terror was growing in her as she realised that her word counted for nothing against that of a nobleman.

Tommaso opened a drawer in the desk and took out a brocade sash which he proceeded to tie around her head as a blindfold.

'What is this?' she whispered, fearful once again.

'You'll see. I won't ask you to do anything that you haven't done a hundred times before, I'm sure.'

There was an ominous pause. Carla heard the rustling of clothes and smelled the faint scent of male musk. She realised what service she was to perform just seconds before the confirmation came, in the form of a thick, rearing cock that was placed between her lips.

'Now suck!' she was unceremoniously commanded.

Although the circumstances were distasteful to her, Carla was relieved that she was being asked to do nothing more arduous than perform fellatio. She set to work with a will, licking at the stubby member with as much enthusiasm as she could muster. It was a relief to find that, even when thrust hard into her mouth, the short cock barely reached her throat although it filled her mouth with its girth.

Soon she developed a technique of alternately licking his shaft and sucking his glans that seemed to please him, judging by his satisfied groans. Absorbed in her work, she scarcely heard the door of the room open behind her until it was too late and rough hands had seized her skirt. She gave a startled cry as her clothes were pulled up to reveal her naked buttocks and her thighs were summarily pulled apart, almost making her collapse.

'Careful, clumsy oaf!' she heard Tommaso say, as she narrowly missed biting on his prick. Unsure whether the crude reprimand was directed at her or the newcomer, she flinched. 'Carry on, Carla!' he commanded her. 'Don't let anything put you off now.'

Obediently she continued to suck at his turgid penis despite the fact that her buttocks were being parted and another cock positioned between them. She was sure the intruder must be Bruno, yet she dared not utter a syllable but could only submit to him. Her mind was in a whirl, trying to understand what was happening. Was the man who, until recently, was swearing undying devotion actually about to take his revenge on her in this bestial manner? Recalling his tender attempts at poetry it seemed incredible, yet she was now convinced that he was the owner of the cock that was attempting to bore its way into her anus while she sucked on his brother's member. Sandwiched between the pair of them Carla felt her flesh mingle with hot, sweaty, maleness.

Carla moaned with pain as the glans entered her arse but the initial discomfort of penetration lessened after a while and she felt the old yearnings return, although she was still bewildered by being at the mercy of the two brothers. Bruno had his hands on her breasts, less for her benefit than for something to hang onto, and he was banging into her as hard as he could, overcoming her resistance and making her gasp as she tongued the length of Tommaso's cock.

Although there was a certain abandoned excitement coursing through her veins, the situation seemed unreal, too weird for her mind to encompass. Giving herself up to the voluptuous gratification of the arse-fuck and the vicarious pleasure of the fellatio, Carla sought refuge from the disturbing thoughts that filled her mind. Instead she focused on the image she had once helped to make in that dark, peaceful chapel, the glowing fresco whose colours she had mixed and applied, working alongside her master. That was another world, a peaceful heaven where she could lose her worldly self and become better acquainted with her soul through contemplation.

Try as she might to enter that rarefied world of the imagination, Carla was brought abruptly back to earth by a hot spewing of liquid into her mouth. She gagged, and then gasped as the pace accelerated from behind and her sphincter fought against the battering she was getting from Bruno's penis. It didn't take him long to come too, and then the human sandwich fell apart and she collapsed face forward onto the rush-strewn floor.

The scent of newly-laid herbs was soothing to her spirit, although her body ached from the punishing double abuse it had suffered. Dimly she heard the two brothers leave the room and, minutes later, one of them returned and dumped something in front of where she lay, utterly exhausted. After a while she opened her eyes and saw the linen bundle which contained all her possessions. The message was clear: take your things and get out at once!

Wearily she rose to her knees and was astonished to see a shiny silver florin on the floor. It was obviously meant for her. She slipped it into her purse and staggered to her feet, picking up her bundle. What a fright she must look! Dragging her horn comb through her hair she attempted to smooth down her clothes, wishing there were some water to hand so she could splash her face at least. She spat on her hands and wiped her grubby cheeks, drying them off with her skirt, then made for the door. The stench from her loins was embarrassing, but perhaps it would dissipate in the cool evening air. With a deep sigh she walked towards the side entrance of the villa which led towards the garden gate and freedom.

She would make for the farm where the woman had been kind to her. With luck she might let her sleep in a barn, and even offer her some bread and milk. It was a while since supper and Carla knew she would be hungry after a long walk in the dark. She was frightened too: were there wolves in these parts? Not many men would risk venturing out at night into open country, let alone a girl. She wished she had kept her old disguise, but it was no use wishing, she must make the best of it.

A hooting owl serenaded her as she began her journey, trying to remember how long it had taken her to walk from the farm to the villa when she had arrived. How long ago it seemed, yet it was only a few months. The thought of returning to Florence both attracted and repelled her, yet she could think of nowhere else to go.

At least she was street-wise now, and knew how to manage things better. She would feel safer on her own for a while. She could go back to painting portraits for a living. Her heart lifted with joy at the thought of plying her former trade once more. How she had missed it!

She had missed Marco too. Her mood saddened when she thought of him, and she was filled with an almost unbearable yearning. Gazing up at the almost full moon she whispered a silent prayer: 'If I should see him again, please let Marco love me this time!'

Chapter Fourteen

*F*lorence. The city seemed to beckon Carla like a fond parent as she stood on the hill gazing down on its gilded splendour. She had spent the night at the farm and the woman had given her a bowl of milk with sops for breakfast. She now she felt strong enough to face whatever the day threw at her.

As she walked along the dusty road her dream of being an artist resurrected itself. She would return to the *loggia* where Claudio plied his trade. He would surely remember the 'boy' who had shown such talent when he drew his portrait. Cheered by the prospect of a friendly face she quickened her pace as she reached the outskirts of the city.

Around noon Carla found herself passing the street where Marco's workshop was. She hesitated, but then remembered that she was still dressed as a girl. Would he recognise her like that? It was tempting to try him, but she feared the consequences. He might be angry that she had duped him, or embarrassed because he was still with Elena, and she could not bear the humiliation. Better to nurture his memory as a beautiful dream than risk shattering the illusion and have no-one to dream about.

When she reached the grand square of the *Signoria*

209

Carla found the place being prepared for a spectacle of some sort. The area where the artists used to congregate had been cleared, so the nobility could have the best vantage point, and she felt at a loss to know what to do or where to go next. Finding some loose change in her purse she bought a pie and some wine near the market and sat down at her old pitch. As she ate the comforting food it seemed to her that she had never been away. As soon as she had refreshed herself she brought out her chalks and began to sketch a Virgin and Child on the stone flags in front of her.

Absorbed in her work, she scarcely noticed when a small crowd gathered around her. The hubbub grew louder, with many more stopping to point and stare or make remarks, and it wasn't long before the gathering attracted the attention of an officer of the law.

'Hey, you!' he called gruffly. 'What d'you think you're doing, defacing the pavement?'

Some of the onlookers tried to defend her. 'She's good – can't you see that? She's as good as a real artist. Let her be!'

But the officer only sneered. 'She should get back indoors where she belongs, or she'll have the Guild on her back. Move along now, all of you. You're causing an obstruction!'

Hastily Carla gathered up her chalks and thrust them back into her sack. She had no wish to attract the attention of the law so soon after her return to the city. Evidently they had tightened up on vagrants since she was last there, or was it because of the festivities that day?

Either way, she was at a loss to know what to do once the man had let her off with a caution. He made it quite clear that if he caught her again she would be thrown in prison and it was not worth the risk. She felt tempted to return to Piero's house and beg for his help, but her pride would not let her. Then she remembered her intention to visit the church of *Santa Maria Immacolata* and view the fresco she had worked on. Her step lightened at the prospect.

The church was full of people since it was a public holiday – the feast of Cosmas and Damian, patron saints of doctors. Carla remembered that the great artist Fra Angelico had painted the saints at his monastery at the request of Cosimo de' Medici. The artist-monk had been reported, ironically, by Piero as saying that anyone practising the art of painting needed a quiet and untroubled life.

In the Verazzi chapel, where the scenes from the Virgin's life were depicted, the atmosphere was one of quiet reverence. Carla fell to her knees, mindful that she had neglected her spiritual life of late, and prayed that the peace she had experienced while working on the fresco would visit her again. She prayed for inspiration and guidance, feeling like a soul adrift, then spent a long time gazing at the work she had done, remembering this detail and that. How perfectly at one with her Creator she had felt back then, creating that work of art herself! Before long the tears began to roll helplessly down her cheeks.

A passing priest noticed her distress and asked, 'Do you wish to confess, my child?'

She shook her head and hurried from the church in embarrassment. The time had long since passed when she would look to any priest for help. If she was to survive on the streets she must count on her own resourcefulness and the help of God – or maybe 'Lady Luck' would be more appropriate.

The festivities were beginning when she left the church and she went with the flow towards the square where a jousting contest was about to take place. Most of the shops were closed so she could not buy any new clothes, but she intended to revert to her disguise as soon as she could. There was a stall in the market that sold second-hand clothes and she would make her way there as soon as the spectacle was over. She would feel safer on the streets once she was dressed as a boy again.

Once the parade began, with the pages in brightly-coloured uniforms twirling their banners and tossing them high into the air, Carla soon lost herself in the pageantry, relishing the sight of so many handsome young men, some of whom reminded her of Marco. As a preliminary to the action there was bear-baiting, but Carla preferred to see the knights on horseback tilting at the quintain or engaging in single combat. It was very exciting to be in the midst of a crowd who were all cheering on their favourites and booing their adversaries, laughing and joking as they outdid each other in oaths, both of encouragement and disparagement.

When the show was over Carla had a terrible thirst and made her way to the market where she intended to buy herself a drink and then some clothes. She found a stall selling grape juice and went for her purse but, to her horror, it was no longer on her belt. With a sinking heart she realised she had been robbed.

The stall-holder witnessed her distress and shrugged. 'You should have taken more care of your money, today of all days. There's cut purses a-plenty about whenever the crowds roll in for a tourney. You should know that by now.'

'It had all my money in, and jewels too!' she moaned. 'What on earth am I to do now?'

'Tell you what, I'll give you a drink anyway.' The man handed her a full beaker and she gulped it down gratefully. She wandered off in a daze afterwards, realising that she could buy nothing now. Everything she had in the world was in her linen bundle: just a few changes of clothes, a mirror, her brushes and chalks and one or two cheap trinkets including the golden tassel she had won from Stefano, so long ago.

At the thought of her cousin Carla wondered if she should return home to her Tuscan village, to throw herself on the mercy of her family once again, but she dismissed the idea scornfully. When she left she had intended to make a career for herself, one way or another, and to return there destitute would be a sign of failure. Once again her pride would not let her risk rejection, so she set off to find a quiet place where she might sit and think about what to do.

When she came across a public garden, she went to enter, intending to rest there in the shade, but she was stopped by a notice on the gate which read: 'Entry to this garden forbidden to geese, women and goats.' She felt like spitting. How dare they lump women in together with mindless beasts! After wandering on she eventually reached a point on the banks of the Arno where there were some trees and she sank down thankfully below their spreading branches.

It was not long before she was asleep and immersed in a strange dream. There was a man making love to her from behind, but she had only a vague idea of his identity. Sometimes he caressed her breasts tenderly and came slowly into her, and then he seemed like Marco. Sometimes he was crude and grasping, which made him more like Giovanni. But then he would nuzzle her neck and spout poetry at her, which made her think of Bruno. When he thrust into her hard, with many grunts and groans, she was sure he must be Piero, and so it went on until she was totally confused as to the identity of her lover.

Carla was soon in such a state of erotic bewilderment that she began to lose sight of her own identity: was she Carlo or Carla? It did not help that she was being buggered by her anonymous lover. The events of the past few months were mashed together into a voluptuous sequence in which she was taken on a pleasure trip of extraordinary intensity. Mixed in with all the physical stimulation was a feeling of euphoria that she couldn't quite identify. Only when Carla found herself contemplating a ceiling painted with the Assumption of the Virgin did she realise that it was the artist in her that was exulting in it all, confusing the physical and sensual with the spiritual.

Up, up went the virgin into the sky and Carla went with her until her dream was shattered by the dazzling

213

brightness of a heavenly sun and a rush of heat that warmed both body and soul. She awoke with a start to find the sun pouring down on her through the branches above, and her body shimmering in the afterglow of her ecstatic vision.

'If I were of a religious frame of mind I would say I have just seen God,' Carla said to herself as she rubbed her aching limbs. It had certainly been a very strange dream, but it had not helped her decide what to do next. With no money and nowhere to stay the night, she seemed to have no option but to ask for alms.

So Carla became a beggar. Just for one night, she thought at first, but when she had enough money to fill her belly and provide her with enough wine to numb her brain it seemed an easy course. Forgetting her hopes of becoming an artist she thought only about where her next meal was coming from, and her horizon shrank to fit her hand-to-mouth existence. There was a hopelessness about her position but she did not despair, only gave in to a kind of dazed resignation.

Soon she was a familiar figure on the street scene, just as the others were familiar to her. There was Blind Bobo, a weird scarecrow of a man who rang a bell aggressively to clear his path and muttered imprecations continually. Then there was Rosetta, an old prostitute who had contracted a venereal disease and was covered with sores. Carla felt sorry for her and often shared whatever scraps she had obtained with the wretched woman.

The man they nicknamed 'saint', *San Michaele,* was anything but. He often made passes at Carla and tried to chase her when he was drunk. Once he caught up with her and brought her to the ground in a flying tackle, when he proceeded to grope beneath her clothes, but another vagrant saved her and after that he didn't bother her again.

It was not the other beggars that she feared most, however. Seeing her ragged clothes and dirty face she was often propositioned by men who could not afford to pay a whore. Thinking she was in desperate straits they offered such insulting trifles in exchange as a crust of mouldy bread, a rotten apple, a piece of rope or an old sack. Carla always refused angrily, but she avoided the dark alleyways at night and always slept near others for safety.

One morning, however, she awoke shivering even though it was a mild autumn day. Pulling the shreds of her clothing around her for warmth she tried to get up but staggered and fell back into the doorway where she had been sleeping. Her head swam and ached as if she had been drinking strong wine, although she had only drunk moderately the night before. Worried by her weak condition, Carla lay there helplessly hoping someone she knew would come along.

After a while she heard familiar voices. Rosetta and a young crippled vagabond called Guido were discussing her plight. Yet although Carla could hear them her eyes were dim and she could only make out their faint outline against the brightness of the mid-morning sun.

'She has some fever,' Rosetta said. 'Swamp fever, maybe.'

'Only if she's been down by the river. It could be an ague.'

'See how she sweats and squints. Fetch some water from the well in the square, Guido. I shall bathe her brow.'

The cooling water helped a little, but did nothing to ease the fever in her blood. Carla tried to murmur her thanks to Rosetta but all that came out was an incomprehensible gurgle.

'She needs a doctor,' Guido said, matter-of-factly. 'Without one she will surely die.'

'Perhaps the brotherhood will help her.'

'Only if they find her.'

'Maybe we could tell them?'

'Tell them yourself. I'll have nothing to do with anyone. You never know who you can trust in this city.'

'All right, I will tell them. We can't just leave her here to perish.'

'Death comes to us all in the end.'

'But she's still young . . .'

The pointless argument wound on and on, making Carla want to cry out in exasperation, but all that issued from her mouth was a faint moan. She felt terribly weak, and all their talk of death and doctors was making her feel worse. After a while the pair moved on, leaving Carla to her thirsty delirium, which only grew more severe as the sun rose in the sky. She began to fantasise about being baked in an oven, like bread, and her skin felt as if it were puffing up like dough. Her mind rambled on through all kinds of fantastic scenes as if she were exploring the dark castle of her imagination, dungeons and all. By noon she had spoken with dragons, danced with angels, and flown over the rooftops of Florence to land on top of the great *campanile* of the cathedral from where she vomited fire upon the people below.

The day crept on and the fever got worse. One or two passers-by stopped to bring her a drink of water from the well, but mostly she was ignored. For most of the day the sun beat mercilessly upon her but by late afternoon it moved round and she was cast into shadow again. By then, however, Carla was past caring. Whatever sickness had taken hold of her was raging in full spate. If the angel of death had appeared in the doorway and invited her to follow him she would have found the strength to rise, but otherwise she had no hope of moving on.

Then, at dusk, a black robed figure appeared and gave her cool water to drink. Carla could barely lift her head, but the stranger supported her and waited patiently while she attempted to swallow. 'I will take you to San Marco nearby,' she heard him say through her delirium. 'The monks shall take care of you until you are well enough to be moved.'

Carla stared up at him but he was wearing the concealing hood of the Brotherhood of Mercy, a band of selfless citizens who helped the sick and needy on the streets of Florence. He lifted her bodily and carried her a few hundred yards to the monastery door. For a while she blacked out, but when she came to she was lying on a narrow bed in a cell with the same, dark-robed figure keeping watch on a stool at her bedside. As soon as she opened her eyes he bathed her forehead with a damp cloth and offered her more water.

Slowly her vision cleared and her thoughts, which had been vague and scattered, began to marshal themselves. Carla propped herself on her elbow to drink cup after cup of the refreshing water and replenish her dehydrated body. Feeling more human again, she looked into the face of her saviour to utter a weak 'Thank you!' and her mouth dropped open in amazement.

It was Marco! The enveloping black hood had been pushed back to reveal his face, but he clearly hadn't recognised her. Carla reasoned that the wracking fever must have altered her appearance drastically. Besides, he had never seen her as a woman, nor with yellow hair. She hesitated, longing to tell him who she was but prevented by the splitting headache which had come upon her suddenly. Feeling too weak to cope with such an emotional reunion, she sank back onto the bed and vowed she would wait until happier circumstances to tell him that he had saved his old friend, 'Carlo,' from certain death.

For two days Carla drifted in and out of consciousness while the fever slowly abated in her. She didn't see Marco again; it was the monks who monitored her progress, fed and watered her at regular intervals and helped her to and from the privy. Morning and night they got her to pray with them, kneeling before the beautiful fresco that graced the wall of the cell. It showed the Annunciation in simple beauty, a pale-robed Mary kneeling before a standing angel in a darker robe of terra cotta. A vaulted ceiling linked the pair with a series of arches, and the harmonious composition was elevating to the spirit. Carla spent long hours in contemplation of Fra Angelico's simple piety and consummate skill, thinking that if she could achieve something only half as good she would die content.

But she wasn't going to die. On the third day, when the turning-point had passed and she was on the road to recovery, one of the monks came to see her early in the morning.

'You must leave us now,' he announced. 'This cell is normally occupied by one of our number who gave it up out of pity for your plight. But you will not be let out onto the streets. The brother who saved you has sent a litter. You are to be taken to his house where he will take care of you until you are completely well. Give thanks to God, sister, who has provided a Good Samaritan in your hour of need.'

As she knelt with him to give thanks, Carla felt joy surge through her bosom at the thought of staying with Marco. Surely he would recognise her and they would be friends again, perhaps even lovers. Despite her illness she felt an unmistakable twinge of desire, a sure sign that her soul was healing as well as her body.

A pair of boys carried Carla on the litter through the early morning streets until they stopped outside the building in the *Via Calimala* that was Marco's home and workshop. It was a modest establishment, its narrow window shuttered on the ground floor, but upstairs there was a larger window with a balcony that would let in the light and she guessed that was where he would have his studio. She couldn't wait to see the work he had been doing since he set up on his own.

Marco came to the door himself when a boy rang the bell. 'Ah, my poor little patient!' he smiled in that old, tender way that Carla remembered so well.

Surely he will recognise me now, she thought, but he showed no sign of it merely waving to the boys to carry the litter in through the door. He helped her up off her portable bed and she sat on a chair while he paid the boys, looking about her. The downstairs room doubled as a kitchen and storeroom but Marco had set up a trestle bed in one corner, near the stove. A black cat was sleeping contentedly on it.

'You were too ill to tell me your name before,' he said, once they were alone.

'It's Carla.'

She waited for the penny to drop, but still he seemed not to know her. Now is the time to tell him, she thought, but she could not summon up the will.

'Well, Carla, as you see I've made up a bed for you down here. I thought you wouldn't be able to manage the stairs. When you're well enough you can come up if you like, though. I could do with some company. I'm a painter, recently set up here, but I've only one apprentice.'

'This is very kind of you,' Carla began, but he held up his hand to stop her.

''We'll hear no more of that. I only did what any right-minded citizen would have done. Besides, I'm not without self-interest. You might be useful to me once you're fighting fit, as I could do with a housekeeper. Sometimes it's hard to stop painting just to prepare food. I confess that more than once I've fainted from hunger at my easel, I was so absorbed in my work that I forgot to eat!'

Carla knew exactly what he meant. She too had entered that timeless world where nothing mattered but light and shade and colour, but she could say nothing. Something else was preoccupying her. Nervously she asked, 'Is there no one else in your household, sir?'

He shook his head. 'None. My name is Marco, by the way, and my apprentice is called Silvio. He's out at the moment but you'll meet him later.'

That should have been me, Carla thought bitterly. But at least there had been no mention of Elena living there.

Marco pointed towards a black pot on the stove that was emitting a homely vegetable smell. 'I have some broth warming for you. If you don't mind I'll join you, I'm starving!'

He drew up a small table and they sat companionably dipping bread into the bowls of steaming, hearty soup. With every mouthful Carla felt her strength returning, and by the end of the simple meal she was laughing and joking with him, just like old times. Several times she saw him frown, or stare at her intently, but she couldn't find the courage to tell him her true identity. Something made her want to start from scratch, to win his love as a woman if she could and not to rely on the friendship forged between them when she was disguised as a boy.

Marco left her after a while to go back to his work, but gave her a little bell to ring if she needed anything. Carla lay on the bed dozing. She was still very weak, and the bumpy journey from the monastery had tired her, but she was very content to be under the same roof as Marco again, this time without the threat of interference from anyone else. When the young apprentice returned with the pigment and paper he had bought he gave Carla such a charming grin of welcome that she felt quite at ease with him.

After that, every day brought advances in her health and strength. She was able to go upstairs and see the work Marco was doing: an exquisite portrait of a noblewoman commissioned by her husband; a small *maesta*, a picture of the Virgin in a little tabernacle, for the head of some grand bed; a cartoon for a fresco showing the Adoration of the Magi that Marco would be painting in a family chapel. It was evident, even from these few pieces, that Marco had found his own style and was no longer following orders from a master. The works had a freshness and originality that was all their own.

'They are very beautiful!' she sighed, wishing she might work on some of them with him, especially the fresco. Her fingers itched to pick up a brush and adorn those crowns and rich robes with gold, or to paint in the tiny tassels on the horses' bridles with infinite pains or bring life to those faces with a slanting brow or a tilted nose.

Marco gave her a searching look, alerted by her wistful

tone, and once again she was sure he would recognise her. 'You know, you remind me of someone I once knew,' he said, thoughtfully. 'You don't have a brother by any chance, do you?'

'Yes,' she answered truthfully. 'I have two. One called Bertoldo and the other Taddeo.'

Marco shook his head, grinning wryly. 'The lad I knew was named Carlo. But no parents would call their son Carlo and their daughter Carla. That would be asking for trouble!'

She laughed with him, but her throat was tight and her heart felt like a lump of undigested food in her chest. Oh, why could she not bring herself to tell him the truth? It wasn't for lack of opportunity. But the longer time went on the more difficult it was because she was so afraid he would chide her for deceiving him. She had dug a grave for all her hopes of becoming his lover. He saw her as a deserving pauper and he pitied her, that was all.

Once Carla was back on her feet again she began to do little tasks around the house. She went with Silvio to the market and came back with baskets of fresh produce, which she delighted in cooking. Marco said he was glad to be getting regular meals again. She washed his clothes and bedclothes at the place where all the washerwomen gathered, on the banks of the Arno, and mended any tears she found.

But when she asked if she could help to mix his pigments, or prime wood with gesso or clean his brushes, Marco emphatically refused. 'That's not women's work,' he told her. 'Stick to what you're good at Carla: cooking and housework.'

Then she grew bitter and wished that she had made it a priority to purchase men's clothes when she returned to Florence. He might have taken her on as his apprentice, as he had promised. As long as Elena was no longer with him all would have been well. Yet if she had done that how could they have become lovers? It was all so confusing.

So Carla resolved to play the housewife and become no more than a quiet observer of the artistic endeavour that went on in the house. She told herself she could still learn by watching and, when she was left alone downstairs, she would often take out her chalks and make some sketches. Sometimes, when she knew Marco was out of the house, she would creep up to his workroom and steal a few colours screwed in paper, rescue a couple of worn brushes from the bin or pick up some torn and grubby paper from the floor. Soon she had a secret collection of materials that she knew he would never miss, and her private hours were filled happily again as she made many sketches and coloured them in, some of them portraits of Marco himself.

'You seem very contented here, Carla,' he said one day. 'I'm glad. It is good to have a woman about the place.'

The very fact that he had spoken of her as a woman gave Carla deep and unexpected joy. She began to dream of him as a lover again, and her hungry eyes fed on him whenever they could. She particularly liked observing him when he was at work, gazing at his easel in rapt attention or sketching out a cartoon that was laid on the floor. Then her longing almost overcame her since she could take in every detail of his handsome face, or gaze uninhibitedly on his round buttocks in their tight hose.

The trouble was, he regarded her as a different person from the 'Carlo' he had once known. Although she longed to share his work as well as his bed, that was impossible and the old intimacy was hard to resurrect now that she was no more than a servant in his house. Carla realised she was in a cleft stick and she could see no way out of it. She was unwilling to risk losing what little she had of him by telling the truth and making him angry.

One night, when Silvio was asleep in the attic, Marco went out to the tavern and returned while Carla was washing herself. Stripped to the waist, she was startled to see him enter with a staggering gait. When he realised that he had caught her half naked his eyes widened and he gave her a look such as he had never directed at her before. She pulled the cloth over her bosom instinctively, but her heart was thudding with excitement as he approached her unsteadily.

'Carla!' he said, his tongue thick in his mouth. 'Lovely Carla! Do you care for me at all?'

'Of course I do,' she replied, without hesitation. 'You saved my life.'

'Your sweet life!' he murmured, taking her into his arms. The cloth dropped from her chest and his mouth bent to kiss each of her hardening nipples in turn. A shudder of intense desire passed through her and she longed to press his head to her bosom, to feel the quickening of his lust for her and to let him take her right there, on the kitchen floor.

But, perversely, the servant girl in her rebelled. She had seen too much of how men took advantage of the females living under their roof and it galled her that Marco was behaving in the same unprincipled manner as the brothers Panzani. This was not how she wanted things to be between them.

'No!' she protested, pushing him away and covering herself up again. 'Please, sir, leave me be. I am your servant, not your whore.'

She was surprised to see a look of respect on his face. 'You're quite right,' he said, lurching backwards and clutching at the table to steady himself. 'I'm not myself. Forgive me.'

'Think no more of it. Do you need help in getting to bed?'

He burped and shook his head. 'No, no, I can manage. Good night, sweet Carla. And thank you for pardoning my – indiscretion. It will not happen again.'

Once he had gone upstairs, however, and Carla lay in the dark room alone, tears of regret coursed down her cheeks. What crazed impulse had led her to turn him down when they might have been locked in passion?

Had she not dreamt of being his mistress almost since the time they met? Was he not the lover she most desired? She had been mad to reject him, and now she might never get another chance.

Chapter Fifteen

Carla was well again. Physically, she had never felt better even though the weather was rainy and she spent most of her time indoors. Marco had so much work that he could afford good food, and she delighted in preparing meals for him and Silvio which they devoured appreciatively.

Yet she was heartsick, and her soul ached for closer contact with the man she loved. She suffered daily torture to have him treat her casually, like a servant, and to see him work long hours when she knew she could ease his burden by giving him a hand in the workshop. She constantly debated with herself, wondering what she could do to ease the situation. Sometimes she was in favour of telling him everything. At other times she thought her best course was to slip away and never return, to flee as she had from home and from Piero's. But running away was no solution to her problems. Older and wiser, she knew that now. You could remove yourself from whatever, and whoever, was troubling you but the tormenting memories persisted and there was no escaping them.

It might have been easier for her, she reasoned, if Marco had found another woman to love but he was so absorbed in his work that he had no time for such frivolities. She knew he sometimes frequented whores. She had overheard him talking and laughing about them to Silvio, late at night, when they drank wine together. But the name of Elena was never mentioned and Carla was curious about what might have happened between them.

One evening, at dinner, she steeled herself to question Marco obliquely. When he announced that he had been given a new commission for a wedding gift, she asked him, point blank, if he had ever been in love.

'Never!' he replied, with a touch of scorn. 'I'm far too busy improving my skill as a painter. I've seen what happens to men who moon after women: they forget everything and follow their dick.'

'But don't you sometimes feel lonely?' she persisted.

'I'm usually too tired to lie a-bed wanting what I can't have. If I get the itch I can go to a whore. But I don't rule out getting myself a wife some day. I'll want a son to carry on my trade, for one thing.'

'Is that all you want a wife for, as a brood mare?' Carla said, her tone bitter.

Silvio looked up from his food. 'I think a woman can be a good companion. When I was at home there was a girl who was my best friend. We did everything together, but then her parents got her betrothed to another who had better prospects than me. I still think about her, sometimes. I used to tell her everything, and she'd understand.'

Carla smiled in sympathy, since his story was similar to her own. But then Marco said, 'It's more lonely being a journeyman than an apprentice. When I take on another boy you'll have a mate to talk to, Silvio. You can complain about me behind my back!'

Silvio laughed, and Carla joined in. They exchanged a sly glance, for Silvio had sometimes crept downstairs to confide in her when he felt hard done by!

Marco didn't seem to notice their looks of complicity. He went on, 'Although I don't regret setting up on my own the happiest times for me were when I was at my master Piero's. It was such fun being with the other lads. There wasn't much trouble, except when a new boy arrived and got on the wrong side of Giovanni, the head apprentice. I think Giovanni was envious of his talent. This boy – his name was Carlo – was untrained but had a natural talent that was astounding. Piero let him do advanced work on the quiet.'

Carla's pulse was racing and her mouth was dry with fear, but she had to pursue it. 'What happened to this – Carlo?'

'Nobody knows. I would have apprenticed him myself – you were lucky there, Silvio, because I couldn't have taken you both on . . .'

Now you must tell him, now! The insistent voice was screaming inside Carla's head but she still couldn't bring herself to admit that she was the elusive Carlo. In her women's clothes, and with her hair longer and bleached, Marco might not even believe she was the same person. Or, if he did believe her, he might be so disgusted at the deception that he threw her out at once. She was so afraid of losing even the little contact with him that she did have.

So Carla continued to glance at him with secret longing every day, even though her soul was split in two. She knew every curve and plane of his handsome face, the way his dark hair curled fetchingly around his ears and the set of his head when he was concentrating on his art. She knew he was feeling anxious when he chewed the corner of his lip. She understood his restlessness when he had been cooped up all day and hurried downstairs to taste the evening air. She knew what he was thinking before he said it. Living so close to him she often felt as if their two hearts were beating as one, and yet he did not know her.

It became more and more impossible to continue in that way and the tension was beginning to tell on her. She found herself taking it out on Silvio in petty ways, snapping at him or accusing him of things he hadn't done. When she screamed at him for stealing the last of the loaf from the larder Marco overheard and came downstairs.

'What is this, Carla?' he asked, frowning. 'Why all the shouting?'

'She says I took some bread when I didn't!' Silvio sobbed in anger.

Marco came up to her and stared into her eyes. 'No, he didn't,' he said, quietly. 'It was I who ate the last crust. I was hungry in the night and had it with the leftover broth. I suppose you were going to accuse him of eating that, too.'

'I'm sorry, master,' she said, her eyes downcast. She could feel the heat in her cheeks and knew she had been wrong to make such a fuss.

'Perhaps you're overdoing things,' Marco suggested. 'You seemed well enough, but maybe the sickness has made you weak in spirit.'

'I am perfectly well, thank you,' Carla said in a huff. She didn't want him to think her feeble-minded.

'Very well. But don't upset Silvio with false complaints. He's a good lad, and I won't have him treated badly.'

Carla sighed and apologised, but she was more careful after that. Marco seemed to treat her more kindly too, perhaps perceiving that she was under some kind of stress. He often invited her up to his workshop to observe him painting, and liked to ask her opinion on his efforts. At first she hesitated to say very much, but as time went by she grew more bold and ended up surprising him by her detailed criticisms.

'You have a good eye, my dear,' he told her, after she had commented on his latest *Annunciation*. 'Much of what you say is very sensible. I shall heed your advice about the angel and make the wings more graduated in colour.'

Some of the old closeness she had known with him was slowly building up again, even though the barrier of gender was still there between them. Sometimes Carla felt he was on the verge of baring his soul to her, yet he would stop himself from going too far. It was frustrating, but all she could do was wait patiently for some development in their relationship.

Carla often thought of the time he had made advances to her and wished she could have welcomed them, but although she was eaten up with desire for him she did not regret the fact that she had rebuffed him. If he ever came to her bed she wanted it to be as her equal, in art and love. She could never be his whore, as Elena had been, to be dropped when she failed to please him, or cast off for becoming too fond.

One morning Carla came back from the market to find that Silvio had left. His father had fallen seriously ill and he had been summoned home. Marco looked troubled.

'I don't know how I shall manage without him, I'm so busy. Now I'll have to go to the apothecary myself, to buy some more materials.'

'I could go!' Carla offered eagerly.

To her disappointment he shook his head. 'No, you wouldn't know burnt umber from raw, nor malachite from verdigris. I'll have to go.'

Carla bit her tongue. She knew she was perfectly capable since she had done such errands dozens of times for Piero, but she could say nothing. As soon as he left her alone, however, she beat her fists upon the wall in frustration and cried aloud, 'Oh, how much longer can I bear this? I am living a lie. I love him, yet I cannot let him make love to me! I know him as a woman, and yet I knew him so much better as a boy! I must pretend to be a servant, yet I'm a better artist than Silvio and almost as good a one as Marco himself! How can I bear to go on like this, day after day?'

She climbed the stairs to the workshop and stood in front of the easel, looking at Marco's current work. His brushes and pigments lay to one side and her fingers itched to pick them up and continue what he had started. It was a portrait of a lady in a pink dress, and she could see exactly how to improve the skin tone of her face and hands, and how to correct the rather clumsy way her arms were half folded in front of her.

Her eye fell on Silvio's discarded clothes in the corner. Evidently he had changed out of his apprentice's smock and into his best clothes for the family visit. With a faint smile Carla went over and picked them up. In a dream she pulled off her dress and pulled on the clinging tights then slipped the loose tunic over her head. She tied her hair up and tucked it under his floppy cap then drew on his belt to secure her waist. It felt good to be dressed as a boy again.

Returning to the easel, she took up Marco's brush and tentatively mixed a warmer flesh tone which she proceeded to apply in minute dabs to the cheeks of the woman in the portrait. There was an instant improvement. Encouraged, she began to work in earnest and soon the picture was subtly transformed into the image of a living, breathing woman.

So absorbed was she in her painting that she failed to hear Marco's return. Only when he gave an exclamation of horror from the stairs did she swing round and confront him.

'Silvio . . .?' He was staring at her in bewilderment. 'No, not Silvio. Then who – Carlo!'

Carla felt a lump in her throat as big as an egg as he came towards her with arms outstretched, then stopped midway between them, his expression changing from one of delight to one of puzzlement. 'Carlo?' he repeated, more doubtfully. She shook her head and the cap fell off, letting her blonde hair tumble free. 'No, Carla! What on earth are you playing at, woman? For a minute I thought . . .'

'You thought I was your old friend Carlo? Well, I am! You know me both as Carlo and Carla, Marco. I can keep the truth from you no longer. Please forgive me for not telling you sooner, but I was in no fit state at first and after that – well, the right moment never seemed to come.'

Although she was glad to have got it off her chest at

last, Carla approached him warily, unsure how he would take the news. There was so much at stake that she held her breath in anticipation. Marco seemed thunderstruck, his dark eyes piercing her face so keenly that she flinched. There were several seconds of agonised suspense, when she had no idea what reaction to expect from him, but then his face broke into a broad grin and she exhaled the breath she had been holding in a long, relieved sigh.

'Carla!' Marco opened his arms wide to receive her. 'No wonder I felt so close to you. Yet I was afraid. Elena broke my heart and I'd vowed not to let another woman get too close.'

She nestled against his warm bulk, pure relief overwhelming her. He lifted up her face and submitted it to long scrutiny, then nodded slowly. 'Yes, I see the resemblance now. But I'm confused. Why did you dress as a boy in the first place?'

'It's a long story . . .'

'We've all the time in the world!'

He drew her over to the truckle bed in the corner and they lay down on it together. As Carla told her tale from the beginning it felt more like a true confession than any she had made to a priest. Her absolution was Marco's caressing hand on her breast and his sweet kiss, deepening with passion as the full impact of her womanliness made itself known to him. The long wait seemed suddenly worthwhile as she realised that all her secret desire for him was made known and that he returned it abundantly.

Soon she could feel the thrusting urgency of his erection through his hose and her longing made her groan aloud. Marco smiled knowingly and pulled down his clothes, letting her touch his rearing member. She fondled it delicately, marvelling at its warm strength, and meanwhile he was stripping her of her gown and underclothes, intent on laying her bare to his sight. When she was completely naked he exclaimed with pleasure at the sight of her small, tumid breasts with their rosy nipples taut with arousal.

'To think that all this beauty was concealed beneath men's clothes!' he gasped. 'If only you'd told me I would have stolen you away at once!'

'You say that now, but I doubt you'd have been so bold at the time.'

He gave her a rueful grin. 'You're probably right. But now is the right time for us, my dear one. I have set up on my own and am beholden to no one. Best of all, my heart is fancy free – or was, until just a few minutes ago.'

'Are you cross with me for awakening those instincts once again?' she asked cheekily, confident now of her own power over him.

He laughed. 'How can a man be cross at getting a gift from the gods? How can he rant against heaven itself? It would be a sin, my darling, to refuse such exquisite pleasure as I know you can give me. And I can give you . . .'

His hands began to explore her then, softly at first but with increasing ardour as she returned the compliment, caressing his cock and balls with a light touch. Her pussy was soon slavering over him, filling up with love juice as he kissed and sucked at her tumid nipples and stroked her tingling buttocks. The desire she felt was stronger than ever, devoid of the old pain which she had come to associate with thoughts of Marco, for now it was swee-tened with the hope of fulfilment.

'Oh Marco, I thought this day would never come!' she murmured.

'Don't think of the past,' he advised her. 'We are together now, and that's all that matters.'

Passion surged up in him and he moved down to kiss her cunny, sending her off on new flights of exquisite joy. Her body was glowing with an energy she recog-nised as love, not merely sex. It warmed every hidden corner of her, turning her flesh into a molten mass of quivering ardour. To desire entirely without fear, to yield totally without resistance, was a new experience for Carla and she relished every second of it.

Marco was probing into her with his tongue, lapping up her juices as if he were dying of thirst, and making guttural noises of satisfaction in the process. She wanted to feel him inside her. There was a fierce contraction in her womb at the thought of it. Now he was dabbling inside her opening with his fingertip, rolling it around her wet entrance and producing the most delightful sensations. The urge to enclose his organ in her streaming vagina was unstoppable, yet she was torn between wanting more and enjoying what she already had. The tension made her squirm and buck her hips, urging him on.

'Stroke me!' she heard him plead faintly, through tumid lips, and soon his hot member was in her palm. She loved the way it responded at once to her touch, swelling and hardening. Her eyes revered it while her fingers delicately explored its surfaces. The skin of its silken shaft moved against the hard rod within and the bulb at the end grew wet and sticky with lust for her. A tender concern enveloped her, as if the penis had some animal life of its own. 'There, there!' she thought, soothingly. 'You shall have my pussy in due course, never fear!'

The moment came when Marco was poised at the door of her sex, ready to enter the portals of bliss. Carla moaned, feeling her cunny expand with longing to receive him and her clitoris pulse with fevered anticipation. At last the head of his member engaged with the mouth of her cunny and she let out a great sigh of satisfaction as he slowly slid into her, inching down into the aroused, sensual depths of her. She clasped him with her vaginal muscles and felt her pleasure intensify, the throbbing nub at the top of her vulva pressing against his solid, moving shaft and prolonging the stimulation that his fingers and mouth had begun.

Soon they were moving in instinctual harmony, their thrusting pelvises synchronised in the primeval rhythm of love. Carla was suffused with pure joy, her heart and soul thrilling to the new subtleties of pleasure that her body was experiencing. Confidently she began to experiment with her movements, lifting her mons and grinding it hard against his to increase her gratification, feeling the blissful warmth of their mutual desire bind them both in a golden web of ecstasy.

Before she reached her consummation, however, Carla had a sublime vision. She saw herself and Marco sinuously entwined as if they had been sculpted from marble, caught in a passionate embrace, their flesh as delicately warm-toned as a tempera fresco. They were floating in mid-air, behind them a glorious sunset like the background to an apotheosis, bathing their bodies with exquisite golden light. In a flash she saw herself and her lover as Adam and Eve, then as Mars and Venus, Dante and Beatrice, Paolo and Francesca ... they were archetypal lovers, old as time and yet new as spring.

The emotions they felt were the same as others had felt, from time immemorial. Carla's identity drifted from her as she became consumed by female energy, all her pulses quivering with pleasure as she interacted with Marco's maleness. The wild stream ran freely through both their bodies, uniting them in one ecstatic dance of the senses. She was being lifted up, up into the vision of perfect love that was itself fading into pure sensation, and soon the delicious feelings peaked in one great explosion of delight, thrilling her through and through until she could take no more of the intense rapture but sank into a profoundly contented daze.

Carla opened her eyes after a while to find Marco staring at her. His eyes were the same ones she had looked into when she was Carlo, but although the familiar friendliness was there she could see another dimension now, one that she had longed to witness. His love for her shone out with unabashed brilliance, transforming his gaze into a soft caress. She smiled and touched his cheek gently. He caught her hand and kissed her fingertips.

'Carla,' he breathed in wonder. 'My beloved. Will you live with me here, and be my wife?'

She nodded, speechless. He pulled her close and let her rest her head upon his bare chest while he stroked her hair. She should have been utterly at peace, but from somewhere in the depths of her mind troubling thoughts arose and Carla knew she must voice them.

'Marco,' she began, tentatively. 'If I live with you, shall I be able to do some painting as I did when I was Carlo?'

'Painting?' He frowned at her, and for a moment Carla feared the shattering of all her dreams in one fell swoop. But then he grinned. 'Of course! You shall draw and paint as much as you like. I shall need no further apprentices with you around.'

'But what of the Guild?'

'Bugger the Guild! We'll find a way to get your work recognised, even if you have to pose as a man again.'

'So you won't palm it off as your own?'

'Never! It would be an insult to your talent, dear girl. Although you may help me with some of the bigger pieces, if you will. There's no shame in that.'

Carla was overjoyed to think that she could practise as an artist once again. 'My first work shall be a portrait of you, dear Marco,' she promised.

'Then you'd better acquire a more intimate knowledge of my anatomy. See how my cock wants you again already. I can't wait to have you "draw" him. There is such skill in your pretty fingers, my sweet!'

Carla thought she didn't know which she preferred, making love or making pictures. It was pure luxury to be able to do both, to her heart's content. This has truly been worth waiting for, she told herself as she reached out to perform her labour of love.

BLACK LACE NEW BOOKS

Published in September

SILENT SEDUCTION
Tanya Bishop

Sophie is expected to marry her long-term boyfriend and become a wife and mother. Instead, she takes a job as a nanny and riding instructor for the wealthy but dysfunctional McKinnerney family. Soon, a mystery lover comes to visit her in the night. Is it the rugged young gardener or Mr McKinnerney himself? In an atmosphere of suspicion and secrecy, Sophie is determined to discover his identity.

ISBN 0 352 33193 3

BONDED
Fleur Reynolds

When the dynamic investment banker Sapphire Western goes on holiday and takes photographs of polo players at a game in the heart of Texas, she does not realise they can be used as a means of revenge upon her friend's cousin, Jeanine. In a world where being rich is everything and being decadent is commonplace, Jeanine and her associates still manage to shock. Dishonesty and double-dealing ensue. Can Sapphire remain aloof from her friends' depraved antics or will she give in to her libidinous desires and the desires of the dynamic men around her?

ISBN 0 352 33192 5

Published in October

FRENCH MANNERS
Olivia Christie

Gilles de la Trave persuades Colette, a young and beautiful peasant girl to become his mistress and live the life of a Parisian courtesan. However, it is his son Victor that she loves and expects to marry. In a moment of passion and curiosity Colette confesses her sins to the local priest but she is unaware that the curé has his own agenda: one which involves herself and Victor.

ISBN 0 352 33214 X

ARTISTIC LICENCE
Vivienne LaFay

Renaissance Italy. Carla Buonomi is determined to find a new life where she can put her artistic talents to good use. Dressed as a boy, she travels to Florence and finds work as a young apprentice to a master craftsman. All goes well until Carla is expected to perform licentious favours for her employer. One person has discovered her true identity however and he and Carla enjoy a secret affair. How long before Carla's true gender will be revealed?

ISBN 0 352 33210 7

INVITATION TO SIN
Charlotte Royal

Father Gabriel has taught the orphaned Justine that it is no sin to worship the Lord with her body. But he has also taught her to obey what he insists are God's laws. When the handsome gypsy, Armand, offers her everything but the blessing of the church, Justine refuses him. Banished from the convent to the ominous Waldgraf castle, Justine is thrown into a life of servitude. But there is a chance of escape – if only she'll accept Armand's invitation to sin.

ISBN 0 352 33217 4

Published in November

THE STRANGER
Portia Da Costa

When a confused and mysterious young man stumbles into the life of the recently widowed Claudia, he becomes the catalyst that re-ignites her sleeping sensuality. But is the wistful and angelic Paul really as innocent as he looks or is he an accomplished trickster with a dark and depraved agenda? As an erotic obsession flowers between Paul and Claudia, his true identity no longer seems to matter.

ISBN 0 352 33211 5

ELENA'S DESTINY
Lisette Allen

The gentle convent-bred Elena, awakened to the joys of forbidden passion by the masterful knight Aimery le Sabrenn, has been forcibly separated from him by war. Although he still captivates Elena with his powerful masculinity, Aimery is no longer hers. She must fight a desperate battle for his affections with two formidable opponents: a wanton young heiress and his scheming former mistress, Isobel. Dangerous games of love and lust are played out amidst the increasing tension of a merciless siege.

ISBN 0 352 33218 2

If you would like a complete list of plot summaries of Black Lace titles, please fill out the questionnaire overleaf or send a stamped addressed envelope to:-

Black Lace, 332 Ladbroke Grove, London W10 5AH

BLACK LACE BACKLIST

All books are priced £4.99 unless another price is given.

---------- ✂ --------------------

Please send me the books I have ticked above.

Name ....

Address ....

....

....

.... Post Code ....

Send to: **Cash Sales, Black Lace Books, 332 Ladbroke Grove, London W10 5AH.**

Please enclose a cheque or postal order, made payable to **Virgin Publishing Ltd**, to the value of the books you have ordered plus postage and packing costs as follows:

UK and BFPO – £1.00 for the first book, 50p for each subsequent book.

Overseas (including Republic of Ireland) – £2.00 for the first book, £1.00 each subsequent book.

If you would prefer to pay by VISA or ACCESS/MASTERCARD, please write your card number and expiry date here:

....

Please allow up to 28 days for delivery.

Signature ....

---------- ✂ --------------------

BLACK
lace

WE NEED YOUR HELP ...
to plan the future of women's erotic fiction –

– and no stamp required!

Yours are the only opinions that matter.

Black Lace is the first series of books devoted to erotic fiction by women for women.

We intend to keep providing the best-written, sexiest books you can buy. And we'd appreciate your help and valued opinion of the books so far. Tell us what you want to read.

THE BLACK LACE QUESTIONNAIRE

SECTION ONE: ABOUT YOU

1.1 Sex (*we presume you are female, but so as not to discriminate*)
Are you?
Male	☐
Female	☐

1.2 Age
under 21	☐	21–30	☐
31–40	☐	41–50	☐
51–60	☐	over 60	☐

1.3 At what age did you leave full-time education?
still in education	☐	16 or younger	☐
17–19	☐	20 or older	☐

1.4 Occupation _____

1.5 Annual household income
    under £10,000 ☐   £10–£20,000 ☐
    £20–£30,000 ☐   £30–£40,000 ☐
    over £40,000 ☐

1.6 We are perfectly happy for you to remain anonymous;
    but if you would like to receive information on other
    publications available, please insert your name and
    address

    _____

    _____

    _____

    _____

SECTION TWO: ABOUT BUYING BLACK LACE BOOKS

2.1 How did you acquire this copy of *Artistic Licence*?
    I bought it myself ☐   My partner bought it ☐
    I borrowed / found it ☐

2.2 How did you find out about Black Lace books?
    I saw them in a shop ☐
    I saw them advertised in a magazine ☐
    I saw the London Underground posters ☐
    I read about them in _____
    Other _____

2.3 Please tick the following statements you agree with:
    I would be less embarrassed about buying Black
    Lace books if the cover pictures were less explicit ☐
    I think that in general the pictures on Black
    Lace books are about right ☐
    I think Black Lace cover pictures should be as
    explicit as possible ☐

2.4 Would you read a Black Lace book in a public place – on
    a train for instance?
    Yes ☐   No ☐

SECTION THREE: ABOUT THIS BLACK LACE BOOK

3.1 Do you think the sex content in this book is:
Too much ☐ About right ☐
Not enough ☐

3.2 Do you think the writing style in this book is:
Too unreal/escapist ☐ About right ☐
Too down to earth ☐

3.3 Do you think the story in this book is:
Too complicated ☐ About right ☐
Too boring/simple ☐

3.4 Do you think the cover of this book is:
Too explicit ☐ About right ☐
Not explicit enough ☐

Here's a space for any other comments:

SECTION FOUR: ABOUT OTHER BLACK LACE BOOKS

4.1 How many Black Lace books have you read? ☐

4.2 If more than one, which one did you prefer?

4.3 Why?

SECTION FIVE: ABOUT YOUR IDEAL EROTIC NOVEL

We want to publish the books you want to read – so this is your chance to tell us exactly what your ideal erotic novel would be like.

5.1 Using a scale of 1 to 5 (1 = no interest at all, 5 = your ideal), please rate the following possible settings for an erotic novel:

     Medieval/barbarian/sword 'n' sorcery ☐
     Renaissance/Elizabethan/Restoration ☐
     Victorian/Edwardian ☐
     1920s & 1930s – the Jazz Age ☐
     Present day ☐
     Future/Science Fiction ☐

5.2 Using the same scale of 1 to 5, please rate the following themes you may find in an erotic novel:

     Submissive male/dominant female ☐
     Submissive female/dominant male ☐
     Lesbianism ☐
     Bondage/fetishism ☐
     Romantic love ☐
     Experimental sex e.g. anal/watersports/sex toys ☐
     Gay male sex ☐
     Group sex ☐

Using the same scale of 1 to 5, please rate the following styles in which an erotic novel could be written:

     Realistic, down to earth, set in real life ☐
     Escapist fantasy, but just about believable ☐
     Completely unreal, impressionistic, dreamlike ☐

5.3 Would you prefer your ideal erotic novel to be written from the viewpoint of the main male characters or the main female characters?

     Male ☐   Female ☐
     Both ☐

5.4 What would your ideal Black Lace heroine be like? Tick as many as you like:

Dominant	☐	Glamorous	☐
Extroverted	☐	Contemporary	☐
Independent	☐	Bisexual	☐
Adventurous	☐	Naïve	☐
Intellectual	☐	Introverted	☐
Professional	☐	Kinky	☐
Submissive	☐	Anything else?	☐
Ordinary	☐	_____	

5.5 What would your ideal male lead character be like? Again, tick as many as you like:

Rugged	☐		
Athletic	☐	Caring	☐
Sophisticated	☐	Cruel	☐
Retiring	☐	Debonair	☐
Outdoor-type	☐	Naïve	☐
Executive-type	☐	Intellectual	☐
Ordinary	☐	Professional	☐
Kinky	☐	Romantic	☐
Hunky	☐		
Sexually dominant	☐	Anything else?	☐
Sexually submissive	☐	_____	

5.6 Is there one particular setting or subject matter that your ideal erotic novel would contain?

_____

SECTION SIX: LAST WORDS

6.1 What do you like best about Black Lace books?

_____

6.2 What do you most dislike about Black Lace books?

_____

6.3 In what way, if any, would you like to change Black Lace covers?

_____

6.4   Here's a space for any other comments:

_____

_____

_____

_____

Thank you for completing this questionnaire. Now tear it out of the book – carefully! – put it in an envelope and send it to:

Black Lace
FREEPOST
London
W10 5BR

No stamp is required if you are resident in the U.K.